*G*loriana Blakely had promised herself she would not cry. She so hated breaking promises, especially to herself.

Her reflection in the carriage window appeared composed and collected, with icy blonde curls caught up in a stylish bonnet and her best travel dress casting a lovely lilac complement to her porcelain skin, but she knew the tears were coming. The warm prick at the corner of one of her lovely blue eyes compelled her to turn her face to the side, so that no one might see it escape and roll down her cheek, glittering like the crystal chandeliers above the final ball of the Season.

This was her least favorite part of the year. Always. And this year was so much worse than the ones that had come before. Why must life be split between vibrant and thrilling Seasons and the slow, dank misery of the months in between?

"They will forgive you before they reach Devonshire," her

cousin Rose assured her from across the carriage, her voice tender, as though she could sense that mutinous teardrop hiding on the other side of Gloriana's face. "You know it as well as I."

"When was it that you gained the power to read my thoughts, Cousin?" Gloriana asked, a humorless smile twisting her lips. She swiped at her cheek and turned to face Rose, a deep sigh escaping her tightly corseted lungs. "And however have I lived without you these past years?"

Rose tilted her head thoughtfully, adjusting the toddler in her lap. She was the same Rose as ever, somehow, despite having become a viscountess since they'd last shared a carriage. Her dark golden curls had been cut stylishly short, just brushing the tops of her shoulders in carefully arranged ringlets. Her lush figure suited motherhood all too well, and as always, reminded Gloriana of just how boyish her own figure was in comparison.

Rose's son, little Lord Reggie Somers, was a year old and bursting with cherubic charm just now. His heavy lashes brushed rosy cheeks as delicate snores escaped his parted lips.

Deep sleep had robbed him of the rambunctious, demanding spirit Gloriana had witnessed in his waking hours. It was a deception worthy of the most devious tyrant, in Gloriana's opinion. The little devil lured people in with his angelic appearance, batting his wide eyes and cooing in that sweet little voice. Yes, no one with a heart stood a chance, and once they were thoroughly in love, the child revealed his true nature, wild and demanding and so very, very loud.

THE SCOUNDREL AND THE SOCIALITE

A STEAMY REGENCY HISTORICAL ROMANCE

AVA DEVLIN

The Scoundrel and the Socialite

The Somerton Scandals - Book 2

Ava Devlin

Printed in the United States of America

First Printing, 2019

http://avadevlin.com

Contact the author at ava@avadevlin.com

Cover art by BZN Studio Designs

http://covers.bzndesignstudios.com

Copyediting by Claudette Cruz

https://www.theeditingsweetheart.com/

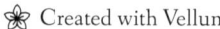 Created with Vellum

Truly, she had to admire it, even if the lad had given her the most serious doubts about the task of motherhood.

"I have written you often," Rose said gently. "Though I have missed you terribly, too. I realize that this venture was not your choice, nor your desire, but I cannot help but feel glad that we are together again. You mustn't worry about your parents. You know any anger at you is always short-lived."

"I know," Gloriana echoed, an emptiness in her voice that she did not like at all. "But it is difficult to request forgiveness for an offense I have no intention of remedying."

Rose chuckled, shaking her head. "You are a stubborn creature. There is no denying that."

"You saw the man! Would *you* have married him?"

"I married Gideon," Rose replied with a raise of her brows. "Another of your castoffs."

Gloriana tutted, waving her hand. "That was different."

It was true, and Rose surely knew it. Gideon Somers was handsome and dignified, a viscount whose standing in Society would have been a boon for any girl, but Gloriana had no desire to be swept off into marriage and locked away in Yorkshire before she could even attend her debut ball, and to a Somers besides.

It was not what Rose had intended, but Gideon was a good reminder that her parents had put her in horrid, unfair, impossible situations just like this one before.

Her blood simmered in her veins. She shifted in her seat, a trail of angry phrases running through her mind that she might pen to Papa at their coaching inn. How dare they do this to her more than once?! How could any loving mother or father want their daughter to marry someone like that corpulent, boorish, barely literate buffoon? Someone twice her age and half as refined!

"Glory," her cousin's voice broke in, placid and encouraging. "I know that you think you are headed into months of misery and boredom, but I assure you that Yorkshire will take your breath away. There is an untamed beauty in the north unlike anything you've seen between Devon and London, and much to do at Somerton."

"Much to do?" she repeated, skepticism plain in her voice. "I imagine the bulk of my time will be spent avoiding whatever hell your dear sister-in-law has prepared for me."

"Heloise doesn't know you are coming," Rose confessed, a note of discomfort trickling into her voice. "She resides in the dower house with her mother and cousin, however, and spends much of her time these days working in the township. It should not surprise me if you go the entire autumn without seeing her at all."

"Working?" Now *that* was a surprise. At school, Heloise Somers had been a no-good layabout whose smugness at her natural good marks in matters of learning somehow offset her abysmal performance in the genteel arts. This intolerability was only amplified by her wicked streak of cruel pranks, the bulk of which had been targeted directly at Gloriana. It was no surprise that the wretch was unmarried, for certain, but who would have expected someone like her to seek out a vocation?

"Mm." Rose nodded, stroking the fine, auburn hair on her son's head. "She has trained under the midwife who delivered Reggie. She attends some of the expecting mothers in the township and often assists at the parish clinic for the poor."

"For the poor!" Gloriana burst out, immediately cringing as she saw a flicker in Reggie's eyelashes.

Both women froze, watching the toddler furrow his brow in his sleep, as though deciding between continuing his nap or punishing them for the noise. After a moment, he turned his face into his mother's side and slumped his way back into dreams, winning a sigh of relief from both women.

"I apologize," she whispered, "it was simply an unexpected revelation."

"Years have passed between your girlish misadventures at Mrs. Arlington's," Rose snapped under her breath. "Perhaps you will find that Heloise has matured in the years apart, just as you have."

"I sincerely doubt it," Gloriana retorted, rolling her eyes at her cousin's naive optimism. "Clearly she's got you fooled."

Rose sighed, squeezing her eyes shut for a moment as they rumbled along, swaying to the movement of the carriage. When she opened them again, clear and golden-brown, she assumed a tone that would broker no argument. "I suggest you put Heloise out of your mind, Glory. The autumn harvest will start within a few weeks, which brings feasts and cider pressing and a small festival in the township that you might like to attend. I am in the midst of redesigning a few of the rooms in the manor if you'd like to help with that. If nothing else, you might at least assist in planning a small celebration for my brother-in-law as he returns home from Oxford."

"Celebration?" Gloriana asked, the word permeating her haze of misery like a sharpened dart sailing toward a target. "Are you arranging a country party? Who have you invited? What are the activities?"

Rose blinked at her. "I hadn't put much thought into it. A small soiree with some of the local gentry should be enough. Alex isn't much for fanfare."

"A small soiree!" Gloriana scoffed. "Don't be ridiculous. Who is this Alex? What are his aspirations now that he is a graduate? Is he looking to become a bursar? To serve on the Parliament? To join the clergy? These things will determine who we invite!"

Rose laughed softly, lifting a gloved hand to her lips. "I couldn't say," she decided after a moment. "If Alex has aspirations of any sort, he keeps them close to the vest."

"Ah," Gloriana said knowingly, giving her cousin a nod. "So he is awaiting the most amenable offer. That is the smart play. Rosie, you should have said something *before* we left London! I don't even have my good stationery handy."

"Why on earth should that matter?"

Gloriana shushed her cousin, rifling through her reticule for her card carrier. "I shall have to think this through," she mused. "How many ought we to accommodate? Perhaps eleven each of ladies and gentlemen? Is Alex Somers married? If not, we must include unmarried young ladies of status along with men of the proper occupation."

"Glory, I don't think that's necessary," Rose insisted. "Of course Somerton can accommodate a great number of guests, but I don't think Alex expects us to—"

"But you must!" Gloriana cut in, her eyes sparkling with sudden zeal. "You must! A noble family does not simply send a son to Oxford and not announce his successful completion of his studies to the world! Let me do this, Rosie. It is the proper thing to do, and besides, it is something I am very, very good at. This changes the entire prospect of an autumn in the country. It could be wonderful!"

Rose did not respond, but judging from the way she released her breath and the begrudging twist of her lips, Gloriana knew that she had been victorious. She stifled a little squeal so as to not disturb the little one, and gazed out the window at the vestiges of the London outskirts. As the last of the taverns and stables sailed past, she thumbed the stack of cards in her lap, her mind spinning with possibilities.

CHAPTER 2

*A*lex Somers was wearing the wrong shoes.

Of course, like most things, he didn't realize until it was far too late to remedy the thing. Bessie Corden gave him a quick peck on the lips, her lovely, plump cheeks bright with excitement as she pushed him the rest of the way out of her bedroom window and flung the curtains shut on his smiling face.

He held still for a moment, long enough to hear her husband, the honorable Judge Corden, burst into the room. The man was excitable at the best of times, but Bessie worked her usual magic, beckoning him into their bedroom and encouraging him to rest after a long day in the courts. It was only when Alex felt certain that no hint of suspicion hung over the judge that he allowed himself to scale his way down their ivy trellis and land in the soft earth of an oft-neglected Oxford garden.

It had been foolhardy to come by and bid Bessie a proper farewell, but Alex had never been much for resisting temptations. Besides, it was his last night in Oxford, and he was truly going to miss the soft hips and sweet smiles of the respectable Mrs. Corden. He grinned to himself, ducking under the boughs of the trees lining the townhouse yard and finding his gait on the bustling cobblestone streets of the city in shoes that were at least two sizes too large.

Bessie had fretted and fussed and smoothed his shock of bright orange hair from his brow in a futile effort to make him look less rumpled as he'd pulled his clothes back on. She must have known, under all that lovely femininity and good intent, that he'd looked rumpled from the start. His own mother had given up on making him into a tidy, presentable lad many years ago, which was all the same when you had Gideon in the family.

He chuckled to himself as he scuffed along, the early-evening breeze picking up as the sun sank lower. If Alex had been born with scabby knees and mud on his cheeks, then his elder brother, Gideon, had been born in a starched cravat, with a budget in one hand and a ledger in the other. His sister, Heloise, would have been born backwards and upside down, breaking rules before she ever drew breath.

There was a bittersweetness to leaving Oxford. It wasn't that this had ever been a real home, but while he continued to halfheartedly plug away at his endless education, he had felt a sort of security here. As long as he was still studying, he wasn't aimless. Wasn't that right? No one frowned on a student with no vocation nor predilection for ambition, but a *graduate?* He'd really screwed the pooch when he'd finished the damned degree, hadn't he? Now he'd have to actually accomplish something to retain any amount of respectability.

Still, it would be nice to return to Somerton. He had missed his brother and sister, and the little ones too. The last time he'd seen wee Reggie, he'd still been a squirming pink thing in swaddling, as cute as he was noisy. Now, Gideon wrote that he was walking upright with no help at all! As for Callie, their precious would-be foundling, she'd celebrated her second birthday already without him, and if Heloise's letters could be trusted, was now big enough for him to toss into the air to his heart's content.

He turned onto Wellington Square, humming softly under his breath. In the morning, he'd load up the last of his things and head north, back home for a spell while he figured out just what in the devil was supposed to come next. For now, there were still plentiful hours ahead to celebrate and bid farewell to his compatriots.

The Lion's Tooth Tavern glowed in the distance as the innkeeper's wife went about the fence, lighting the lanterns. The sky shone purple and orange, with the faintest twinkle of early stars hiding beneath the veneer of late-summer clouds.

Alex inhaled deeply, promising himself that he would remember this moment, even if the revelry and spirits erased the remainder of the night from his memory. He shoved his hands into his pockets, curled his toes in his too-large shoes, and made his way to his own farewell party, hoping against hope that tonight was not the final night of his youth.

THE HANGOVER WASN'T so bad as he expected. He imagined if he weren't crammed into a stagecoach at the crack of dawn as it rumbled and bounced over holes in the road, he'd be in tip-top shape. He'd also still be asleep, which would be lovely.

Still, he'd had a hearty breakfast and two strong cups of tea, and while the headache was not completely gone, he certainly had experienced worse mornings. It was worth it, anyhow, to have enjoyed such an epic sending-off. His purse had enjoyed a fattening over several rounds of cards, and he'd made one of the barmaids cry when he confessed that it was his final night in town.

If nothing else, he'd at least left Oxford with a few new friends and knowledge of the best haunts in the city. The education was fine, he supposed, for what it was. The attitude of most of his classmates had been that the entire affair was nothing but a formality, and as such, required no real passion or devotion to the actual lessons.

Of course, there had been one or two that were true academics. A squirrely little fellow named Peter Applegate had taken nearly three terms of effort to coax out onto the town for a spot of fun. Even when foxed, the man got a zealous gleam in his eye and talked endlessly about their proud British heritage and his dreams of publishing tomes that regaled readers with the thrilling exploits of their national history. Luckily, the ale provided just the right amount of lubrication to turn the tone of his fact spouting a little more salacious than usual. Besides, bringing him along always turned up some unexpected morsel of entertainment.

He enjoyed the challenge of a chap like Applegate. Drawing someone like that out of his shell was always one hell of a puzzle to unravel, followed by a never-ending wealth of surprising moments once the deed was done. That's why he'd been determined to take local transport back to Yorkshire.

Gideon would give him an earful when he found out that he'd opted to take a stage rather than send for Graham to retrieve him. Still, Alex loved this sort of thing. There were always such interesting people on coaches, and it was always a bit of fun to engineer a cheery, social atmosphere along the way. This particular journey, however, was looking less than promising.

Across from him, a governess of middling age had somehow found her way back into the enchanted land of dreams, her head tilted back on the seat cushions, mouth sagging open to accommodate her snores. On either side of her were bored-looking children shooting one another increasingly incendiary looks.

Next to Alex was a portly fellow in tweeds, doing his best to take up as little space as possible. He had his face practically smashed into the window, as though the passing early-morning scenery were of utmost interest, and his legs tucked toward the door.

Of the available company, Alex thought the children had the most potential to be entertaining. He flashed them a grin and nodded toward their guardian with a rise of his eyebrows. Curious, they turned their attention from antagonizing one another to the strange man across from them, who set about doing an imitation of a collapsed, snoring woman in short order.

He used his hand to mime the large feather in the governess's hat, as though it were billowing violently back and forth every time she drew breath. The resounding giggles from his companions were a satisfactory result, and all three settled into speedy camaraderie.

The portly man glanced over at them, curiosity battling with what appeared to be a crippling case of shyness, and caught Alex's sparkling green eyes with his own hesitant brown ones.

"Say," Alex whispered to the children, "if we can convince this official-looking fellow to join us, we might play a game of charades! It will make the journey go by much faster."

"Oh!" the younger of the boys gasped, turning his hopeful gaze to the portly man. "Would you, sir? Would you consider it?"

"I ..." The man cleared his throat, a hesitant smile finding its way onto his lips. "I surely would, though I cannot promise I'll be any good."

"That's all right," the elder boy responded. "That just means we're more likely to win."

"Oho," Alex replied, rubbing his hands together, "that's a challenge if I've ever heard one."

The governess snorted in her sleep. It was anyone's guess whose team she was supporting with such commentary.

CHAPTER 3

*G*loriana would not admit it, but the Somerton estate was far more impressive than she had anticipated.

It was true that the land had become progressively wilder as they'd shambled farther north. The neat emerald horizons of the midlands had given way to rolling, chaotic dales, with rocky outcrops that produced some of the most stunning wildflowers she'd ever seen in her life.

The air had taken on a crisp, cool quality almost as soon as Rose had announced that they'd passed into Yorkshire, and the villages and towns they'd passed had become far more rustic than anything Gloriana had seen in the southern part of the nation. Yes, it had its charms, but the farther along they got, the more concerned she became about the impression such a place would make on the genteel people she'd so carefully chosen to invite for this country party.

It was beautiful here, yes, but in the same way a wild creature is beautiful, with graces best admired from a distance, lest that allure transform into unpredictability and danger.

She knew Gideon Somers was a viscount, and as such did not likely live in one of these stone-and-earth lean-tos that seemed de rigueur in the countryside, but the truth of the matter was that she had never asked. The estate could very easily be only as luxurious as one of the public coaching inns where they'd spent their nights along the way. A title did not mean a fortune, as any good debutante knew.

In fact, the only thing she truly knew about the Somers family was that it had produced Heloise Somers. Hellish Heloise, whose wild ways and utter lack of refinement could very well have been the result of living in some prehistoric hut at the ends of the Earth for her entire life.

But then came Somerton. Oh, but it almost made Gloriana regret the choices she'd made on the night of her debut.

In another life, this vast mansion, this sprawling estate that wrapped its way around the Yorkshire moors so elegantly, might have been her own home and hearth. Her pale blue eyes had grown wide as they passed through the gates and approached the drive. It was an enchanting design, modern and classic all at once. All concerns she'd been nursing about the impression it would make on her Society connections evaporated like so much Yorkshire mist.

Her fingers were stained with ink beneath her muslin gloves, as she had sacrificed a goodly amount of sleep over the last several nights, bent over writing desks at coaching inns along their route and scrambling to have the missives posted before they set off again at sunup. She had never attended a country party, but she had heard tell of plenty.

She was determined to excel at organizing such an affair, even if the entire endeavor was on behalf of a man she had never met nor thought of prior to stepping into her cousin's coach.

Yes, this was a perfect venue. She was confident that everything would be exemplary when hosted in such a place. Mentally, she was already doubling her guest list, agog at just how many things might be possible under such a large and fashionable roof.

The carriage slowed to a trot in the circular drive of the manor, where Lord Somers awaited the return of his wife and child with the rigid formality of a man about the most dire of business. He was tall and handsome, with burnished auburn hair and an undeniably refined bearing. He was flanked on either side by members of the household staff, but did not await a footman as the carriage came to a halt.

Instead, he strode forward, a smile blooming on his stony face that mirrored the one worn by Rose.

"Look, it's Papa!" she cooed to little Reggie, her eyes flashing in the afternoon light as Lord Somers pulled the door open and opened his arms just in time to catch his enthusiastic son and heir.

The driver grumbled as he stomped over to the door, shooting his hand out in a way Gloriana found most impertinent. However, it only made her cousin laugh.

"I'm afraid Lord Somers could not wait for you to do your duty, Mr. Graham," she sighed, accepting his calloused hand as she stepped daintily from her perch. "You mustn't take it to heart. He is only eager to see his son."

"To heart?" the man replied, meeting his mistress's eye, bold as you please. "The day has not yet arrived where my heart is affected by any lord."

"Mm," Rose replied without comment, stepping away from the driver to peck her husband on the cheek.

Gloriana started as the driver spun to her, squinting up at her with considerably less petulance. "Might I help ye down?" he asked, his voice softer.

"Yes, please," she replied, hoping the relief at his shift in demeanor was not overly plain on her face.

The soft leather of her traveling boots sank into the gravel of the drive, her legs aching from the hours of inactivity beneath her confection of skirts. She put a gracious smile on her face and braced her hands in front of her, awaiting acknowledgement from a man she had once thought she'd be forced to marry. "Lord Somers," she said with a polite curtsy. "Thank you so much for this generous invitation to your estate. I am much looking forward to my time here."

"Are you?" Gideon replied, the corner of his mouth twitching. "We are pleased to have you, Miss Blakely. I hope that you consider Somerton your home while you are here."

"Oh, she will." Rose laughed, her hands curling around her husband's arm with an affectionate squeeze. "Gloriana has already taken it upon herself to offer Somerton up to the *ton* in her efforts to organize a celebration for Alex."

"For Alex?" Gideon repeated, confusion evident on his face.

"To celebrate the completion of his degree," Rose replied, with a meaningful tilt of her head. "Glory is quite right that this is an opportunity to showcase his achievement to the right sort of people, so that he might pursue whatever vocation his ambitions may favor."

"Ah," Gideon replied, his tone cryptic. "I am eager to learn exactly what those ambitions are myself."

"I discouraged her from inviting the clergy," Rose whispered, winning a chuckle from her husband.

He turned and gestured to his staff, sending them into motion. "Let us withdraw inside so that you ladies may rest, and we will discuss plans for this event over supper, hm?"

"Oh, yes please." Rose sighed, leaning into her husband's body as the nanny swooped forward to gather Reggie. She beckoned with her free arm that Gloriana might follow them as footmen filed past with their luggage in tow.

The grand double doors opened into a marble and gilt foyer, with a large staircase curling up along the right-hand side of the room. There was much that Gloriana thought she might take interest in examining at some point, but for the moment, she was rooted on the spot by a curling bramble of horror that had sprouted in her stomach and made its way rapidly into her chest.

She had not expected to be confronted with such unpleasantness so immediately.

The first thing one saw when entering Somerton was a large portrait hanging just opposite the entrance. A portrait of Heloise Somers, as it happened, the girl who had tormented Gloriana through her tender years as a young woman at finishing school. Hellish Heloise, who had been the most unfathomable bully, the most unspeakable wretch.

The portrait was a fine thing, she had to admit, clearly done by a master of the craft. It depicted a glorious perception of Heloise, seated in a room of sunlight, her hair loose and vibrant around her shoulders as she stroked the head of a tiny orange kitten. Her eyes were so real, so sharp and calculating gazing out from the canvas in that wicked poison green that for just a moment, Gloriana felt as she had back at Mrs. Arlington's. Catching the eye of Heloise Somers always meant that something was not as it should be, often at great expense to her personal dignity.

She shivered, knowing she was being foolish, and tore her eyes away. It had been years, after all. She was not the easy target she once had been. If Heloise sought to torment her now, she'd find a much more formidable opponent in a debuted and adult Gloriana Blakely.

To her relief, Lord and Lady Somers were so caught up in one another that neither had noticed her reaction to the portrait. She had time to turn her back to it, refusing to give such a thing power, before she spoke.

"I may take a nap, if there is time," she said sweetly, the message that she required a bedroom clear. "I have much I wish to discuss with both of you very soon, of course. Will it, erm," she hesitated, clearing her throat into her glove. "Will it just be the three of us at dinner?"

"It will," Gideon replied, something knowing in his voice. "I shan't subject you to my siblings until you've had time to settle in."

She smiled her gentlest, most practiced smile. "I can't imagine what you mean," she demurred, pleased at how convincing the lie sounded on her lips.

~

Sir Reginald Blakely, Gloriana's esteemed papa, had always insisted that if one dedicated herself to a task, time would jump in tempo, speeding past in the blink of an eye. Of course, like most of Sir Reginald's sayings, Gloriana found her father's wisdom to be right on the mark. Somehow, almost a week had passed at Somerton already, despite her being certain that she'd only just alighted from the carriage.

She had spent days absorbed in party planning, and yet it felt as though she had barely begun true preparations.

On her second night, Rose had burst into her bedroom in a flurry of authority and disapproval. She'd brought with her an extra lantern, a slim but sturdy leather ledger book, and stern instructions that Gloriana should not sacrifice the integrity of her eyesight nor curve her spine into a grandmother's posture at the behest of party planning.

It was impossible to resist Rose when she had set about solving a perceived problem. For most of Gloriana's life, this had been a delightful boon, a shining knight in chiffon and lace who always made the bad things disappear. She was ever grateful for her cousin's caring and capability, but some small part of her bristled that she was not yet adult enough to require no rescuing.

It wasn't that she wished to outgrow Rose, but rather that she had hoped to be her equal by now, partners rather than lioness and cub. Still, she knew Rose was right, and it was an honest relief to be ushered into a small reading room, complete with a desk and sturdy-backed chair in which to continue her business. The little library was conveniently located on the same floor as her bedroom, and she was told to consider it her private study for the remainder of her tenure at Somerton.

The ledger book had neat notes in the first few pages from Gideon Somers himself, expressing with delicate tact a limitation on spending. Of course, he seemed savvy to the fact that such events did not come for free and that it would be a disservice to his family name and to his brother to skimp on amenities. In fact, Gloriana rather got the impression that he was keen on the prestige and positivity that would come from hosting a clutch of esteemed guests.

While she had not spoken to him directly, Viscount Somers had allocated funds for additional temporary servants added to the staff as well as a stipend for food and one for limited entertainment. Gloriana noted that while this would not be the lavish free-for-all she might have imagined, there was some pleasure in the creative challenge of staying within the budget.

While the viscount himself had left only written notes, the Somerton housekeeper, a Mrs. Laughlin, had offered a wealth of advice and assistance in the planning process, often alongside delivering some morsel of sustenance or a cup of tea to ensure that Gloriana did not wither away at her work.

The housekeeper was a cheery woman with an encouraging buzz of energy about her, and yet again Gloriana found herself deferring to the authority of a more experienced woman and the comfort that came with that reassurance. They had agreed on sourcing additional staff from the nearby township and, of course, had crunched the numbers regarding the expectation of vails for the current staff as they were saddled with additional work.

Gloriana didn't like to flatter herself overly much, but she did rather get the impression that Mrs. Laughlin's enthusiasm for the party was in part inspired by Gloriana's skill in creating a truly enjoyable affair.

Letters had finally begun to arrive from those she had written on the road from London. Her dearest friends from school had sent their acceptance in letters gushing with enthusiasm. The two would travel from Oxfordshire under the guardianship of Eleanor's brother. Both ladies were unmarried and would make fine prospects for Lord Alex should he be wise enough to consider them.

The other early acceptance had come from Mr. Nathaniel Atlas, a darling of Society, known for his firebrand speeches in the House of Commons, his diplomatic dealings in the West Indies, and an undeniable charm that lit up the likes of Almack's this past Season. Mr. Atlas happened to be particularly handsome as well as young and unmarried. In fact, Gloriana rather hoped that his attentions focused upon her rather than Tia and Nell, no matter how dearly she loved her friends. After all, she had engineered an equal number of eligible ladies and gentlemen, hadn't she? Why shouldn't she use the opportunity to improve her own prospects? Didn't a dedicated hostess deserve that much?

Rose had teased her about her guest list, of course. "Whose party is this, really, Glory?" she'd laughed, tucked into the corner of the little library with her needlework. "Tell me, what other handsome young bachelors will be in attendance?"

"Why, all of them, Rosie," Gloriana had quipped, a smile carrying in her voice.

It was yet to be confirmed, of course, but she had indeed curated a list of mostly unattached young people. Nell's brother was still in his studies and by all accounts just as much of a wallflower as his sister, if men could be wallflowers. Still, he was from a good family and was necessary for the presence of her schoolmates. Nell guessed he would never truly leave the university and would instead morph seamlessly from student to professor as the years passed by. Next to his name on the ledger, Gloriana had noted: *possible prospect - academia?*

She had invited Sheldon Bywater, the Marquis of Moorvale, whom she had met in London a few years prior. He was an ideal guest, as he was already an intimate of the Somers family. Moorvale was an incorrigible flirt and rather fun in a social setting, though Gloriana couldn't imagine being married to such a very, very large man. If Alexander Somers was interested in a career in the military, Lord Moorvale would be an excellent contact toward those ends. He had sold his commission just this last season after returning from the Continent, practically plastered in medals and accolades.

She could only hope that the numbers of ladies and gentlemen who accepted her invitations would be close to equal. As she'd ticked off tallies of those who might attend, and found more men than women, her cousin had gently reminded her that Heloise Somers also lived at Somerton, and might very well make an appearance at her brother's celebration.

"None of these young men would suit Heloise," she had

clipped, lifting her chin. "I am not acquainted with any lion tamers nor adventurers who could stand to such a challenge."

"I do not think Heloise is much concerned with marriage," Rose had laughed. "She is very much her own woman, and you will have to face her soon. Perhaps you should make your peace with silly feuds in the past."

Gloriana hissed at the memory, pushing herself back from the desk and to her feet. Silly feuds indeed. Heloise had put ink in her tea the night before she was meant to be presented to a visiting duchess! A duchess with young, eligible sons! She'd had to hide in her room for almost two weeks as she waited for her teeth to go from dark purple back to their customary pearly white.

Dratted Heloise. Like hell she'd put it in the past. One didn't turn her back on a viper, even if it had been a long while since it last struck.

She sighed, shaking her head to clear those thoughts and stifling a long yawn.

She had long since kicked her slippers off, and they sat askew against a pretty blue ottoman. She inhaled and stretched her arms over her head, urging her spine to climb back into healthy alignment as her toes burrowed into the soft fibers of the carpet. Her hair was still pinned tight against her scalp, and she was eager to change into the unconfined luxury of her night rail and massage her curls loose and free. Nothing could have been more seductive to her in that moment than the idea of slipping between the cool sheets on her plush bed and sinking into a dark, dreamless slumber.

She had no idea what time it was, only that it was well after dark. There was something more aggressive about the nighttime here in the country, something more wild and forbidding. Back home in Devonshire, one could hear the bustle of mankind around her family's townhouse at all hours, whether it was the clatter of the market in the mornings or the constable's bell and the smell of baking bread at night.

Here, there was no human life outside of the walls of the manor, not for miles. Here, there were only sounds of wind ripping through the trees and the mournful cries of owls and falcons swooping down on unsuspecting little creatures in the dark. The wilds overtook the power of men out here. The stars shone just a bit too harshly, and the moon seemed somehow just a little too close to the ground. She imagined all manner of mythic beasties roaming through the tall grasses and misty forests here, and wondered how anyone ever felt safe venturing out alone.

Perhaps that's why hunting was such a popular sport this far north, she mused. Perhaps venturing out on horseback with hounds at your heels and muskets in your hands was the type of thrill that couldn't be matched in a more civilized place. She imagined the foggy uncertainty of a forest must awaken some primal force in men who hunted, reminding them that humans once came from the wilds too.

She slipped the letters she'd received into the ledger, tipping the cover shut with a satisfying *thump*, and gathered it into her arms. The lantern was burning so low that she feared moving it would extinguish the flame. She must stop forgetting to replenish the oil.

Could she find her way back to her room in the dark? What

might she encounter without the protection of visibility to guide her way? Were there ghosts in the halls of Somerton?

She laughed to herself, shaking her head, and crossed the room toward her shoes. She was being a silly girl, wasn't she? Grown ladies organizing country parties didn't fear walking in hallways at night. There was no such thing as ghosts.

She froze, the hairs on the back of her neck rising as the lantern sputtered, casting eerie shadows around the little room, each one dancing menacingly, drawing closer as the pool of light retracted.

Grow up, Glory, a voice in her head chided, seemingly disconnected from the way her heart surged at a creaking of wood just beyond the window, accompanied by a mysterious thumping that seemed to be moving closer. *Get the lantern and go!* the voice screeched, panic giving itself over to even her most adult instincts.

She would go in just a moment, she told herself, sinking to her knees next to the ottoman. The flame was almost doused and she'd just sit here, safe and still, until her eyes adjusted to the dark.

She winced at another thump, her fingers digging into the edges of the leather-bound book. She willed herself not to shiver at the howling of the wind, though she felt like a child with the book drawn tight to her chest and her jaw clenched against chattering teeth. She held her breath as the room faded to black, leaving only the dull glow of the wick behind and the shallow sounds of Gloriana's breathing.

CHAPTER 4

The problem with drunken endeavors, Alex found, was that if they took too long, one began to sober up before the task could be completed. Such was the case tonight as he shuffled down the dirt road from the nearest inn to Somerton, a walk of enough miles to take one from a tipsy, cocksure swagger to the plodding gait of a man whose higher functions had returned far too early.

It wasn't that he'd never made this walk before. He had, plenty of times, and often in the dead of night. Was it simply that he was getting older? No, it couldn't be that. It must be the fact that he was sleep deprived and sore from all those days cooped up in the stagecoach. That and he'd skipped dinner in favor of ale, and as the cheery stupidity of intoxication had shrouded his senses, he'd become nostalgic for a time when he'd had to sneak out of the manor to make merry in the township.

One should never be forced to experience this type of regretful, self-chiding pain until the sun was up again. What had he been thinking?!

He tilted his head back, squinting up at the moon, which was fat and bright tonight; a harvest moon to usher in the autumn. He had no idea how late it was, but appearing bedraggled and smelling of spirits in the dead of night was not a prospect he relished. He'd have to hear it from Mrs. Laughlin, then Gideon, then Rose, then probably damned Reggie at this stage. The lad's first words would be "Oh, for God's sake, Alex! What now?"

No, he'd best keep to the nostalgia of those youthful excursions and sneak in the same way he used to sneak out. He'd worry about waking up the following morning without any of his belongings nor a change of clothes if he ever made it that far.

The large, wrought-iron gates of Somerton appeared in the distance, cheering him enough to invigorate his pace. Perhaps he wasn't getting old after all. Wasn't it only a few steps ago that he'd begun to feel tired? Yes, he was still in his absolute prime!

He slipped between the iron bars and took his time on the gravel path as he approached the house. As expected, it was all dark in the distance, save for the porch lights near the stables and on either side of the main entrance. That meant it was indeed quite late.

The grass had grown long and lush in the summer sun, and he could feel the soak of evening dew lashing at his trouser legs as he ducked around to approach the right side of the house, where no stables nor crofter huts shone light on his business.

God, but he hoped he had enough time to sleep some of this off. Maybe he could just hide in one of the bedrooms all day tomorrow and sneak back out again at nightfall. He'd be hungry, certainly, but that was better than being humiliated, wasn't it?

He locked eyes on the window with the loose hinge and took a deep breath. Hopefully the trusty thing had managed to continue to evade notice of the staff and household in the years since he'd last used it.

It was only one floor up. Hadn't he recently had some practice scaling exterior walls anyhow? He grinned to himself, sparing an affectionate thought for Mrs. Bessie Corden, and slapped his hands onto the protruding stones of the wall face, looking for a good foothold.

He tried to stifle his grunts of effort, just on the off chance that someone was about and would hear him, but it was a surprising amount of effort pulling one's own body upward this way. The house might as well be a mountain, treacherous and forbidding, as he scaled its craggy peaks.

His fingertips found their way into the corners of the window's ledge. Pressing it inward sent it creaking back outward again on its faulty hinge. He pushed once, twice, three times, each time a little harder than before, until he heard the satisfying *click* of the pane sliding off its latch. A final push revealed a glorious crack of opening, and he was able to pry the whole thing open.

Now all that was left was to heave himself through the little portal to safety and perhaps take a quick nap on the library carpet before he attempted to navigate to his bedroom. Oh, but bed sounded lovely just now, didn't it?

He stifled a yawn and shook his head. One more pull and it'd be over. The muscles in his arms and back groaned as he leveraged himself up and over that final vault. True to plan, he simply allowed himself to tumble forward onto the carpeted floor in a pile of exhaustion.

The wind whistled through the open window, stirring up his hair and sending a rather refreshing, if loud, breeze along the back of his neck. He sighed, rolling over to his side and forcing himself to use what little strength remained in his arms to push himself to his knees.

He was moments away from making his way to his feet when an explosive force of pure pain slammed into his cheekbone, knocking him right back onto his back again. He didn't know what he'd been hit with, but he knew it had been swung by another human being.

He reacted on instinct, his arm lashing out and gripping whatever was within reach—in this case, the very delicate ankle of his assailant, who went scrambling to the ground with a scream of such terrorized volume that it overpowered all of the pain and dazed confusion with raw panic.

"No!" he rasped, scrambling to his hands and knees as she went tumbling to the ground. "No! I live here," he heard himself saying nonsensically. "I live here!"

She was crawling forward, reaching for the desk chair with what he was certain was full intent to brandish it as a weapon, perhaps swinging it directly into his body in her own defense. As much as he regretted startling this mystery woman, he did not think he could bear another injury while his eye and cheek were still throbbing in pain from the first blow.

"Miss!" he cried, grabbing at her bare foot again and dragging her backward as she clawed for the chair. "Miss, please! I mean you no harm."

She screamed again, abandoning the chair in favor of rearing up to slash at him with her fingernails. "Back!" she choked, a strangled sound of misery escaping her throat as he caught her wrists in his hands, just a whisper from his face. "Stay back!"

He could see the impression of her features from the moonlight streaming in from the window. This was no housemaid, dressed as she was in fine white silk with what looked like silver ringlets framing a stunningly beautiful face. Who was this girl hiding in Somerton in the dark? Had he caught himself a ghost?

She was frozen in place, her hands still clawed and primed to shred him to pieces if not for those dainty wrists captured in his hands.

He opened his mouth with the full intention of attempting to explain himself again, but was interrupted by a sudden flood of light and sound as the doors burst open, revealing every single person he had hoped to avoid.

"What in the devil!" Gideon bellowed, thrusting his lantern into the room. He stood in the center of the orb of candlelight, wearing nothing but a pair of absurd striped pyjama trousers. "Release her at once!"

"Oh, for God's sake," Rose echoed from behind him, only moments ahead of Mrs. Laughlin's more fevered exclamation of "Oh, for God's sake!"

In such situations, when things looked much, much worse than they truly were, Alex had learned that the best tactic was to close one's mouth and, if applicable, to unhand the maiden. And so he did both, with all fantasies of a warm, soft bed scattering into the dust along with his hopes of remaining undetected.

She retreated immediately, rubbing her wrists as she scooted backward across the floor, wide, icy-blue eyes focused on him with the most potent accusatory glare Alex had ever seen. She scrambled away until she was forced to stop, her back coming up against one of the desk legs.

Gideon immediately offered her a hand and a whispered apology. She seemed reluctant to take it, glancing up at her savior for a moment before turning those heavily-fringed eyes back upon him. She rose to her feet without wavering from that intent, as though any attention taken off the intruder might once again make her vulnerable to attack.

Whoever this chit was, she was even more exquisite in the candlelight than she had been in the dark. It was just his luck that she was now terrified of him, whoever she was.

Alas, her identity was destined to remain a mystery as Rose floated forward to wrap her in an embrace and led her out of the room, with Mrs. Laughlin trotting close behind.

Alex attempted to grin up at his brother, but could only manage a wince over the throbbing pain in his face. The leather-bound book lying on its face an arm's reach away on the carpet seemed like the most likely weapon that had met his visage with such impressive force. He absently lifted his fingers to the area of damage, but drew them away quickly at the tenderness he encountered.

All the while, Gideon stood like a damned statue of judgement, glowering down at him.

"I say," Alex croaked, hoping he looked sufficiently abashed, "might you give me a hand up as well?"

Gideon narrowed his eyes, fury building around him like thunderclouds, but in the end, he did extend a hand and helped his little brother to his feet.

Now THAT THERE was light in the room, Alex could appreciate that there had been some changes to it since he had last sneaked in this way. Things seemed tidier, more carefully arranged, though perhaps it only appeared so because he was currently half blind. One eye examined the surroundings while the other was covered with a cool, wet cloth that Rose had slapped onto his face with all the fanfare of a fishwife tenderizing the day's catch.

She hadn't even stayed to lambast him. She'd given him a rather terrifyingly firm peck on his uninjured cheek and retreated back to see to the young woman he'd traumatized, leaving him alone with Gideon. At least she had thought to bring Gideon a dressing gown, which the latter had dutifully knotted around his waist.

Alex didn't fancy being lectured at the best of times, but if it had to happen, he preferred his brother not be half naked for the affair. He'd also prefer to have both of his eyes functioning and to not be suffering the early stages of a spectacular bottle-ache to boot.

Gideon had gathered up the weapon which had befallen the fragile bones of Alex's face and was flipping through it with what appeared to be genuine interest, rather than acknowledging the existence of Alex or the conversation that they both knew must happen next.

Alex had never been much for patient waiting, nor did he relish the prospect of being awake for much longer. It had been a spectacularly long night already, hadn't it? Still, when he opened his mouth to deliver the expected prompt for lecture commencement, instead he heard himself ask, "Who is she?"

"Hm?" Gideon replied, his head coming up from whatever was written in that dangerously sturdy book. "Who? The girl who bested you in clandestine combat?"

"Oh, I would hardly say she bested me!" Alex huffed. "I did have the upper hand when you came bursting through the door. I was just on the cusp of explaining myself to the damsel."

Gideon sighed, slapping the book closed. "She is Rose's cousin, come to stay with us for the autumn season. Do you know what this is?"

"A murder weapon?"

"This book is the ledger that the girl you just got into a bout with has been using for hours on end to plan a celebration. A celebration for *you,* in honor of your graduation from Oxford."

Alex raised his one visible eyebrow. "A party for me? Interesting concept. Whoever will come?"

"I'm inclined to let her reveal her plans to you if she so desires," Gideon replied. "Though I imagine she is presently regretting her charitable endeavor."

He considered Alex for a moment, a flicker of amusement passing over his typically stern countenance. "I'd never say it to the girl herself, but I've often hoped that the reality of the expenses incurred on your behalf would someday slap you right across the face."

"Oh, what a wit," Alex replied dryly, ignoring the responding chuckle that took hold of his brother. He reclined back on the chaise, draping the cloth over the throbbing pain in his eye and considering the ceiling. "Rose's cousin," he said wistfully. "They don't look much alike, do they?"

"No? I think they have many similarities," Gideon replied easily. "Perhaps if you see her in the daylight with an expression other than abject terror, you will observe the same."

His casual tone and the ease with which he chuckled these days only served to discomfit Alex. Gideon should already be delivering a tongue-lashing for the ages, ranting about how Alex should know better and be better and do better and so on. It wasn't that a married Gideon wasn't a welcome improvement, but one simply didn't know how to prepare for battle when the opponent had changed so much.

"Will you please just shout at me so I can go to sleep?" he said, sounding childish even to his own ears.

"You want me to shout at you?" Gideon replied with a raise of his eyebrows. "It's rather late to be making a ruckus, even if everyone is already awake. Besides, I suspect even if I did rally myself up to a good rant, you already know everything I was going to say."

"What were you thinking, Alex? We have a front door, Alex. Where did you come from? Where are your things? Must you always cause trouble, Alex?" Alex recited, sarcasm dripping from each word.

"Interesting. And?"

"I didn't want to wake you. The inn. Also the inn. And yes, evidently."

The two men sat in silence for a moment before the air was punctured with a light chuckle from Gideon followed by a sigh of amused defeat from Alex.

"We'll send Graham for your belongings in the morning," Gideon said, pushing himself to his feet. "You ought to rest up and contemplate exactly how and when you are going to apologize to Miss Blakely before your guests begin arriving. You've rather made a mess of first impressions."

"Blakely? Not d'Aubrey?" Alex said curiously. Miss Blakely. Why did that name sound familiar?

"They are related on Rose's mother's side," Gideon explained. "You might also want to formulate an apology to Rose, come to think of it."

"And one for you?" Alex suggested, rolling onto his side. "And perhaps one for Mrs. Laughlin as well?"

"Well, be careful with that," Gideon remarked, lifting one lantern and motioning to the other for Alex's use. "If you start apologizing for every time you've made an ass of yourself, it shall consume the remainder of your natural life."

"It's good to see you too, Brother," Alex said to Gideon's retreating back, an affectionate smile finding its way onto his face despite himself.

He was home.

CHAPTER 5

*G*loriana did not rise until the sun had arrived firmly in the center of the sky, and she did so with great difficulty, clawing back the blankets. She had thought for certain she wouldn't sleep at all after the fright she'd had, and yet she had apparently dropped into the deepest, quietest slumber of her life just after drinking a tincture of warm milk and honey from that housekeeper.

So heavily had she slept that even the movement of her eyelids felt like a feat of strength. Her limbs were heavy as logs, and the haze of blissful unconsciousness weighed heavily throughout her body.

She forced herself to blink, the shafts of sunlight breaking through the corners of her curtains sliding from hazy, wide globs of gold to thin beams scattered along the carpeted floor. She lifted a hand to her head, pushing her loose hair over her shoulder, and forced herself to sit upright.

Perched at the foot of her bed was yet another intruder,

watching her with the steady, judgmental gaze of a creature born to higher things. Gloriana had seen this cat lurking in the corners of the manor before, but this was the first time he had deemed her worthy of direct consideration. His big, yellow eyes met hers with unwavering, unapologetic steadiness that seemed to her like an offer of friendship.

"I think the housekeeper drugged me," she said to the cat. "What does laudanum taste like?"

The cat yawned, his long pink tongue curling outward between his sharp teeth, but did not otherwise answer.

"Yes, I suppose it tastes like sleep," Gloriana allowed with a sigh. "Perhaps I ought to be grateful instead of scandalized. Come here, you snob."

She crawled forward, extending her hand tentatively until the cat gave an impatient sigh and pushed his head into her fingers, allowing her to pet him. She couldn't repress a little grin and scooped him up and into her lap, leaning back against the headboard as he slumped, purring into her embrace. Perhaps she could remain like this, bundled in her sheets with this handsome orange tomcat, until winter arrived and it was time to go back to Devon.

Yes, that would be preferable to facing the Somers family after what she'd done last night.

How was she supposed to know that a strange man, creeping in through the window, wasn't a brigand or burglar?! And she'd done her level best to subdue him, hadn't she? Though the entire humiliating experience had been a stark reminder of the physical disadvantages of her sex. Perhaps she might ask Papa for fencing lessons or the like, just in case she ever found herself in such a situation again.

Alex Somers had been so strong, those big hands locked around her wrists, his handsome face lit by the shadow of moonlight, his wild, alarmed eyes intent upon her face. She had been helpless to fight him off, and certainly would have succumbed to ruin had he harbored any dastardly intentions. His tousled hair and open collar had not been those of a gentleman, had they? A gentleman would not have knocked her to her feet or restrained her. Gentlemen did not crawl in through windows under moonlight and overpower helpless girls.

She shivered, her memories sending a strange curl of excitement into her belly.

A rap at the bedroom door interrupted her reverie and sent that foreign spark of something she couldn't quite name dissipating into the harsh necessity of the day. Rose did not await an answer, slipping in through the smallest possible crack in the door and clipping it shut behind her.

"Good morning," Gloriana said, unmoving from her spot with her newfound ally.

"Good afternoon," Rose returned, taking brisk steps across the room to toss the curtains open.

Gloriana's hand flew up to shield her eyes from the bright sunlight while the tomcat huffed in outrage and leapt from the bed to crawl beneath it.

"Oh, Rosie, look what you've done!" Gloriana pouted. "Just when I was making headway!"

39

"He'll recover," Rose said with a flip of her hand. She glowed in the afternoon sun, a halo seeming to form around her neat golden ringlets. She gave Gloriana an encouraging smile and took a seat on the corner of the bed. "Nero could never resist a pretty girl."

"Nero?" Gloriana wrinkled her nose. "What a singularly horrid name! Who would name such a sweet creature after Nero?"

Rose tilted her head and bit her lip, turning her big brown eyes onto her cousin with a sparkle of amusement.

"Oh," Gloriana replied. "Of course she would."

"You missed breakfast," Rose said, "but you ought to appear for luncheon. Might as well clear the air as quickly as possible, especially with guests arriving soon."

"I can't," Gloriana whispered, the mortification she felt evident in her voice. "I can't face him after last night."

"Of course you can," Rose corrected. "He is the one who ought to be embarrassed, not you."

"I assaulted him!" she squeaked. "I was hiding in a dark room in the dead of night and did bodily harm to a member of the gentry! Furthermore, if anyone other than you had found us together thus, my reputation would have been utterly shattered."

"Your reputation is intact, I assure you," Rose said, patting her hand. "Alex is hardly a staunch gentleman, in any event. I am certain he wishes to make his apologies to you as quickly as possible so that we might all put this mess behind us. Now get up!"

Rose pushed herself to her feet, marching over to the armoire and tossing it open. "Let's put you in something angelic so that his sense of chivalry-laden regret is further piqued, hm? Come on now, I won't broker any argument."

Gloriana groaned, wanting nothing more than to flop back into her pillows for the remainder of her life, but she had long ago learned that arguing with her cousin when she was in a mood like this one was a losing battle. "White, then?" she said begrudgingly. "And you'll have to pin my hair up. I haven't time to curl it."

"Yes, naturally," Rose said, choosing a dress from the hanging array and holding it out for retrieval. "And perhaps pearls at your ears?"

Gloriana pushed herself from the soft comfort of her bed and paced reluctantly across the room to retrieve the gown. "What did he say? After everything, I mean," she asked, draping the gown over the foot of her bed and moving to her trunk to dig out underthings. She kept her face turned toward her trunk, not wanting her cousin to see the flush that rose on her cheeks. "Did he ask after me at all? Or was he very outraged?"

"I wouldn't know," Rose replied airily, selecting hair pins and a comb from the vanity table. "I gave him a cold compress for the bruise that was blossoming on his cheek and bid both Somers men goodnight. I can assure you, however, that insofar as Gideon is concerned, Alex is completely and solely at fault."

"Oh God, a bruise?" Gloriana moaned, spinning to face her cousin with a selection of underthings clutched to her chest. "Is it awful? He must loathe me! Must I face him, Rosie?"

"Yes." Rose sighed. "I'm afraid you must."

THE BRACING BREEZES of these early-autumn mornings had put the entire household into merry spirits. The windows of the ground floor had been thrown open to allow the temperate atmosphere to sail through the house, reminding everyone from viscount to scullery maid that the brutal heat of summer was well and truly past.

Gloriana did not find the cool air much of a relief for her nerves, though it at least provided a plausible excuse for the gooseflesh on the back of her neck. She was pacing in the hallway near the dining room, working her thumbnails along the insides of her fingers as she willed her heart to slow.

A large mirror captured her anxious ritual, the silver threads in her gown flashing like little claps of lightning every time she passed. She forced herself to stop, bracing her hands on the little table and looking hard at herself in the mirror. She wouldn't be so beside herself if Rosie had stayed to accompany her into the lion's den. But no, she had a child to look after now, and wanted to retrieve little Reggie for a luncheon *en famille* with everyone in such a jolly mood.

Glory pulled a face. Some little part of her whispered that she missed being Rosie's only concern, but she knew it was in bad taste to envy a toddler, especially for the attentions of his own mother. At least she had assisted in pulling together an attractive presentation before scuttling off to maternal duties.

Gloriana's wispy, platinum hair was swept from her brow

into a loose bun with tendrils framing her heart-shaped face. In white and silver and pearl, she did think she looked rather angelic. She pinched at her cheeks to raise the color, giving her lips a quick bite to raise the blood. Yes, she looked just fine, and what else was there to do if not adjust her appearance to delay the inevitable?

She could hear their voices from where she stood, carried on the cool gusts of wind through the open door of the dining room and into the halls around. There was laughter and the clink of silver on ceramic and enough conversation that individual words were difficult to parse.

She looked down at her hands gripping the table and forced herself to loosen her grip, allowing the blood to return to her knuckles. She gave herself one final glance, urging a smile onto her lips, and stepped out and into the open, nearing the open doors where the Somers family sat at their meal.

She was uncertain whether to be relieved that no one immediately noticed her. Gideon and Rose had their heads together, deep in some secret conversation with their plates forgotten before them and Reggie sleeping soundly against Gideon's chest. On the other end of the table was an amalgamation of all the things Gloriana dreaded.

Of course this would be the first time she'd see Heloise, disadvantaged as she was. She was holding a berry high in the air, teasing another child, this one a girl, who was standing on a chair with a frown of concentration as she reached for the food.

"Go on, Hel," Alex laughed from next to her. He was at the foot of the table, watching the display with amusement. He looked devastatingly noble and well-groomed this morning, not a trace of the rumpled rogue who had toppled her to the carpet the night before. He was turned slightly away from where she stood, and as such she could not tell if his face was marred or not from her ill-conceived blow to his person.

"There you are!" Rose called, her bright and cheerful voice immediately drawing the attention of everyone at the table to the door.

The little girl saw her opportunity to swipe the berry, and plopped down on her chair while slapping fruit into her mouth with the palm of her hand. She was the only one who appeared uninterested in Gloriana's arrival.

Alex immediately shoved his chair back and came to his feet, turning to face her in full.

She did her best not to wince at the sight of him, where there was very clearly a shiny, purple bruise around the curve of his eye. She had done that. She had marred that lovely face. She would never have predicted that anyone might distract her from a reunion with Heloise Somers, but she could not tear her eyes from Alex's face.

"Miss Blakely," he said, his voice somewhat throaty. "I had hoped you would join us. You must allow me to apologize at length for our last encounter."

"Oh," she replied, sounding meek even to herself. "That isn't necessary. It is I who ought apologize."

"Yes, yes," Gideon said with impatience. "Everyone sit and we'll get to apologizing in good order. Thank you for joining us, Miss Blakely."

Gloriana tore her eyes from Alex, who was still standing

stock-still as though at attention for a commanding officer, to nod to the head of the house. "Lord Somers."

She imagined the wind was pulling her inside, weaving its way around her body, teasing at the fine hem of her skirt and tugging her toward the chair opposite Heloise. There was nothing for it. She would have to greet her nemesis.

Heloise Somers looked like a cat who'd snatched her owner's prize canary right from its cage. She wore a curious half smile as Gloriana approached, and had not adjusted her posture at all.

To Gloriana's distress, Heloise looked very well. Her long mane of ruby-red hair was flung over her shoulder in a long braid, and she wore a fashionably casual cut of deep-blue cotton. She seemed to have grown out of the spindly, bony figure she'd sported through their teen years, and now had a modestly feminine figure that made Gloriana all the more resentful of her own slender frame.

"Lady Heloise," she said tightly as a footman drew back a chair for her. "You are looking well."

"Gloriana," Heloise returned with that infuriating amusement in her tone. It was just like her to refuse proper address. "You are looking the same as ever."

Unwilling to rise to the bait, Glory turned her eyes onto the little girl who sat between the two Somers siblings. She looked to be a little older than Reggie, with hair of burnished auburn and big, dark eyes. "I'm Gloriana," she said to the child. "It is a pleasure to make your acquaintance, Miss...?"

The little girl caught her lip between her teeth and looked quickly to Heloise for guidance.

"Go on," Heloise said in a voice so sweet and soft that Gloriana could scarce believe its origin. "Tell Miss Blakely your name."

The little girl didn't look as though she wished to do anything of the sort, but under the unflinching gaze of the elder lady, she finally squirmed herself into squeaking "Callie!" and immediately hiding her face in Heloise's side.

"Oh, goodness," Gloriana said, glancing at her cousin. "I didn't mean to upset the child."

"It's all right," Rose replied. "Caroline is learning to not be so shy, isn't that right, my love?"

An inaudible affirmation came from the girl's muffled face.

"She is our cousin, from the Americas," Alex explained, his bright green eyes drawing Gloriana's across the table as he slid back into his seat. "She was tragically orphaned as a babe and taken in as a ward to House Somers."

"Oh, have you family in America?" Gloriana asked politely, her heart racing in her chest.

"Our mother is American," Heloise said for him, still smiling like a sphinx. "The Cunningham Steel heiress. Surely you recall commenting on that connection at length?"

A forkful of eggs was just the thing to avoid having to formulate a response. Gloriana gave a noncommittal nod as she turned her focus to her food. Misery at the memory of her own schoolgirl taunting rose up in her throat. How was she going to survive this? If Heloise told her brothers about the barbs she'd tossed, they would surely hate her just as much as their sister did. Suddenly, that prospect distressed her very much.

She must find a way to speak to Alex Somers in private and explain why she had been lurking in the dark. It was humiliating that she had maimed him so just before a party in his honor. All of those people would arrive to see that shining black eye and ... well, someone would have to give an explanation. Surely it wouldn't be the truth!

"Gloriana Blakely!" Alex exclaimed suddenly, as though it were the solution to a puzzle and not her name.

The outburst drew the attention of everyone at the table to him. Rather than shrink from the attention, he grinned broadly, revealing a set of even white teeth, and slapped the table happily.

"Alex," Gideon sighed.

"That's why your name sounded familiar!" he said, with no care at all for his brother's disapproval or Reggie's sleepy blinking. "Gloriana Blakely! You're the one who tormented Hel at school! Ghastly Gloriana!"

"Alex!" both Gideon and Heloise snapped.

"I?" Gloriana gasped indignantly. "*I* tormented *her*?"

There was a beat of silence as members of the table exchanged glances. Rose sighed, pressing two fingers into her temple, as though it had suddenly begun to throb.

Heloise cleared her throat, placing a hand on little Caroline's head. "Perhaps we shouldn't—"

"I agree," Gloriana said quickly.

Alex's grin only grew, glancing between the two ladies. "Oh, this is going to be delightful," he decided, snatching his fork back up to return to his lunch. "Simply delightful."

"I hate you," Heloise muttered.

"No you don't," Alex returned, still smiling.

CHAPTER 6

The cool breezes of the day swept into a warm and colorful sunset, rustling the late summer grasses that flourished between the manor house and the cliffs to the north.

Alex had left his jacket behind for this walk in the twilight. The warmth of his sleeping niece burrowed into his side was doing just fine to ward off the light chill in the air. She clung to his neck, her legs wrapped around his middle, with her precious little head nestled into his shoulder. Introducing her to Gloriana had been the first time he'd had to tell the lie of her origins, and even as the story had left his lips, he'd felt it sounded wrong.

It was unnatural to deny her the truth of her place in the family, but what choice did they have?

"I told you she was dangerous." Heloise sighed, brushing her fingers against her face in the spot that mirrored his bruised cheekbone. "Though in this light I can barely see the damage."

Her easy gait alongside him, with the wind pulling tresses of her red-gold curls loose from her plait, struck him in a way he hadn't expected. She smiled as though she hadn't a care in the world, as though her future hadn't been taken from her, and as though she had somehow found the wisdom of adulthood hidden in some secret hideaway at Somerton while he was gone.

It seemed impossible, but somehow, while he had been wrapping up his infernal degree back in Oxford, his little sister had become a woman grown. Of course, becoming a mother, even in secret, likely had that effect on many a girl. Still, she strode with the easy confidence of a lady born to walk on Yorkshire soil, the wind nipping at her in an affectionate way, as though she were part of the moor itself.

He shrugged with the shoulder that was not serving as a pillow to a wee girl and shot her a look out of the corner of his eye. "Perhaps you've all been dramatizing how bad it looks from the beginning, hm? My honor couldn't stand if I had truly been beaten blue by such a little thing."

"Honestly," she laughed, "I'm somewhat impressed. I would've never guessed she had that kind of strength."

"Mm, perhaps it's best your feud never came to fisticuffs, then?"

Heloise scoffed, flicking her braid over her shoulder. "I'm only impressed as a woman whose strength is evident. I would be well armed in such a confrontation. Better than you were, I daresay."

"Hel, you wound me!" he replied with his customary cheer. "After all, I was taken quite by surprise in the dead of night."

She made a noncommittal sound, shaking her head affectionately. "I still say we ought to have taken Boudicea," she said, stretching her arms over her head. "It's a lovely walk, but a long one this late in the day. You'll have to take a lantern on the way back."

Even with the first hint of an autumn chill, Alex found the walk between Somerton and the dower house a pleasant endeavor. Heloise's bay mare was wholly unsuited to such a quick and banal journey, anyway. Long, aimless walks over the grounds were the hallmark of the twilight hours, as far as Alex was concerned, and he'd be damned if that uppity horse was going to take this experience from him.

"The moon will be plenty bright," he assured her. "It was fat and full last night, and I managed to walk from the gate to the approach with as clear a view as you'd find any summer afternoon."

"Hmm," Heloise responded, "arriving by the light of the full moon, only to be locked in passionate embrace with a beautiful maiden. You know what Tatiana Everstead would say about that."

"Who the devil is Tatiana Everstead?"

"Oh, you'll meet her soon enough. I'd bet my life on her inclusion in the guest list." Heloise sighed. "She's Gloriana's shadow, dark and mysterious where Glory is light and angelic. Mrs. Arlington used to say that they were one another's most fetching accessory."

"I see," Alex said, curiosity clear in his tone. "And she has beliefs about the full moon, does she?"

"Oh yes," Heloise laughed. "And the new moon and the crescent moon and for dropping salt on the table or lighting a candle the wrong way. She is nothing but nonsense superstition, parceled up in a pretty package. The rumor at school was that her grandmother was a gypsy."

"Fascinating," Alex said, his mind failing to build this dark temptress that could match the light of Miss Blakely's angelic glow.

The arrival of some appealing young maidens might be just the thing to break the awkwardness he'd caused in the household. The reality of beautiful women was more powerful than his failing imagination anyhow.

"She's most certainly invited her as a temptation for you, unmarried as you are," Hel continued. "That girl does nothing without some manner of conniving behind it, and Tia is just your type of woman."

"What, married?" Alex laughed. "What do you know about my type of woman?"

"Only what I hear in the township," she responded tightly. "Which is altogether too much information for a sister to hear, I assure you."

"I don't meddle with debutantes," he told her, the honest tone of his voice offset by a twinkle in his eye. "Married ladies make far less fuss and tend to know their way around the boudoir. Far superior, if you ask me."

"Well, I didn't," she clipped, making him chuckle.

"Why should the Blakely girl try to tempt me with other women?" he asked, shifting Callie's weight on his hip. "She herself is unmarried. Surely she aspires to capture a man such as myself in matrimony."

Heloise cut her eyes to him with a sharpness that could split wood. "Do not even joke about such a thing. You know she was originally to wed Gideon? She wouldn't have him."

"Naturally," Alex replied without thinking, the joke softening the tension in her shoulders. "Wait, what are you on about? He has been smitten with Rosie from the start."

She shrugged. "I do not know how the story unfolded, simply that he set out to wed Gloriana and came home with Rose. From what I understand, Miss Blakely has already turned down a great deal of proposals, and, if you'll forgive me, from men with far more status and direction than you, my beloved brother."

"How dare you!" he gasped theatrically, grinning at the way she rolled her eyes. "So what is her game, then? Ever a spinster?"

"How should I know?" she snapped. "Do you think the wretch pours her heart out to the likes of me? If you're so interested, go ask her yourself."

"I might," he replied, just to irk her.

She responded with an icy silence that was more affectation than true annoyance.

The crickets sang lower tonight than they had for the weeks prior. Soon they'd go to ground and the green would fade to orange and red and yellow. Soon the soft grass that swished beneath their boots tonight would turn to the crunch of fall foliage, and the whisper of a chill in the air would darken into a robust and frosty gale.

The dower house towered in the distance, only a few lights on within as the staff went about their evening duties. It had always unsettled him, that house. Perhaps because it had always been vacant. His paternal grandmother had never used it, opting instead to live out her golden years in the estate proper. So, even in the days of his father's reign, there had been no dowager to light its halls. Instead, it had stood a foreboding husk, much like one might imagine a viscountess without her lord, watching with empty eyes over the grounds that led back to the manor house, the seat of Somerton.

When their father died, they had never expected Ruthie Somers nee Cunningham to trade her Philadelphia mansion for a dower house in the country. She did not even bother returning to Yorkshire for her husband's funeral. What a surprise that she had taken up residence in the dower house after all, some years later, and at the behest of a bastard grandchild rather than the passing of her spouse.

He shivered, whether from the cold or thoughts of his mother, he could not say, and stopped just short of the pebbled drive.

Heloise turned to him with an impatient frown. Sternness was new to her, a necessity of rearing a little one. When she scolded Callie, Alex had found, a little line appeared right between her ruddy eyebrows, like an exclamation point on her face to punctuate her authority. This little line had made itself present as his sister regarded his hesitation to proceed.

"She isn't home," she snapped, propping her hands on her hips. "She's been in York for weeks, up to her personal business. When will you cease this nonsense?"

"I don't know what you mean," he replied easily, shifting forward to hand the sleeping toddler over to her mother.

"You know very well," Hel hissed back, mindful of her volume. She gathered Callie into her arms and shot Alex a hard look over her daughter's ringlets. "You ought to come in. I can get you a lantern and a cup of tea before you walk back in the cold."

"I'd rather not," he said, shoving his hands into his pockets. Perhaps it had been a mistake to leave his jacket behind, after all. The wind swirled around him, rustling his cropped shock of hair around his face and raising gooseflesh along his neck.

"Fine," Hel replied with a roll of her eyes. "Do be careful walking back. I would hate for you to get yourself beaten senseless again."

"Would you hate it, though?" he wondered as she turned on her heel to walk toward the front door.

She looked over her shoulder with a little smirk, silhouetted by the warm light from within. "I would hate to once again miss the entertainment, Brother," she replied sweetly. Then, in a flash of skirts and the click of a door, she vanished into the house, leaving Alex alone with the night and his thoughts.

By the time Alex re-entered the manor house, his fingers and toes had come to acknowledge the sudden power of a Yorkshire autumn. Had it always arrived like this? With a few puffs of cool air and then the theft of all warmth?

He frowned. It was only old men who grumbled about the weather. The cold had never bothered him before. It must be other things on his mind making his constitution fragile. He was not accustomed to this constant flutter of anxiety in his chest, nor any manner of discomfort over a woman.

Women loved him, didn't they? And he loved them right back.

This one was very easily one of the most beautiful he'd ever seen, and better than that, a wonderful means to antagonize Heloise. Yet here he was floundering like a nervous damsel in her presence because of that damned embarrassment of a first encounter.

He mounted the stairs with a sigh. He had walked himself through an eloquent apology speech throughout the morning hours, and yet when she'd appeared like a beam of pure sunlight in the doorway of the dining room, he'd barely managed to expel a monosyllabic plea for forgiveness before her attention was stolen by the others.

He had concocted a reason for his midnight antics that sounded respectable and plausible, and had woven in a humorous compliment on her brawn. The whole speech had transitioned artfully into a gracious thanks for her efforts to celebrate his achievements and his eager thoughts of the revels to come.

But no, he had mucked that up. He couldn't even remember what he'd said to her, only that she'd cut him off about three words in. Damn it all. What a waste of his oratory talents! Was anything worse than composing a speech that would never be delivered?

Without even really thinking about it, he found himself

wandering toward the second-floor library. That room had been largely ignored throughout his lifetime, save for the odd spot of rainy-day reading. What was this girl about, suddenly making use of it?

He found himself in front of the door, a solid slab of warm, lacquered wood, and debated between knocking upon a possibly empty room or barging in on Miss Blakely for the second time. He sighed, all his rebellious instincts currently licking their wounds, and rapped smartly upon the wood.

"Enter!" a melodious voice called from within.

Well, it was too late to reconsider now, wasn't it? He straightened his shoulders and turned the doorknob, pressing it gently open, the low lamplight spilling out into the hallway as he stepped within.

She was bent over the little secretary desk next to the fire-place, her quill scratching away in that little ledger. Her elegant neck was bare, her hair spilling over one shoulder in a glorious mess of platinum ringlets. From here, the aura of firelight created a glow about her body, creating the illusion that she and not the flames were the source of light in the room.

He noticed with a twist of something dangerous in his gut that her feet were bare, peeking out from the hem of her gown, their slippers discarded on their sides next to a nearby ottoman. There was something unbelievably intimate about being in a room with a woman whose feet were bare.

"Mrs. Laughlin," she smiled without lifting her head. "I told you I would be all right. I doubt I'll be ambushed again."

"One can never be certain," Alex replied. He leaned against the doorway, crossing his arms over his chest, biting down on the urge to chuckle at the way she startled, like a white rabbit set upon by a fox.

"Lord Alex," she said thinly, dropping her quill neatly into the center of her ledger and turning those otherworldly blue eyes onto him. "I apologize for my presumption. How may I help you?"

"You needn't do anything in particular," he responded, sounding more flippant than he felt. "I only wished to offer you a proper apology, without the audience of my brother and sister creating an air of polite artifice."

She raised her eyebrows, but did not otherwise respond, her body still half turned toward the ledger.

He took a deep breath and did his best not to sigh on the exhalation. "I am unsure if Rosie has told you aught about me, but I'm afraid I have a bit of a reputation as the reckless one in the Somers family. Last night was an unfortunate testament to that assessment. I never dreamed that anyone would be in this room, and when I realized I had frightened you, the last thing I should have done was attempt to restrain you."

"Indeed?" she murmured, her expression unreadable.

He nodded. "While I am quite used to making an ass of myself within the confines of my family, I am deeply uncomfortable with having subjected you, a guest, to my foolishness. I am truly sorry to have frightened you so. I only hope you will forgive me, and perhaps, given time, allow me to make a better impression upon you."

She pressed her lips together, her eyes assessing him where he stood. After a moment, she sighed, turning herself from her work to face him fully. "I am not entirely without blame, you know. After all, I did give you that striking bruise you're wearing."

"Striking, is it?" he laughed, raising his fingers to brush the swollen flesh. "Perhaps it's not all bad, then."

"Perhaps not," she replied, gracing him with the fairest hint of a smile.

Alex could see why this girl unsettled Heloise. A creature who kept her true feelings so carefully contained was a dangerous thing, particularly when combined with the type of beauty that made people want to talk without end.

He cleared his throat, his heart beating slightly faster than he thought it ought to. He'd gotten the apology out, hadn't he? And now she was looking at him with calm expectation as though he might deliver some interesting performance for her amusement.

"I also wanted to thank you for that," he said, gesturing toward the ledger. "Gideon said you have put in a great deal of work to arrange for a celebration. I can't tell you how much I appreciate it."

"Oh." She flushed, her veneer cracking just a little as she pushed a handful of curls behind her dainty ear. "It is nothing. I was staring down a long few months of inactivity and this gave me an opportunity to make myself useful."

Inactivity? Did that mean that she was not here of her own accord, then? That would make sense, wouldn't it? For why else would she agree to spend so long within spitting distance of Heloise?

"Might I ask who you've invited?" he asked, not trusting himself to step closer and peer at the ledger himself.

"An assortment of connections in various fields," she said with a slight frown. "Your brother was not very helpful in explaining your particular ambitions to me, and so I'm afraid I attempted to create a varied guest list rather than a focused one. I did include Lord Moorvale, though. I understand he is an intimate of House Somers."

"Sheldon is coming?" Alex grinned, pleasantly surprised. "I didn't know he was back from the Continent."

"Only just," she replied, nodding to a stack of letters on the desk. "He was a friend during my debut Season, and I am much looking forward to seeing him again."

A flash of something like discomfort sent a ripple of warmth through Alex's middle. Sheldon liked pretty girls and had always done quite well for himself in his pursuits. Had he set his hat at the delectable Miss Blakely during their acquaintance? Furthermore, had he enjoyed any success in the endeavor?

She pushed herself from the desk with a little moan of relief as her bare feet sank into the plush carpet. "Oh," she breathed, letting her eyes flicker shut and rubbing one little hand over the back of her neck. "I have been sitting for far too long. Rose says I'm going to give myself a scholar's hump!"

Alex had opened his mouth to respond, but couldn't quite force the words out. Standing as she was in front of the light of the fire, the diaphanous white dress she wore created a sort of translucent shroud about her shapely legs. He could see them clearly through the fabric, spread slightly as she pushed herself up onto her toes and back to stretch her languid little body.

What would be the appropriate response? If she'd let him, he'd happily rub the tension from her neck and shoulders, though he supposed that would exacerbate the trouble he'd come here to relieve.

"You seem tired," he managed, though his throat was completely dry. "Might I walk you back to your rooms?"

Her eyes fluttered open, focusing on him from across the room under hooded lids with a kind of sanguine familiarity. "I'm not sure that would be proper, my Lord," she said, her lips curling into a teasing smile. "We should both be grateful that our little escapade last night didn't compromise me completely."

He hadn't considered that, but he realized immediately that it was terrifyingly true. Being caught tumbling about on the floor with an unmarried girl in the dead of night should have lowered the gavel completely on his future. He shook his head, a nervous chuckle escaping him.

"I imagine you are just as relieved that it did not as I am," he said. "Unless you'd rather have caught a prospectless second son in betrothal, of course. If that's the case, we could always give it another go."

She glanced up at him in surprise, and he forced himself to smile reassuringly, raising his hands to indicate that he'd only been joking. Why had he said that? He'd been here to apologize, not to continue to demonstrate his impropriety. It was simply hard to think straight with her standing there, cool as a queen, looking the way she did.

"It is a little unfair, don't you think?" she mused, turning to tidy up the desk, innocently unaware of the way her body was revealed through the shadow and light from the fire. From the side, he could see the pert roundness of her backside glowing through the fabric of her dress, a fact that did little to slow the thud of his heartbeat.

"It seems unjust that such an event could cost a girl her virtue," she continued, oblivious. "Why, it's all the consequence of being ruined and none of the fun."

"The fun?" he croaked, painfully aware that he needed to flee this room before his baser urges took complete control of him. *Fun!*

"Mm," she replied, biting her lip as she arranged her work into neat piles. Glancing up at him with a mischievous twinkle in her eye, she said, "If a girl must needs be ruined, she hopes it is through passionate embrace, not tragic misunderstanding."

"Ah, of course," he replied cautiously. Would it have been tragic, then? Being stuck with him? Or perhaps the tragedy was that his hands were on her in defense and not seduction. That particular fact was indeed seeming more tragic by the moment.

She smirked to herself as though she could hear his thoughts and returned to her task. She kept her gaze locked on her tidying as she spoke, elegant white hands adjusting things just so. "You are quite strong, you know," she said softly. "If you *had* harbored roguish intentions last night, I'm well aware I'd not have escaped them."

All of the blood in Alex's body seemed to drain directly to his groin at that sentiment. It was too much, and the naive little thing likely thought she was paying him a compliment for his chivalry rather than putting filthy scenarios into his mind.

"I will bid you goodnight, then," he said tightly, grabbing the doorknob and wrenching open his means of escape.

He saw her lift her head in surprise, imagined he heard the beginnings of her returning his farewell, but by the time she spoke, he was already well away, fleeing to his room like a man pursued by the most ravenous of demons.

CHAPTER 7

*W**here in the blazes is Alex Somers?*

She hadn't seen hide nor red hair of the fool since dinner two nights prior. Never mind that he hadn't deigned to speak to her beyond crisp formalities in almost two weeks. If she had offended him that night in the library, he very well had been given plenty of time to get over it or demand recompense. His absence just now was the cruelest sort of revenge!

It was a perfect autumn afternoon. The sun was shining a glorious gold over Somerton, with only a few fat clouds for garnish. Light breezes sent colored leaves in charming whirlwinds about the property. If not for the missing guest of honor, it would have been a nigh ideal day to begin the festivities.

Several of the guests had arrived already. In the company of Rose and Gideon, they had first welcomed Lord Felix Benton, his wife, and their two daughters from their coach early enough this morning to invite the whole lot for breakfast. The Bentons were a prodigious family, with social sway that even the Regent himself would envy. They certainly had taken note of the absence of their host, though were far too well-bred to comment upon it.

A few hours thereafter, a coach had arrived from the township carrying a few important figureheads, added to the invite list by Viscount Somers himself—the vicar and his curate, a stately physician, and a man who Gloriana gathered served in a capacity similar to a mayor.

The inclusion of these four had upset the balance of gentlemen to ladies that Gloriana had so painstakingly engineered, and so as a solution, Rose offered to invite some eligible ladies of middling status from the surrounding areas for the organized events. It would have to do, of course, but the fact that her event had now expanded to include the *demi-monde* did not particularly thrill Gloriana.

They were only hours from their first revelry, an old-fashioned country ball, and yet the prodigal, enigmatic, *infuriating* Lord Alex Somers was nowhere to be found! Who were they here to toast if not him? What sort of ingrate was he?

Gloriana had never been a nervous girl. She had never paced or fretted before big events. Even as a child, she had never stayed awake the night before Christmas, nor trembled at presentations and tests of skill. However, today she was wringing her hands like a harried matron, gritting her teeth against the urge to bounce her leg as she waited, staring out the large, sunny windows that overlooked the drive.

Rose, in her eternal tranquility, was perched beside her,

making steady progress on a bit of needlework embroidery, as though she hadn't a care in the world. She was humming softly to herself, some manner of lullaby, lost in her task as her needle flashed in a steady rhythm.

Gloriana wasn't sure if she wanted to shake her cousin or beg her for reassurance. Her own needlework was discarded on the cushion next to her, replaced by Nero, who had appeared only to crawl into her lap and promptly fall into a deep and oblivious sleep. Usually, stroking the soft fur of a sweet feline would do wonders for her mood, but she was certain her heart was going to leap out of her chest if the fool didn't reappear soon.

"He is likely with Heloise," Rose said, softly enough so as to not startle either girl or cat. "She has had run of the dower house for the last few weeks, which has plenty of extra room."

"I see," Gloriana replied, the tightness of her tone reflected in her posture. "It might have been well to inform us of that."

Rose giggled, setting her project aside and tilting her head to take in her cousin. "I've never seen you so fussed, Glory. It's a little unseemly."

"I agree!"

Rose sighed affectionately, reaching over to give Nero a scratch between the ears. "Alex has a way of getting under people's skin without intending to. I assure you he is oblivious to the implications of his absence this morning. He is a fool for certain, but a harmless one."

Gloriana narrowed her eyes at this minimization. How

could he possibly not realize that he should be here? "You know he propositioned me," she snapped.

She told herself that she was desperate to channel her own outrage into Rose, but the truth was that she'd been dying to tell someone about that encounter for weeks. She had been unable to stop it playing in her mind since it happened. "The night after the mishap," she continued. "He came into the study to apologize and said if I was unhappy with not being ruined, he'd be willing to give it another go!"

"Oh, he's propositioned me too," Rose said with a toss of her hand. "He doesn't mean anything by it."

"Rosie!"

Rose's laughter drowned out Gloriana's shock. She had changed very much since becoming a woman wed. The old Rose would have furrowed her brow and taken Gloriana's hands in her own, determined to make everything all right. At least, that's how Glory thought this exchange ought to have gone.

She didn't even have time to formulate a response, as the cadence of horse hooves on earth and the crunch of carriage wheels on gravel alerted them that more guests had arrived. The only thing to be done was to check her appearance once in a hallway mirror and hurry after her cousin to the grand double doors to greet this next set of well-wishers for a guest of honor who was nowhere to be seen.

Two coaches had arrived. The first was modest and practical, pulled by a pair of geldings that looked more durable than well-bred. The other was a glossy, black affair with a coat of arms painted on either door and a set of horses that wouldn't be out of place in a royal parade.

Evidently the driver at Somerton, that surly Scottish fellow, took great issue with one of these two coaches. He was striding across the green with his finger pointed in their direction, bellowing something unintelligible to a slight little woman who hurried after him, grinning from ear to ear.

Gloriana rather thought that if that man was carrying on so in her company, she would not look so pleased about it.

Her oblivious gaping at the spectacle meant she only heard her name when it was called a second time, more insistently from a familiar voice behind her.

She spun on her heel, her sky-blue dress belling out around her legs and, seemingly with pure instinct, found herself running toward Tatiana Everstead, her arms outstretched, and a glow of giddy excitement in her chest.

The two collided in a warm embrace, their squeals of excitement as intertwined as their arms. Tia's blue-black hair and crimson traveling kit swirled into a beautiful chaos against Gloriana's coloring and dress. It had been only a little over a month since they'd last seen each other, but to Glory, it felt like a lifetime apart. There was nothing she needed more than something of her own world here in the strange, alien life at Somerton.

"Oh, Tia, I'm so glad to see you!" she sighed, pulling back to take in the lovely face of her closest friend, who beamed in response, clearly sharing the sentiment.

"We would have been here sooner," Tatiana responded with a throaty little sigh, "but Lady Bluestocking and her twin insisted we stop at York to look at a pile of rocks for half a day!"

"It is a fort," the prim voice of Eleanor Applegate corrected as she stepped daintily from the coach, her petite form coming nearly a head shorter than the other two girls. "And it's a thousand years old, Tia! How can you not feel excited about that?"

Nell pursed her lips when she disapproved of her friends, drawing her pixie-like face into something that could never quite pull off sternness. Gloriana always thought that the more worked up Nell got, the more one wanted to pat her on the head and feed her biscuits, which only inflamed her temper and made her all the more adorable. It was a vicious cycle, truly.

Her mousy brown hair had clearly fallen askew from its arrangement into a bun and sagged too far to the right of her head. She was wearing her wire-frame spectacles, which meant she must have been buried in a book right up until the carriage door opened. Gloriana sighed. She really was quite hopeless.

Her twin brother was much better suited to their bookish interests, having had the good sense to be born a man. He was a tall, thin fellow who climbed out after his sister, squinting against the sunlight with hair that had also been disrupted during the ride. If she had to guess, Glory would assume that they'd both fallen asleep with their heads bumping against the coach windows while Tatiana glared at them, adrift in torturous silence.

"Miss Blakely!" Peter said with a shy smile. "It is lovely to see you again."

"And you," she returned warmly. "We missed you this Season in London."

He blushed, scratching at his disheveled hair. "I'm certain it was more festive for my absence," he said with a crooked smile. "I'm looking forward to festivities here, though! I know Lord Alex from Oxford, as it happens. I consider him a friend."

"Do you?" she said, her eyebrows lifting.

Now what on this green earth could Peter Applegate and Alex Somers *possibly* have in common? The urge to take Peter by his arm, whisk him back into the carriage and interrogate him was stronger than she might have anticipated, if one could ever anticipate such an unlikely pair of friends.

The boom of a barking dog caught the attention of their little ensemble, turning them all to see a large brown bloodhound leap past the driver of the more well-appointed coach and come tearing toward them at a terrifying speed. Even if there had been a moment to react—and there was not—the dog's burst of movement would have eclipsed any action they might have taken.

The dog, however, was uninterested in them, and bounded right past toward the Scots driver on the lawn and the little woman with him, both of whom knelt in enthusiasm to receive what looked to be a very sloppy greeting from said canine.

"I don't recall inviting a dog," Gloriana murmured, watching the display with curiosity. The grumpy Scottish fellow was allowing the dog to lap at his face with what appeared to be genuine pleasure, while the woman had knelt down to scratch it on the head. Never would she have imagined the man had such a soft spot, particularly not for such a common creature as a hound.

She turned over her shoulder to see what else might emerge from the mysterious carriage and witnessed the shiny, black boots of an exceptionally large man land with a spray into the gravel as he maneuvered his frame out of a vehicle that appeared entirely too small to accommodate him.

He was a startling sort of handsome, with a shock of dark hair and a shadow of stubble over his jaw. He sighed in seeming relief to be free of his confines and locked his eyes on Rose, a brilliant smile blossoming on his face. "My Lady Somers!" he boomed, marching over to greet her. "You are looking very fine!"

"It's the Marquis of Moorvale," Gloriana sighed in relief. "Which means *that*," she jerked her thumb over her shoulder, "is his often-lauded pet, Echo."

"Rather a large chap, isn't he?" Peter commented, watching as Moorvale planted hearty kisses on each of Rose's cheeks.

"Moorvale," Tatiana echoed, her dark eyes narrowed and still affixed on the carriage rather than its occupants. She lifted her arm to point to the painted crest that adorned the still-open side door. "What is that on his coat of arms?" she demanded, forcing everyone to look. "A crow?"

"It's a bat," both Applegate siblings said in unison.

Tia's face seemed to drain of color. She bit her bottom lip and turned in a sudden fluster, dark red skirts gathered up in her fists, and took off in a trot to the manor house without any of her entourage in tow, black curls bouncing in time with her haste.

Nell and Gloriana exchanged a look. Whatever omens were foretold by a bat on a carriage door would likely be revealed to them in due course, but one often hoped Tatiana could mask her eccentricities for at least small moments of societal obligation.

There was no time to dwell upon it, however, as the Marquis of Moorvale had noticed them standing there and was excitedly making his way across the green to be introduced.

"Miss Blakely," he cried, "you are looking beautiful as ever!"

Gloriana put on her most brilliant smile, rising to a proper posture, introductions brewing in her mind. Somewhere deep in her soul, a spark flew, igniting a fire that the machinations of Society could inspire within her. The party had begun, she realized, with or without Alex Somers.

"You don't think this color washes me out?" Gloriana frowned. She was plucking at her gown, which hung on a door hook, pulling the skirt this way and that under the light opposite the pallor of her forearm. "It looked so glorious in the shop, but in the candlelight, I just don't know."

Tatiana just rolled her eyes through the mirror on her vanity table, refusing to engage in such nonsense, while Nell murmured the requisite assurances that the color suited Gloriana's skin very well until Gloriana gave up on her appraisal and dropped the fabric with a huff.

The three of them had retreated into the room that Tia and Nell would be sharing during their stay to dress for tonight's ball. As a result, they'd had to watch from the window as the devastatingly handsome Nathaniel Atlas arrived, just around sunset. Though it was all from a considerable distance, and with only the low light of late afternoon illuminating the scene, none could argue that his manners and graciousness were exceptional when greeting Lord and Lady Somers at the threshold. All three of them had sighed wistfully as he doffed his hat and made his way into the manor with the impeccable swagger of a man truly refined.

Nell was already as dressed and primped as she intended to get, and was curled on the bed, sorting through the things in her valise. She had packed what appeared to be an equal quantity of reading and clothing, and was cradling one of her books in her lap, considering it rather intensely.

"You ought to take your spectacles off now," Gloriana told her, "so you don't have a red rivet on your nose throughout the dance."

Nell scrunched up her nose in annoyance. "I bet Peter will wear his spectacles to the ball."

"It's true," Gloriana sighed, pacing over to the bed and crawling in across from her friend, her loose ringlets draping down around her elbows, "and he'll forego the stays and petticoats too, I wager. Come now, I'm only looking out for you. What's that you're so enamored with, anyhow?"

"Oh, it's not mine," Nell said, blinking up at Gloriana, her eyes magnified behind the frames of her glasses. "It came for Heloise shortly after she left Mrs. Arlington's. I always meant to forward it along to her and never did. I was hoping to see her tonight before the ball."

"Give me that," Glory snapped, snatching up the volume curiously. It wasn't a very expensive thing, from the looks of it, the bindings made of some hollow material with a scratchy surface. The title was inked across the front in spiky, bold letters: *Caesar et Cleopatra: Un Histoire d'Amour*.

"Erm," Gloriana snorted, turning her eyes up to a pinch-faced Nell. "Are you certain this belongs to Heloise? It looks rather salacious."

"It arrived from France. A gift," Nell said, "and I'd thank you to give it back."

"Just a moment," Glory snickered, carefully cracking the cover open. Inside was an inscription in a hand that was decidedly masculine, if not particularly elegant.

Thinking of you Always ...

Forever Yours - C.L.

"Fascinating," she murmured, passing the book behind her for Tatiana's inspection.

"Oh, you two!" Nell cried as Tia spun away to conduct her own investigation. "I'm sure that's private!"

Nell had never been the target of Heloise's mischief, and though she'd observed plenty of it, she seemed to lack the natural mechanisms of sororal solidarity that should preclude any sort of good relations with the harpy. The two of them had been cordial at Mrs. Arlington's, friendly even, despite the open hostility between the others. Nell's effortless ability to move from one social circle to the other had never ceased to irritate Gloriana.

"My, my," Tatiana cooed, flipping through the first few pages, "it's from a sweetheart! Heloise Somers has a paramour! Can you imagine? It must be an officer, having shipped from France."

Gloriana scoffed. "I'd wager it's some deck swab with no refinement to speak of."

"It doesn't matter!" Nell huffed, shoving herself from the mattress to snatch the book back. She clutched it against her chest, glaring at her friends. "It isn't for us to know, nor speculate. I simply brought it because I thought I might finally give it to her."

"Very curious indeed," Tia teased, her dark eyes sparkling with mirth. "Have you had to see her very much, Glory? Why, it must be dreadful! I'd be afraid of every meal served in this house with her in it."

"Ugh, you've no idea," Gloriana groaned, tossing herself back on the now-empty pillows. "She doesn't live in the manor, thankfully, but rather in the dower house with her mother ... you know, the American."

"Ah, that's right," Tia nodded. "Perhaps that's why she never debuted? Is she caring for an elderly parent?"

"I haven't a clue." Gloriana shrugged. "The dowager has been in York since before I arrived. It's possible you've seen her before I have, as you just came from there. I've always assumed she thought the whole endeavor beneath her."

"Oh, who cares about Heloise?" Tia grinned, pushing Nell back onto the bed and crawling in after her. "Tell us about the brother. Alexander, is it? Is he very handsome?"

"Peter says he's a bit of a cad," Nell replied. "Apparently quite the debonair throughout Oxford proper."

"Well, if he's a cad, then he's got to be good-looking," Tia decided, wrapping one of her glossy black curls around her finger. "And he's unattached still?" she asked Glory.

"Entirely," Gloriana responded, uncertain why her tone was suddenly icy.

A cad, was he? Well, that shouldn't surprise her, especially after what Rose had said earlier.

"And the marquis is unmarried as well," Nell added, watching Tia carefully. "The large fellow with the bat on his carriage door. You recall, don't you?"

Tatiana shrugged, looking for all the world as though she couldn't recall her outburst earlier. "And what of Mr. Atlas?" she said quickly, reaching for Gloriana's hand. "He was so obviously smitten with you by the end of the Season."

Gloriana blushed prettily, allowing herself a delicate sigh. It was the proper reaction, she knew, but truth be told, in that moment, she could not properly conjure Mr. Atlas's face at all. In fact, her entire mental process seemed consumed by Alex Somers giving her that damnable, dashing grin across the library floor and the words *bit of a cad* echoing in the air.

CHAPTER 8

"*I* cannot believe you spent the entire day hiding in the nursery," Heloise taunted, dropping herself onto one of Gideon's armchairs in a rustle of chiffon. "You'd still be in there, dressed like a farmhand, if I hadn't stopped by to check in on Callie."

"I wasn't *hiding*," Alex snapped, sounding guilty even to his own ears. "Is it a crime to want to spend a day with my nephew and niece?"

"Your nephew and *cousin*," Gideon corrected, adjusting his cravat in the mirror. "You must be careful not to say something telling, especially with all these people in the manor."

Gideon kept his back turned, fussing with the starched fabric, though Alex got the distinct impression that his brother was fully aware at the sour faces tossed at his person by his siblings at the rebuke.

He glanced down at his own cravat with a sinking sort of resignation. He could have spent the whole day folding the damned thing and it still wouldn't look as perfect as

Gideon's. This talent, he suspected, was one either you were born with or not, and could not otherwise be acquired. Of course, one hoped that in the absence of one talent, something different was hiding in the wings, waiting to announce itself as consolation. Hiding too well for its own good, in Alex's case, whatever the mysterious talent was.

Heloise pulled her legs up under her billowy satin skirt and regarded her brother with a keen tilt of her head. "Was it the children you were looking to spend time with," she wondered, "or one of the pretty, young nannies?"

"Alex, please don't compromise the staff," Gideon sighed, turning from the mirror with a frown. "It took such a very long time to find the right caretakers for the children."

"I haven't!" Alex said, a little louder than strictly necessary. Gideon's sigh and Heloise's giggle only raised his ire. "I wasn't going to!"

"Remember that parlor maid? The one who stole a bottle of gin on the way out?" Heloise laughed. "Gemma, was it?"

"Emma," Gideon responded flatly. "Really, Alex, you ought to know better."

"I do!" he cried, then corrected, "I do know better *now*."

The truth was he'd barely noticed the nannies, or he might have very well taken an interest. What sort of omen was it that he'd taken no notice of two pretty girls in an unattended room with him for several hours? Certainly he'd seen them, tending to the little ones, and yes, they were comely enough, but he couldn't remember their particular features just now, nor their names. He had possibly not said a word to them other than a cursory greeting.

Why, perhaps it was alarming that he hadn't even felt a slight flicker of interest. He frowned, crossing his arms and turning to face the window. He wondered again if he was becoming one of those surly old men who groused at the weather and snarled at pretty girls. Heaven forbid!

The Somerton front lawn looked ablaze, glittering like a Yuletide brazier with torches arranged along the cobbled pathway. Carriages from the neighboring towns wound through the lantern-lit grotto, horses' flanks glowing from the flames flickering on the ground. He couldn't remember Somerton ever being host to a party like this, nor looking quite so merry and welcoming to outsiders. In fact, he couldn't rightly remember visitors *ever* gracing the halls of this place in his lifetime.

He wasn't sure he liked it.

Somerton, after all, was a sanctuary. It was the place waiting to embrace you in peace after a night of revels. It was the place your instinct drew you to when you'd get into trouble. It was a cool, quiet bed to climb into when you'd grown weary of music and conversation and movement. So where the devil was he supposed to go if said revels were incessantly happening here henceforth?

"I'm only teasing," Heloise muttered, clearly disappointed in his lack of reaction. "The truth is, dear Alexander was dead asleep in a rocking chair when I arrived. The children had long forgotten him and were amusing themselves with toys on the opposite end of the room whilst Alex dozed the afternoon away. No lechery to be found."

"Hm," Gideon grunted, still frowning. "Perhaps you lot can take your teasing and bickering elsewhere rather than rattling my nerves. Why are the two of you congregating in here, anyhow? Surely, my bedchambers are not a site of particular interest."

"Oh, I'd disagree with that," sang Rose as she sailed into the room on a cloud of jewel-toned silk, fastening a garnet earring closed as she moved. "This is my favorite room of them all."

"Well, now." Gideon smiled, the stern patriarch dissolving away to reveal a strange, happy fool Alex still found jarring. Who was this relaxed, joyous Gideon who reached out for his wife and shared a quick, familiar kiss on the lips as a greeting, *in front of people?* What had he ever done to deserve a woman like Rose d'Aubrey, besides?

"I recognize that dress!" Gideon said softly, taking her in.

"Yes, you know, I never returned it to Glory." Rose laughed, taking a little spin in a confection of deep-plum silk. "I'm surprised it still fits as well as it does. And, between us, I think it might just be good luck!"

She turned with a sparkling smile to the other Somers siblings and clasped her hands together. "Oh, Heloise, you look beautiful in that minty green! I hardly recognize you with your hair done up."

"I hardly recognize myself," Hel muttered, giving her pinned-up hair a shake for emphasis, a pair of matching red ringlets brushing her cheeks. "It'll do for a few hours, though."

She did look different, Alex thought, all neat and primped like a proper lady. A few years ago, he might have laughed to see it. He certainly would have teased her about it.

Tonight, he simply didn't feel up to the task. There was some sort of nauseous unease brewing in the pit of his stomach that he couldn't shake, and he was certain it had put a damper on his usual jovial self.

"I saw my cat on the way in," Heloise said. "At least, I think it was my cat. Someone's tied a rather expensive-looking blue ribbon 'round his neck. Who on earth would do such a bizarre thing?"

Rose chuckled, lowering her lashes.

"Oh," Heloise sighed. "Of course she would."

"You might wish to take Nero to the dower house for the duration of the party," Rose suggested. "I don't know what might happen if he encounters Echo in the halls."

"Echo is staying in the house, is she?" Gideon said, doing his best to refrain from marked disapproval. "I suppose I ought to have known. I shouldn't be surprised if he puts her in a bodice and brings her to the dance."

"Now *that* would be a truly dignified guest." Heloise laughed. "And perhaps the only woman in the room brave enough to spend the whole evening with Sheldon Bywater."

"The guest list is rather dignified already," Gideon said thoughtfully. "I am rather impressed that an unmarried debutante has managed to secure such a grouping of elites."

"Oh?" Alex said, a sudden spark of interest permeating the haze in his mind, though he knew damn well that it was more to do with hearing Gloriana invoked rather than the possibilities of this dratted party.

He had been doing his level best to be a proper, respectful, polite copy of his elder brother these last weeks, ever since he'd had to flee the library for fear of completely losing his head. Meals in particular had been torturous, with her sat there beside him, always aglow with some fascinating bit of gossip or simply lighting the room up with her smile and wit.

Rather than attempt to charm the girl, some horrendous part of him, the part that was definitely related to his brother, had frozen him from tip to toe in icy formality and awkward silence. No wonder he preferred it in the nursery!

"Yes," Gideon said, studying him in a way that made Alex want to squirm under the carpet. "You'd know that if you'd made yourself present for the arrivals."

"Well, who is it we're talking about, then?" Alex replied impatiently. "I've been scolded well enough already."

Gideon nodded, turning to check his appearance one last time as he spoke. "I imagine Miss Blakely was competing with many other invitations to both Atlas and Benton so near the end of the Season. Atlas is a coveted bachelor and accomplished statesman, which puts him in very high demand. Benton ... well, he is certainly well connected, but for the life of me I can't fathom him being the sort of bloke who strikes up friendships with fashionable young women."

"He has unmarried daughters," Rose pointed out. "Glory likely appealed to them rather than their papa. Alex, I know this is all a bit overwhelming, but it truly is a singular opportunity for you to explore some promising options for your future."

"Which options?" he scoffed. "Some mysterious vocation for which I've a talent that's sat latent my whole life? Or options for marrying one of the daughters of a terrifying, mysterious man who's likely got the power to have displeasing sons-in-law quickly and quietly disposed of?"

"Such dramatics," Heloise tutted with a roll of her eyes. "Who says either Benton girl would have you, besides?"

"Hel, you know as well as I do that I'm irresistibly attractive," he intoned gravely. "Once they see me, I'm as good as marked for death."

Gideon sighed loudly, offering his hand to his wife and motioning toward the door. "Let's make our way downstairs before I throw myself from the window," he said, winning a muffled giggle from Rose and a begrudging exchange of amused glances between Hel and Alex, who obeyed the order, all the same.

GLORIANA WAS WELL aware that she was drinking too much champagne.

It was too full a glass, consumed too quickly after such a spirited dance. She could hear the rational part of her brain screaming "no, Glory, you'll get foxed," and yet here was the bubbly, tipping past her pretty pink lips and dancing past her tongue, sending warmth and reassurance into her belly in place of the restless irritation.

He had finally appeared, apparently at the behest of the lord of the manor, and he'd done so with none other than his hellish harpy of a sister on his arm, looking more elegant and beautiful than either of them had any right to.

How had Heloise managed to avoid every single demand

expected of a modern, well-bred girl? Furthermore, how had she managed to acquire a shapelier figure, complete with bosoms, so late in life, hm? Glory had always resented her own lack of bosoms.

"You are glaring," Tatiana whispered to her, sweeping the champagne flute away with a playful but firm grip. She lifted it to her own lips, studying her friend's face. "He *is* very handsome."

"Who?" Gloriana snapped, blinking at Tia with a sudden wide-eyed innocence. "Mr. Atlas is a very fine dancer indeed."

"Oh, bag Mr. Atlas. I see you staring at the Somers chap," her friend whispered with a knowing smirk. "I don't blame you."

"If I am staring, it is only because I wish to beat him about the head with a heavy object," Gloriana muttered, then added, "again."

Tia raised her eyebrows, but did not otherwise inquire as to the meaning of that suggestive bit of commentary.

Gloriana knew she was being ridiculous. This was *her* party, created by the labor of her own imagination. The couples swirling about the dance floor were only here at her behest. The musicians had been chosen by her finely tuned ear. Even the flowers and candles had been arranged with her oversight.

The golden glow of this perfectly elegant evening should have put her into an euphoric mood. Leave it to a Somers to ruin absolutely everything! She hadn't even been able to properly enjoy laying the foundations of her snare for

Nathaniel Atlas, who seemed very keen on being caught, as it were. She thought he seemed keen, anyway, but who could say when her mind was elsewhere?

"Shall we persuade him to dance?" Tatiana mused, tipping the last of the champagne into her mouth as she watched Alex laugh at some wretched quip made by his sister. "He looks as though he might move just as elegantly as Mr. Atlas."

"Do as you wish," Gloriana said with a shrug. "I have other aspirations for the evening."

"Oh? Like getting yourself soapy-eyed and collapsing on the floor in front of the entire congregation?" Tia snapped. "No. Look at me!"

Glory winced, allowing her friend to grip her shoulders and turn her about. "What?" she whined, unable to resist looking directly into Tatiana's unsettlingly intense gaze.

"You look beautiful tonight, *radiant*," Tia said sternly, her dark eyes flashing with feeling. "We laced you into that lilac love song of a dress for a reason. I shan't stand by and watch you waste it sulking over some ungrateful man, no matter how handsome he is. If you wish to punish him, do so by presenting the most desirable, unattainable version of Miss Gloriana Blakely that ever graced a dance floor!"

Glory knew she was pouting. She wanted nothing more than to stomp her slippered foot on the polished floor and stalk off to her room to sulk in peace. All this agonizing over a missing guest of honor had utterly ruined her excitement about everything. She didn't care about dancing. She didn't care about the guests. She didn't even care about pursuing Nathaniel Atlas and the marvelous future such a man could provide as a husband. She wanted to crawl into bed, eat cake, and have a good, angry cry.

Yes, of course she had danced with Mr. Atlas, but it had felt disconnected somehow, lacking. She had spent the entirety of this ball staring at the doorway, waiting for Alex Somers to arrive, and now that he was here, she was trying her hardest not to stare at him.

Couldn't Tia see? The night already felt forfeit.

The fact of the matter was that both girls knew the unspoken rules of Society, and Tatiana was right. There was no acceptable way forward other than to aggressively enjoy the evening festivities. She sighed and gave a begrudging nod, strangely comforted by the clawed fingers holding her arms so firmly.

How lucky she was to have such sensible friends!

"Good!" Tia smiled, allowing her grip to loosen. "Do sort yourself out quickly, though, because he is walking this way."

The practiced mechanisms of a good finishing school education seemed to overtake Gloriana, softening her features, brightening her eyes, lightening her spirit. When she turned to greet the approaching object of her eternal disquiet, it was with all the poise of a woman greeting her most cherished friend.

"Lord Alex!" she said brightly. "I'm so happy you've arrived! Allow me to introduce my dearest friend, Miss Tatiana Everstead, who joins us from Norwich."

"Pleasure," Tia demurred, performing an exquisite little curtsy and a dazzling smile. "Lord Alex, I would love to converse at length, but I'm afraid I've promised the next dance to Mr. Applegate and must hasten to my spot. You must sweep our Glory into the waltz before anyone else can claim her!"

"Oh, that isn't ..." Gloriana trailed off, knowing she was stuck as Tia scampered away and Alex extended his hand out to her in wordless invitation. "Thank you," she decided, putting her dainty gloved fingers into his large, warm ones. "Of course I'll dance with you."

"She doesn't mean Mr. Peter Applegate, from Oxford?" he wondered as they made their way to the center of the floor. His bright green eyes scanned over Gloriana's head until they settled on Tatiana, likely informing an oblivious Peter of their impending waltz. He looked back down at his partner with eyes full of wonder. "I know him! How could you have known that?"

"I didn't," she laughed, surprised to find herself feeling amused amidst all the complex feelings of angst. "Much as I'd like to embrace the mysterious air of the omniscient socialite, I must confess that it is simply one of life's funny little coincidences. As it happens, I am an intimate of his sister, Eleanor, who attended Mrs. Arlington's. Are you great friends with Mr. Applegate?"

"Yes, I think so," Alex replied with a little smile of his own, settling them into place and sliding his hand around her corseted waist. "One can never be entirely certain with the bookish sort. Still, I'm rather chuffed to see him amidst all these strangers. A familiar face dulls the anxiety of swimming in an unknown sea, at least a little."

"Anxiety?" she whispered back, her voice swept away by the

rise of the music as the waltz began. She didn't have a chance to repeat herself, as she was suddenly drawn in very close to Alex Somers, their bodies warm and buzzing with energy as the first steps of the waltz sent them spinning.

She found herself momentarily speechless at the elegance with which he moved. Of course, it shouldn't be surprising. He was a man of breeding, after all. There was just something about Alex Somers that hinted at rebellion, she supposed, and so his flawless adherence to this social ritual was unexpected.

"You look stunned," he said with a chuckle. "Were you expecting me to be counting the steps aloud as we danced?"

"Of course not!" she sputtered, heat flooding to her cheeks. "I was taken aback by your confession of anxiety. It had not occurred to me that your absence today could be explained by nerves."

The look he gave her was unreadable, as though he himself wasn't sure how he felt about this morsel of information. He took advantage of the pause in conversation to spin her on the dance floor, her lilac skirts blossoming around her like a morning glory on the vine, exploding into bloom, and gathered her back against his chest in a single breathless tug of his strong arms.

She blinked away the dizziness that gripped her, a reminder of that sweet, treacherous champagne, and allowed herself to be swallowed by the music and its dance. The steps were second nature to her, after all. The most exclusive soirees of the Season will bestow that upon a girl.

She suddenly felt comforted. His vanishing act had in no way been inspired by a dislike for her as a person, nor by offense at her awkward attempt at flirtation that night in the library.

It was humbling bordering on offensive, really, that he'd reacted with such disgust at her tiny, harmless reference to the ribald. After all, hadn't he just suggested a second attempt at compromising her virtue? And anyway, her comment could convincingly have been dismissed as simple observation rather than flirtation, couldn't it? That was the mark of a well-crafted coquetry.

No man had ever reacted that way to attention from Gloriana Blakely. No, in fact, most men ate any favor she was kind enough to bestow upon them as though it were a gourmet delicacy on a golden spoon. Of course, beguiling men was no trick. It was proposals that were difficult. Marriages were a matter of cold bureaucracy, and the only men who had ever actually offered Gloriana a ring had been … lacking.

That, of course, excluded Gideon Somers, who she'd ensured never had the opportunity to actually ask for her hand face-to-face. Well, she'd had Rose to ensure it, anyhow, and that had turned out beautifully, had it not? For Rose, anyway.

The younger Somers brother really was a handsome sort of devil, she thought, gazing up at him as he swept her around the room. His hair was shorter than was strictly fashionable, which at least minimized its shocking red color. His eyes were that glittering, mischievous green, and his lips were so very well sculpted.

That, of course, was just his face. She'd experienced his brawn firsthand, that night in the dark. She glanced over at her own hand, gloved as it was in white satin, held so gently in his big, strong grip. His hands that had held her in place by her wrists without even the necessity of true effort.

She shivered, forcing the thought from her head, but when she looked up again to meet his eyes, she thought for one horrifying moment that he'd been able to read every salacious thought that had just gone through her mind.

She found herself quite unable to look away, locked within the thrall of his suddenly hot gaze as his hand tightened around her own and their bodies seemed to draw closer together as they spun toward the crescendo of the waltz.

His eyes roamed her face, lingering upon the curve of her champagne-sweetened lips before rising to meet her wide, blue-eyed gaze. Surely she wasn't imagining it. He looked just as taken by improper memories and scenarios as she was.

Was he thinking about that night? Was it possible he'd had the same shameful fantasies in its wake that she had? She wanted very much to reach up and touch the cheek she'd bruised with her fingertips, though tonight it looked as though nothing had ever happened. It had healed without a trace in the last weeks.

Her lips parted, her breath coming shallow as the music lowered to silence, their bodies stilling on a dance floor that suddenly seemed as large and vast as the whole of the world.

"Miss Blakely," he said huskily, one hand still wrapped around hers as they parted from the waltz.

"Gloriana," she corrected breathlessly, without thinking. "Call me Gloriana."

He smiled then, a genuine smile of happiness. It was softer, more sincere somehow than the way he grinned at his own jests that day at luncheon. "Gloriana," he said softly, in a way that sent a shiver of pure sensation through her body.

He opened his mouth, ready to share whatever thoughts had descended upon him during that dance, but the words never came. His body stiffened, his hand dropping hers as though it were suddenly offensive to touch, and his smile dissolved into that mask of blank formality she'd been suffering through at every meal for weeks.

"Alex?" she started, but he gave a slight shake of his head, his eyes locked behind her.

She turned, expecting something heinous at her back, but instead found only a slim woman of middle age, with a chin just as sharp as Heloise's and eyes that sparkled a familiar mischievous green.

"Ruthie Cunningham Somers," the woman announced in a broad, flat accent, jutting one bare hand out to be shaken. "And you are?"

"Oh, erm," Gloriana fumbled forward, grasping the lady's hand and giving it a quick, albeit limp shake. "I am Gloriana Blakely. Lady Somers's cousin. Maternal cousin. My father is Sir Reginald Blakely."

Ruthie sighed heavily, as though this were a great disappointment. "Well," she said, "it is lovely to meet you, Miss Blakely, but I'm afraid I did not come over here to make your acquaintance. In doing so, it seems my hopes of stealing my second-born for a dance have expired."

Gloriana glanced back to the spot where she was certain Alex Somers stood to find nothing but empty air. He must have turned on his heel the moment his mother arrived and made a quick sprint toward the exit.

All soft, sensual feelings she'd been harboring toward the man during that dance hardened into cruel, little spikes that pricked at her insides. In the space of a breath, the sweetness of the waltz had turned to bitterness.

How dare he! How dare he flee his own ball!

She turned back to Ruthie Somers with the most apologetic face she could muster, scrambling to think of a way to explain away this behavior. "Madam, you must accept my apologies," she began.

"Oh, think nothing of it, lovely," the dowager cut over her with an impatient roll of the eyes. "The boy is prone to running away. Don't let it spoil your party."

"But it is *his* party," Gloriana said softly. "Not mine."

"Is it, dear?" The dowager gave her a sympathetic pat on the hands. Any upset at her son's behavior seemed nothing but a momentary disappointment, quickly remedied as she snatched a glass of champagne off a passing tray and marched resolutely into the crowd, chestnut curls bouncing to match time with her steps. She acted as though this flagrant act of rudeness had not impacted her in the least, and within moments was having a spirited, apparently joy-filled conversation with Lady Benton.

Well. It might not upset his mother, but Gloriana would not

stand for it! She'd had her fill of confusing highs and lows and inexplicable slights from Alexander Somers. This was the last time she'd allow it to happen!

She gathered her pretty purple skirts in her hands and made her way through the crowd, avoiding the eyes of the guests, blending and weaving her way to the hall. He wasn't going to do this to her all autumn long. No, sir.

As her father always said, bad behavior must be nipped at the root lest it flourish.

She caught the flash of his tails turning the corner as she exited the ballroom. He was headed toward the staircase, she wagered, which meant she was as well.

This nonsense had to stop.

CHAPTER 9

*A*lex briefly considered heading down the final flight of stairs to the ground floor, making his way to the double doors, and fleeing into the night. He could saddle up Boudicea and be in the township in under an hour, he wagered. The local innkeep knew he was good for credit. He could lay low, drink himself into a merry stupor, fall asleep on a hard cot above the pub, and forget he'd ever even made the first attempt to play at Society.

Sure, Gideon would immediately know where he'd gone and likely come to drag him out by the ear first thing tomorrow. Of course. But what was one more humiliation just now? He'd just made a complete ass of himself, *again,* in front of perhaps the first person he'd ever truly wanted to impress in his life.

That was the way of the universe, wasn't it? Play a fool all your life and when you think you're finished with the act, the stars align to remind you that you'd stopped pretending long ago and a fool you were, now and forever.

Why did he care so much what she thought of him, anyhow? She wasn't the first beautiful girl he'd ever met. Hell, he'd bedded girls just as pretty, hadn't he? Though none of them had spent so much time devoted to projecting confidence in his future. None had nearly knocked him unconscious by way of introduction, either.

It was perhaps some bone-deep memory of that first humiliation that led him past the stairs and onward toward the little library with the broken window. He certainly hadn't intended to make that particular room his destination. If he'd stopped to think about it, his own bedchambers certainly would have made a more appealing sanctuary. Alex had never much been one for stopping and thinking before acting.

The room was dark at this hour, with only the glow of the torchlight from the lawn casting shadows through the windows. The fireplace was cold and the lanterns unlit, with all souls who cared to experience this glorious night doing so in the ballroom. That ballroom had sat dormant for his entire life, but tonight it was pure gilt and glitter, alive with laughter and conversation and the swish of fabric dancing to the tune of musicians.

She had made that happen. She was a gilded sorceress, capable of conjuring the divine and impossible, of assembling a crowd and compelling them to dance, and he'd just shattered the first moment of true kinship by acting on instinct at the appearance of his reprehensible mother.

One would think that being avoided for over three years would be a sufficient indication that one's company was not welcome. His mother surely didn't believe that strolling into a ball thrown in his honor would somehow undo the years of neglect and disappointment! He had stayed away from her for a reason, hadn't he? What true need was there for him to expressly communicate his disinterest in a relationship at this stage? She knew damn well he wanted nothing to do with her, and now she'd gone and ruined something special, once again. It was almost impressive how utterly destructive that woman managed to be.

He found himself slumped on the carpet, the window he'd used to climb into this mess at his back, and his elbows balanced on his knees as he stared at the blank darkness of the room across from him. Should he go back? *Could* he go back now?

Miss Blakely must think him an utter boor for behaving as he did. Would she care to understand his reasons, had he the courage to return, tail between legs, and take the time to explain them? No, likely not. For girls like Gloriana, decorum and acting the way one ought to were more important than the air one breathed.

He kicked his feet out with a grimace, dropping his head back against the wall to stare up at the ceiling.

Perhaps she should have married Gideon after all! Gideon would have stood and borne the indignity of that interruption as certainly as a mountain is unmoved by a windstorm. Perhaps she regretted spurning the unfailingly appropriate Lord Somers now, he thought bitterly. Perhaps she saw all the rigid respectability of his elder brother and thought yes, that is what a man should be.

He scowled, digging his fingers into the carpet. Why was he layering phantom jealousy onto an already horrendous fit of shame?

A sharp click and the door flying open brought his head up in alarm. For the briefest moment, he was certain he was imagining her there, wreathed in light from the hall without. However, surely if he were to summon the spectre of Gloriana Blakely, it would be with an expression about her lovely face that didn't bode murder.

"You," she hissed, knocking the door ajar with her hip as she stalked toward him.

Backlit as she was by the stream of secondhand candlelight from without, she appeared to glow with that same angelic aura that had accompanied her the last time they'd been in this room together, though he wasn't altogether in the right frame of mind to admire it as thoroughly tonight.

He pushed himself to his feet to meet her, his head swimming with the rapid-fire emotions he'd been dealt in the last quarter hour. At least if he were standing, she would not tower over him. At least he could afford himself that small dignity.

"What are you about, running off like that?" she demanded, coming a breath away from him, her shadow slashing across the carpet to intersect his own. "Why would you do such a thing!"

"Gloriana," he started, unsure even where to begin, but she cut him off with a sharp hand slicing into the air between them.

"I was ready to overlook the way you've treated me," she said, her delicate shoulders squaring behind her as she raised her eyes to meet his own. "The way we met was folly for us both, but leaving me mid-sentence the next night? Refusing to look at or speak to me for weeks? *Disappearing* for the entire day leading up to the festivities I've spent *over a month* planning, well into the witching hour, night after night, *for you!"*

She exhaled sharply, turning her face as though to spare herself from having to look at him. When she spoke again, it was softer, but no less condemning. "I simply do not understand it," she murmured.

"I didn't ask you to do any of that!" he retorted, his own voice subdued in the wake of her rage. He didn't know why he was reacting with anything other than abject apology, but as he spoke, he felt the heat in his face rise at the truth of his words that seemed to formulate of their own accord. "I didn't even know you existed when you began shaping my return to Somerton! Perhaps I wished to come home and enjoy peace and solitude before leaping into the world with both feet!"

"Oh, how horrible for you!" she scoffed. "How dare your wealthy, titled family ensure you have every advantage! The struggle you must endure to be catered to so! Goodness, it must be a horror, for even the sight of your own mother sends you scampering off into the dark, as though everyone is so lucky to have parents that wish to launch them into life with only the best."

"You don't know anything about my mother!" he snapped, taking a step forward. "You are an outsider in my home!"

She didn't flinch nor shrink away, lifting her chin in welcome to his challenge.

It immediately humbled him, and he turned instead of going farther, dropping himself onto the couch where he'd recovered from their last miscommunication. He dropped his head into his hands and sighed heavily, wishing for all the world he'd taken his first instinctual choice and fled to the township.

"And despite both of those things, you are right," he sighed, cursing that for all the world he sounded like a scolded child when he wished to be nothing but dashing and impressive to this particular woman. "I do not know how to apologize to you."

"Why, you might try the usual way," she suggested, crossing her arms across her chest.

He glanced up at her, tapping at her elbows with gloved fingers, and almost wanted to laugh. Yes, saying the words would be a decent start.

"Miss Blakely," he began.

"Gloriana," she corrected immediately.

"Gloriana," he said, somehow comforted that he still had permission to use her Christian name. "I am beyond sorry for my behavior. I would love the opportunity, some day, to explain to you the motivations behind every stupid thing I've done over the last month, though I fear such a feat may take quite a while. Please, if you are able, forgive me and allow me to start again."

She was silent, staring down at him with those lovely eyes and her pouty mouth drawn into a grim, horizontal line. "I do not believe in starting again," she said, after a moment. "Perhaps we might do better from this point on, hm?"

She hesitated, a look of distress flickering over her face, and held her hand up to forestall his response. "Oh no," she breathed. "I sounded just like *my* mother just then. Good heavens."

She took an unsteady step forward and spun on her heel, lowering onto the settee next to him as her skirts billowed out over the two of them. She mimed his earlier pose, putting her head in her hands, and laughed shakily. "Forget what I've just said," she decided, peeping at him through her fingers, "starting again is just fine."

He felt a little pang of relief permeate the large ball of anxiety in his chest. He opened his mouth, ready to lighten the mood with some sort of jest and perhaps suggest they make their way back to the party, but the sound of approaching voices froze him in place.

Gloriana's head shot up, her eyes wide in alarm as the rumble of conversation drew nearer. It hadn't occurred to either of them that they'd put themselves in a compromising position, yet again, in the very same room as the first occurrence. This time, it wouldn't be Gideon and Rose who found them. This time, there would be consequences.

"This door is open. Let's talk in here," a male voice out in the hall suggested to his compatriot, making Glory hiss in alarm.

"There's a linen closet," Alex said quickly, offering her his hand as he shot to his feet. "Quickly, now!"

She hastened after him, whipping her skirt up into her free hand, what he could see of her face stricken with panic.

He tugged her into the linen closet, squeezing his back against the sharp press of the shelving, and wedged the door shut just as the interlopers made their way into the library, light suddenly flooding through the cracks around the doorframe.

She clung to his lapels, attempting to make herself as small as possible in the tight space as footsteps came near. The click of the door shutting made it clear that these other people might be making use of the room for quite some time.

"No one followed us?" a female voice asked, breathy and anxious.

"Of course not," the male voice from earlier snapped. "Why should they? Surely we aren't the only people who've sneaked away for some privacy."

"That is not why we are here, sir," the female voice gasped, seemingly affronted by the suggestion.

Gloriana tilted her head up to meet Alex's eyes, her expression just as quizzical as his own. Certainly not every opposite-sex pair who sneaked into empty rooms during a ball were looking to tryst, as the two of them, jammed into the linen closet, could attest, but any other reason was a damned rarity.

Truly, he should be relieved. He wasn't sure how well he'd handle the sounds of lovemaking through the thin closet door with Gloriana pressed so very firmly into him. It would either be unspeakably awkward or very, very suggestive, and he couldn't trust his body to avoid reacting to the second option in such close quarters.

"I should certainly hope not," commented a *third* gentleman.

Just what in the devil was going on here? If not for the commentary specifying otherwise, Alex would have thought something very salacious indeed. He gave a small shrug to Gloriana, meeting her eyes in a shared expression of puzzlement. At the very least, he thought, the mystery of it all was something of a distraction from suddenly having her held very firmly in his arms.

She bit her lip, perhaps thinking something along the same lines, though undoubtedly with more innocent connotation. It was a challenge bordering on cruelty not to move his hands whatsoever, looped as they were on the slight flare where her waist gave way to her hips. He could feel the strings of her stays beneath the fine, smooth fabric of that purple dress, and the smell of her perfume coiled around him like a hangman's noose.

For some unfathomable reason, she took it upon herself to explore the cut of his lapel with her gloved hands, running her thumbs under the fold, that pretty bottom lip still caught between her pearly teeth. She seemed to have lost her curiosity for the goings-on without, instead choosing to study him with those pale blue eyes, which managed to shine even here in the cramped darkness of a silent hideaway.

He became very aware of the lines of her body, of her hips pressed into his own the way they were crammed together, of the sweet smell of champagne on her warm breath, and the smooth expanse of her perfectly pale bare shoulders that rose from the daring cut of her ballgown.

Christ, he needed to get a hold of himself. He could feel the damning proof of his interest in this level of proximity to Miss Gloriana Blakely stirring to life at an alarmingly quick rate. He slid his hands up from her waist to grip her wrists, gently detaching them from his lapels.

He slid his thumbs into the palms of her hands, recalling the last time he'd held her this way.

If you'd harbored roguish intentions last night, I'm well aware I'd not have escaped them.

He swallowed. Hard.

Had she known how she sounded when she'd said that? Just after referring to losing one's virtue as *fun*? She must. A girl who navigated the social games of the *ton* so easily would not have escaped a single Season without men doing their level best to compromise her in a shadowy nook very like this one.

Had she ever let it happen? Had this glorious creature allowed some *ton* rakehell to kiss her? To touch her? He wasn't sure if the idea that she had filled him with jealousy or excitement. He also wasn't sure that moving his hands from her waist to her wrists had done anything to calm the intensity of his desire in these close quarters.

She studied the way his hand looked around her wrist, so much larger and somehow more primitive-looking than the delicate bones of a lady's wrist. The contrast was enhanced by the way said wrist was wrapped in ivory satin. She curled her fingers around his thumbs and lifted her eyes from the spectacle of his gentle restraint to once again meet his gaze.

This time her curiosity had taken on a far more dangerous hue. Her lashes fluttered against her cheeks, her breath quickening within the confines of her gown, petite breasts swelling over her decolletage. She raised herself onto her toes, tilting her head back to brush her lips against his jaw.

He froze, utterly stunned by this development. His grip on her wrists tightened, but he did not push her away. The flutter of her flower-soft mouth sent jolts of shivering shock through his body in a way he wasn't entirely sure he'd ever experienced before, even when stark-naked and enjoying a lady to her fullest.

Was he expected to simply stand there and control his baser urges while she teased him so? This was the trouble with debutantes! One never knew for certain what messages they intended to send. Still, lips to skin were hard to misinterpret. Surely?

"Alex," she whispered, her voice breathy enough to only carry to his ears. Any farther and it was lost under the droning of whatever those damned interrupting guests were babbling about in the library. She spoke for him and him alone, and breathed again, helplessly, "Oh, Alex."

He wasn't certain whether she wanted a verbal answer, but he was pretty damned convinced that by this point he wasn't particularly capable of giving her one. He pulled her wrists up, looping them around his own neck with no resistance to speak of from the lady herself.

She caught her breath prettily, resting her cheek against his own as he slid his fingers down the length of her arms. He could not resist gathering her close, taking full advantage of their current confines to grip her in a way most unacceptable for a first kiss. Still, one must take advantage when life provided the rare, unexpected gift.

The truth was, he'd been an utter failure at fighting off fantasies about this exact thing. He'd tossed and turned at night, telling himself to think of someone else, attempting to conjure Bessie Corden's lush curves and dark hair. Time after time, the women he pictured would ripple and fade, their bodies drifting into smoke in favor of angelic pale features and the slight, elegant build of the woman he truly wanted, who haunted the periphery of every fantasy, both waking and abed.

This was why he hadn't spoken to her for weeks, why he maintained an icy formality at meals. He didn't trust himself to look at her, to listen to her laugh. It would only provide his wicked imagination more fuel with which to torture him.

Night after night, he'd ached in the twisted confines of his coverlet, waking from fevered dreams about rolling around that night on the carpet, and the encounter coming to a much more pleasant conclusion as skirts were pushed up and the only collision was that of their bodies.

He could feel the heat of it swimming in his head, putting fire in his belly. When they were dancing such a short time ago, he had thought only of her beauty and the pleasure of her smile. He had contained the beast within him so well. But he was only human, wasn't he? A man. And she was everything a woman could possibly be. The ultimate temptation, warm and willing in his arms.

He kept one hand at her waist, just like he'd done during their waltz, and with the other, cupped the back of her neck, brushing his thumb along the soft line of her jaw as he brought her mouth up to meet his own.

She was pliant and willing for certain. The first breathless moment of contact sent her into the same frozen shock that she'd inflicted upon him moments earlier, but it took nothing but the lingering taste of her lips to thaw any hesitation. She melted within his arms, clinging to him in this dark, hidden place as she tilted her head, seemingly experimenting with the brush and friction of her lips against his.

It was all he could do not to groan in pleasure, the satisfaction of finally having her like this, of tasting her like this, surging through him with a power that was almost frightening. He allowed his fingertips to tease at the bottom of her coiffed hair, not disturbing the style, but indulging in just a brush of discovery, a desperation to know how that glistening wealth of white gold felt against his fingertips.

Somehow, despite the heady grip of the moment, he knew he must exercise restraint. As it was, the limited ability to move in the tiny closet, with barely enough room for their bodies amongst the shelving, served as a reminder that no matter how delectable she tasted, carrying her off to bed was not a possibility at this particular moment.

He flicked his tongue into her mouth, pleased at the way she gasped, the way she gripped her arms around his neck to pull herself closer. Yes, this girl had been kissed before. Jealousy might come later, he thought, but the naughtiness of her skill and how she might have come upon it only stoked the flames within him.

He wanted to grip her hair and pull her head back. He wanted to taste the column of her throat. He wanted to pin her to the carpet like he could've that first night, and this time turn it into the fantasy encounter that would make all that ruin and compromise worthwhile—*fun,* she had said. He was dizzy with it.

She pulled away so suddenly that he almost stumbled, her brows drawn together in concern.

Had she just come to her senses? Please, God, no. He was not satisfied yet. If anything, this sampling had only made his cravings more keen.

He stroked the back of her neck, inhaling the scent of her hair in the hopes that this pause in her fervor was only temporary. He opened his mouth to say her name, to beg her to fall back into insanity with him.

Her eyes snapped up to meet his, her hands unclasping from about his neck and coming up over his mouth in a clear command to be silent. As tempting as it was to nip at her fingers playfully, he gathered that she had a sudden fear of being discovered, and as such complied with this sudden and forceful demand for silence.

It took him a moment, but the voices without came into sharper focus. They began to sound like words rather than a buzzing drone, and they were saying his name.

"As I've said before, I can't sanction so much fuss and expenditure over the likes of Alex Somers. I could have had him killed weeks ago," one of the men said casually. "That is how one ought to deal with traitors, isn't it?"

CHAPTER 10

Gloriana's blood seemed to freeze within her veins. This was quite a feat, for moments ago she had felt so warm as to burst into flames. Her palm slackened over the mouth of Alex Somers, though she could not say whether she was reacting to the accusation of treason or the off-handed way the man beyond the closet door had just suggested cold-blooded murder.

She shuddered, leaning into Alex instead of away from him, as though he might comfort her from the threats against his person. Absurdly, he seemed willing to do so, his warm, strong hands coming around her and stroking her back in a way that was reassuring rather than seductive. If she swooned right then and there, she trusted him to catch her.

"You know we don't approve of your methods," the second male voice snapped. "It is entirely unnecessary to react with the ultimate extremity when we do not even know how he came by the papers."

"As far as I'm concerned," the woman piped in, "we don't

even know for certain that he has them. How reliable is your contact?"

"I have more faith in my contact than I do in either of you," the murderous voice responded coldly. "I do not see how else Alex Somers might have left Oxford with such sensitive cargo short of being an agent of the enemy. You know as well as I do that he has an extensive history of traveling the Continent for reasons that have always been abstract at best. The veneer of the wastrel cad is a smart one for a man who collects coin in exchange for betrayal."

"It does not look good," the woman agreed begrudgingly. "But until we have proof that he is a spy or a traitor, I do not sanction a lethal retaliation."

"If he is dead," the other man said, "he will have a hard time returning what was taken, and I understand the cargo is still extremely valuable."

"He can't sell it if he's dead either," the murderous one barked. "The lives of British battalions are at risk here. What is the life of one fool opposite two hundred heroes, hm? We are wasting time here, playing at a country party when war is surging due south."

"We are maintaining responsible cover, gathering intelligence, and working toward a solution," the woman responded. "During the grouse hunt in two days' time, I will conduct a thorough search of his room—a task I *could* be performing right now if you had any patience at all. If I can recover the package with a simple search, you can conceal it and we will leave this gathering before he realizes it's gone."

"I agree," the second man said. "We will observe Somers closely moving forward, until we are certain he is not an enemy asset. If he is, we will turn him over to the Crown, *not* conduct brigand justice."

The room quieted as the chimes of the grandfather clock announced the hour, each gong vibrating through Gloriana's chest in the most fearsome way. She clung to Alex, resting her cheek against his chest and squeezing her eyes shut, praying to God that this be over soon.

"Our absence will soon be noted," the woman said. "I suggest the two of you return together. I will retire separately."

"If you do not find that package," the cold man said, his voice deepening with impatience, "we will have little choice in the matter."

"Go," she responded quietly. "Go. We will discuss that matter if it comes to necessity."

There was a rustle of movement, the squeak of the door being pushed open, and then a long, heavy silence. Gloriana supposed they might have left the door ajar, the same as it was when they entered, which was a dratted inconvenience in knowing for certain they'd gone.

She glanced down at her feet, looking for the glow of their lanterns under the door. There was only a faint light, though she could not say absolutely that it was just as it had been before. She lifted her cheek from Alex's chest and gazed up at him. Yes, it was dark now. She could barely make out that incredible mouth.

"I think they are gone," she whispered as softly as she could. "Alex?"

He gave a short nod, leaning to the side with his arm still around her and twisting the door knob with agonizing slowness, allowing the closet door to peep open bit by bit, just in case. He sighed in relief at the empty room and allowed the door all the way open, providing their escape into open air.

Gloriana gasped in the night air like a woman who'd just surfaced from the sea. Her head was swimming with all that had happened. She walked to the settee and gripped the back of it, drawing breath deeply and deliberately, her heart thundering in her chest.

Alex paced over to the door, peeking out of it into the hall. He cursed under his breath, turning to her, and said, "Whoever it was is gone now."

"Whoever it was?" she repeated shakily. "It was a murderer and two agents of the Crown! They think you're a foreign spy!"

He frowned, rubbing at the back of his neck. "Yes, I know. Gloriana, you must believe me when I say that I haven't the faintest idea what could have given them that idea. I should be offended at their description of my reputation for a flighty fool, but it truly is all I am. I'm restless and reckless at times, but not treasonous!"

"I have to get back," she replied, barely letting him finish his spiel. "Alex, I've been gone far too long!"

He nodded, motioning for her to come to the door with an extended hand. When she arrived, placing her hand within his, he closed his fingers and looked desperately into her eyes. "Tell me you believe me," he pleaded, his voice raspy and urgent. "I am no traitor, Gloriana. I swear it."

"I believe you," she said, knowing it was a foolish thing to say and an even more foolish thing to believe. She must be a fool, then, for she willingly did both. "I must go."

He nodded, sighing heavily as he released her hand.

She leaned forward, for reasons she could not quite justify to herself, and placed another soft, sweet kiss upon his lips. It was perhaps the only way to assure him that she spoke truly. She blinked at him as they parted, the curl of panic in her chest reflected in the confusion on his face. And then she ducked under his arm and out of the little library, hurrying as fast as her slippered feet would carry her back to the simple revelry of the ball.

GLORIANA BRIEFLY WONDERED if the housekeeper might consider drugging her again if she asked politely. How else was she supposed to get a wink of sleep after the night she'd just had?

She threw the sheets back off her body, balling her fists at her sides as she stared up at the ceiling. The second half of the ball seemed nigh unreal in the wake of the penny dreadful she'd found herself living through earlier in the evening. It had been damn near herculean the way she'd managed to navigate the remainder of the night.

Rosie was certainly none the wiser. Tia and Nell had stopped only for a few scraps of gossip amidst their own whirlwind of an evening. Even Mr. Atlas was blissfully unaware, as Gloriana had put on her most placid and mysterious guise for their second waltz. She couldn't remember a single thing he said, to be fair, but all the same, she was certain his suspicions had not been piqued.

No, no one knew she had vanished for a time. No one suspected that she had found herself folded in the strong embrace of Alex Somers, her wrists once again locked in the strong circle of his grip. No one knew he had kissed her so thoroughly. To them, it would sound absurd that he was suspected of treason and in danger of being murdered.

No. Everything was as it should be to all who'd managed to dance the night away without visiting the little library on the second floor.

It was a little disappointing, somehow, that the most thrilling night of her life had gone past without any proof whatsoever. No one would be chattering excitedly about the mystique and romance of it all come sunrise. No one would know how tight the line of tension had been drawn before it came crumbling down about them in a fiery argument followed by a flurry of heated kisses.

She supposed that was for the best. It was a strange thought anyhow. She'd never wanted anyone to know about silly little kisses before, had she? No, becoming compromised before she was good and ready was a disaster to be avoided at all costs.

What was different this time, other than the obvious? It was hardly the first ball she'd attended where a few stolen moments in a dark corner had added a spot of variety to the evening.

The only sensible conclusion to draw was that it was not the heat nor fervor found in the attentions of Alex Somers that were keeping her awake, but rather the bone-chilling implications of the conversation they'd overheard. A little kissing couldn't possibly be responsible for this restlessness, after all! Not for a girl like Gloriana. Never.

She huffed, tossing herself onto her side. She didn't even have Nero with her tonight to provide a bit of comfort. Heloise had stolen him away as she passed the night in the manor. Wicked girl, always making things harder for those in her wake!

Alex had returned to the ballroom almost half an hour after she did, looking a bit rumpled, as though he'd nipped away for a drink and a snooze following their dramatic experience. She hadn't rumpled his hair and lapel, had she? Certainly in the crush of the closet, it had been possible, but ... no! She shook her head, forcing her memories back to the ballroom.

It had taken an unbelievable amount of self-control to not march right over to him the instant he'd come back through the double doors, grab his arm, and drag him into a quiet corner wherein she might demand all manner of answers from him.

Is it answers you're after from him? a little voice tittered inside her head.

She sighed, for one sweet moment allowing herself to remember the delicious ferocity of his kisses, the strength of his arms around her. He had tickled the nape of her neck, teasing little curls loose from her chignon as he'd held her so tightly to him, she thought she might melt. Oh, but what right did such a fool of a man have to kiss so skillfully?

She folded her pillow over her ears and squeezed her eyes shut, groaning dramatically. Surely sleep would never come! Why must humans live through a single torment and then replay it again and again once the sun had fled and only night and shadow remained to keep them company? There must be some evil ether, some unspeakable thing about darkness that signaled to the mind, that spoke to the thoughts in the secret voice of the shadows and said, "Hello, please share with me all the things that cause you distress!"

She had gone into the library tonight to lambast Alex Somers, *not* to make love to him! It was all his fault, wasn't it? He knew she had improper thoughts about the way he'd held her in thrall that first night. What was he thinking, repeating the gesture? She'd scarcely been able to breathe when he'd done that, and had thought to content herself simply with inhaling his scent, with brushing their cheeks together.

Of course, such things were never enough for men. How much further might it have gone if they hadn't been so shockingly interrupted?

Tomorrow, Alex must find a feasible way to relay what he'd overheard to Gideon. If her own involvement in the eavesdropping weren't so morally condemning, she'd have taken care of that herself, immediately upon returning to the ballroom. She'd had half a mind to go tell Rosie right away and consequences be damned, but something had stopped her.

Yes, something, laughed the teasing voice in her head. *Whatever could it be?*

CHAPTER 11

*T*he choices for Alex had come down to drinking himself unconscious with whatever he could pilfer from the now-empty ballroom or staring wide-eyed out the window of his bedroom until dawn whilst contemplating his own fragile mortality.

While neither option was particularly appealing, fatigue would be easier to mitigate than alcohol poisoning come the morrow, and so, stay awake he did, at least in spurts. He must have nodded off here and there while attempting to be somber and brooding, because before he knew it, the sun was rudely rolling its fat arse into the window pane directly opposite his favorite eyeball.

Had he not closed the damned curtains? Must he ruin *everything* in his own life? In the chaos, it had been such a gift to fall asleep, only to be so rudely awakened. He'd been having such a lovely dream too, wherein the cool satin of a lilac dress was cast in a puddle on his bedroom floor while long tresses of platinum-blonde hair adorned the pillow at his side, crowning the silhouette of a moon-pale body, breathing peacefully in the embrace of contented sleep.

Alas, there was nothing in the bed with him but his own woes, and with those, it was plenty crowded, wasn't it?

He hoped to God above that the girl hadn't said anything to Rosie or Gideon just yet. He needed more information before he could decide upon how to act. He needed to be absolutely certain that the entire thing was real and not some elaborate jest engineered at his expense. Could it possibly just be a jest?

It sounded like one, for certain. As though he had the mental and emotional fortitude required for espionage! He could barely navigate a game of chicken hazard with Rose without being taken for all he was worth, for the love of God!

It was true that he had spent a fair amount of time meandering around the Continent. He enjoyed purchasing unusual bits and bobs, especially to give to Heloise upon his return. Nothing substantial, however. He much preferred interesting local knickknacks to pricey baubles and artistic investments.

Was it possible he'd grabbed something deceptively valuable last time he'd been abroad? If so, surely someone would have come for him by now. After all, he'd been in England since Callie was born, determined to finish that blasted degree to appease Gideon.

Maybe he'd been walking around Oxford for going on three years with some infernal state secret tossed on a table in his rooms!

For a brief moment, he thought perhaps he'd have been better served erupting from the closet and confronting the mysterious trio head on. It was potentially the only opportunity he would ever have to do so. But that would have endangered Gloriana too, and while he might frequently be a horse's ass, he'd never put her in danger.

Well. He'd never knowingly put her in danger. Not much, anyway. Kissing her wasn't dangerous, was it? Even if they were caught, the worst thing that could happen would be a compromised reputation, leading to a hasty marriage, ergo life at his side.

Perhaps that was dangerous after all.

Would the likes of her even have him?

He huffed, tossing himself out of bed and stomping toward the armoire. She had been *horrified* at the idea of being compromised that first night. Nothing had changed, had it? She'd kissed him, but from the skill of that kiss, it was not a thing she was reserving for her one true love.

He gave a begrudging half smile, ruffling the short strands of his hair. Implications aside, it had been a very good kiss.

THE LAYOUT of the dining room made it difficult to tell for certain who had congregated within before making one's presence known.

Alex's only means of ensuring that his mother was not perched at the dining table like a hawk at its roost, ready to swoop down and dig her talons into him, was to listen for a bit from the hallway before making himself known.

Most of the guests would be taking breakfast in their rooms following the dance, if they were eating at all. He wasn't surprised to hear his brother and sister-in-law at the table, overseeing the meal, despite the excuse they might've used to stay in bed. Gideon would have insisted on being a good host.

The rest of the voices spoke in such a low murmur that he couldn't place their identities to their voices with any certainty. The fact that none of said voices were loud, brash Americans was enough for him to feel safe and secure striding into the breakfast with his head held high.

Of course, one or more of those assembled might be planning to kill him, but that was genuinely preferable to a confrontational breakfast opposite Ruthie Somers.

He made quick eye contact with Gloriana Blakely, who was nibbling rather conspicuously at a scone while a petite and somewhat mousy girl whispered in her ear. She gave him the slightest nod of acknowledgement before turning to her friend, feigning a sudden and strong disinterest in his appearance.

"Alex!" Rose said in a tone of pleasant surprise, her fork halfway to her mouth. "Good morning to you! We were just discussing you."

"Shall I make myself scarce, then?" he joked, pulling out a chair to the distress of a footman who hadn't acted fast enough. "I shouldn't want to interrupt a good roasting."

"My brother is quite the wit," Gideon explained to the vicar seated to his left. "When Rose was putting together the Somers family line, she said she very much expected to find the famous Will Somers, jester to Henry the Eighth, within our legacy. Alas, there is no proof that Alex descends from the man."

"If I did, that would mean you do as well," Alex replied easily, scanning the offerings on the table. "One can still hope."

Lord Benton sniffed in disapproval, raising his keen gray eyes to meet Alex's. He spoke in the flat tone of a man who is certain that all he says is infallible truth. "Surely you would not be proud of such a connection? A fool in the ancestry?"

"The fool survived King Henry and both daughters," Alex responded with what he hoped was a friendly smile to a truly terrifying man. "A feat not shared by the likes of many, nor accomplished by giants like Cromwell, Neville, and More. I'd say it's a matter of pride if we are indeed kin."

One of the daughters giggled into her teacup, deepening Benton's frown. "As you say," he allowed, though Alex thought his commentary had quickly and permanently been etched into some mental ledger the man kept of those who crossed his path.

"If you eat quickly, you can join us on a walk of the grounds," Rose put in, folding her napkin over an empty plate. "The weather is brisk but not unpleasant, and the turning foliage is quite spectacular."

The mousy girl with Gloriana brightened at this. "Oh, I've heard the botany this far north rivals the gardens in Chelsea," she breathed. "Do you keep a garden, Lady Somers?"

"Only on canvas, I'm afraid," Rose responded with a laugh.

"I've no talent with earth and seed, but am rather a keen hand with watercolors."

Gideon patted his wife's hand affectionately. "My mother keeps a rose bed at the dower house, though I'm certain it's out of season by now. I will ask Heloise how it is faring."

"Yes, I was hoping to see her this morning," the mousy one replied, meeting Gideon's eye with a calm sort of confidence one didn't often find with debutantes, especially not the wallflowers. "Heloise and I were friends at Mrs. Arlington's."

"Were you?" Gideon replied in genuine surprise.

Gloriana made a huffy sound and tossed her own napkin onto her plate.

Alex resisted the urge to chuckle at her pouting like that. She was in a right snit over Heloise, all these years later. It was hard to believe that this was the girl who'd caused such a tangle of admiration and rage in his little sister. What he wouldn't give to have witnessed the exchanges between them at this school for girls. He shouldn't say it out loud, but he rather thought the idea of Gloriana with ink-stained teeth to be a charming one.

He followed the group out onto the grounds, refreshed by the crisp autumn breeze that stirred through the grasses around the manor.

His instinct, of course, was to make a beeline for Gloriana and find enough space to discuss the goings-on of the previous evening before she might share the details of their adventure with anyone else, *particularly* his sister-in-law, who would, without a second thought, share it with his elder brother.

Oh, how he wanted to go put his face into a pillow for the remainder of eternity. But no, here he was, strolling down a gravel path, listening to the ladies sigh over leaves dying in pretty colors. Perhaps it was rather pretty, he thought begrudgingly, shoving his hands into his coat pockets as the wind tickled his hair.

At present, Gloriana was with her mousy friend, though she did toss a look over her shoulder at him, likely encouraging him to pick up his speed.

He resisted the urge to just flee back to the house and forget the whole endeavor and trotted up to the ladies, putting on his most charming smile.

"I don't believe we've met," he said to the mousy one. "I'm Alex Somers."

"Eleanor Applegate," she replied evenly, though she made no move to shake hands or otherwise cement their introduction. "You are intimates with my brother, I believe."

"It's a pleasure, Miss Applegate." Alex smiled. "I am very fond of your brother. You know, it took me almost three terms to coax him out of the library and into the pub."

"Was he much different from one setting to the other?" she asked, tilting her head. "I cannot imagine he would be."

"A few pints of ale can sometimes reveal parts of us we'd never have met otherwise." Alex chuckled. "I find him quite different at the pub than the library, yes."

"Nell," Gloriana said softly, linking her arm into the other girl's. "Did you know that Lord Benton studied horticulture in the Netherlands? I imagine his expertise would enhance your particular desires for this promenade."

"Did he really?" she asked, her clear gray eyes turning to Gloriana's. "Would you forgive me if I were to leave you for a bit, then? I will only ask if he is willing to share his observations. Or you might join me?"

"Oh, I am no botanist." Gloriana laughed. "I shall be fine with Lord Alex at my side. If you learn anything particularly interesting, do save it for the recital tonight."

"Yes, of course," the girl answered absently, already pulling away and looking to make her way up to Lord Benton.

Alex thought it rather impressive that such a little thing would ask the formidable Lord Benton for a botanical tour of the hedgerows. "Quite the little bluestocking, isn't she?" he said curiously as the girl caught up to Benton and his daughter.

"She is whip smart, yes," Gloriana sighed as she watched her friend, "and fearless too. Look at the way she commands a man who influences kings and armies. She is always a bit of a surprise."

"She's bolder than the brother," Alex observed, offering his arm to Glory. He didn't dwell on the warmth that spread through him when she took it, nor the way her scent wove around him as they walked.

"Peter is a man," Gloriana replied with a wave of her free hand. "The rules of the world allow him his foibles. Nell is not so fortunate and must demand any experience she wishes to have, lest it pass her by."

"That Lord Benton, though," Alex said softly. "He is a dangerous, well-connected man. Gideon was notably surprised that he accepted the invitation to our little country party. Perhaps he did so because it suited a separate agenda."

She bit her lip, considering it. "He certainly seems to have the disposition for such matters," she allowed. "Though I take exception to any surprise at his acceptance of my invitation. I intervened to save one of his daughters from a compromising position at Almack's this spring. He has expressed a personal thanks to me, and the girl considers me something of a role model now. It is no surprise to me that he would accept my invitation, independent of any potential desire to snuff you out."

"Snuff me out!" Alex laughed. "I see you are unaffected by the threats to my person, to refer to them so glibly."

"Nonsense," she said, shaking her head. "I barely slept for how seriously I've taken what we overheard."

"How can you not think Benton the most likely to be a member of our trio? The whispers about him alone are almost an implication in espionage. He influences the very powerful, runs in the elite circles behind the curtains, does he not?"

"He does," she agreed, turning those pale blue eyes up to him. "Which is why it seems strange that he would be involved in such a petty matter as retrieving some parcel you don't even know you have."

"What about that Atlas chap?" Alex suggested. "Gideon also mentioned that he was an impressive addition to our roster. He's a diplomat, isn't he? Hand in lots of foreign interests?"

"Mr. Atlas has attended because it was I who invited him," she replied stiffly. "Have you not noticed how he attends me? We are courting."

Alex narrowed his eyes, a sudden discomfort settling in around his midsection. "I haven't noticed any such thing."

"Perhaps you should be more observant," she clipped, lifting her chin. "Besides, the *ton* guests are not the only strangers at the manor right now. Who is to say we did not overhear members of the serving staff last night? Mrs. Laughlin hired a host of temporary staff with the promise of generous vails. It seems a most opportune place for a spy to lurk in plain sight, no?"

He hadn't considered it. It seemed immediately absurd to cast suspicion on the servants when established and talented political players were gracing the rooms of Somerton, but perhaps that was the best cover for one with nefarious intentions.

"If I were a spy," he said thoughtfully, "I should be very disappointed if my assignment was as a servant and not a party guest. I would be useless at stoking fires and serving luncheon."

She giggled, giving him a nudge of playful rebuke for jesting about such a thing.

For just a moment the tension eased in its iron band around his ribs. He inhaled deeply, taking the liberty of pulling her just a touch closer to his side. He enjoyed the feeling of her warm little hand tucked into his elbow and the graceful sway of her gait matching his own.

"Alex," she said softly. "We must not take this lightly. Have you spoken to your brother yet?"

"No," he said, the band of concern snapping itself firmly back around his middle. "And I don't intend to until I know exactly what we are dealing with. Gideon is known to over-react, and his plans for mitigating disaster are often not very well thought out."

"Oh," she said, blinking up at him.

"You mustn't say anything to Rosie either," he added. "Not yet. At the very least, this whole blasted affair gives me an excuse to skip the bloody grouse hunt."

"Skip it?" she repeated, furrowing her pale brow. "You mustn't do that."

"I will feign a grippe or some such." He shrugged. "I cannot think of an activity I am worse suited for than lying in the hedges, planning to shoot some poor bird. If I'm in my room all day, the female villain cannot conduct her search."

"Exactly!" she said, stopping dead in her tracks, her grip on his arm forcing him to stop too.

She looked ahead at the group, which had gathered around Lord Benton as he pointed to various trees along the route, seemingly concerned about being overheard.

"If she cannot search your rooms, the murderous one will potentially take action against you," she hissed. "Let her search! If she finds whatever it is they are after, this whole affair may conclude quietly."

Alex frowned. "But how will we know either way?"

"What if," she considered, pulling away from him for a

moment. "What if we speak to Mrs. Laughlin? Would she aid us in examining the temporary staff?"

"She'd tattle to Gideon in the space where you drew breath," Alex said. "Consider her on par with the viscount."

"Drat!" She paced back to him, taking his arm and nodding to the group, which had gone quite far ahead. "We must keep up appearances," she muttered, a frustration in her tone that Alex felt right down to the soles of his shoes.

He gathered her back to his side, matching her pace to close the gap between the two of them and the others. Her presence there was reassuring. Somehow, despite the topic of their conversation, his heart was not in his throat with panic. Discussing the matter with her made it feel more like a challenging puzzle, an amusing riddle rather than a threat to his life.

It seemed, however, that this calming effect was not mutual. Understandably, he realized. His own reassurance was as irrational as they came.

"I did look through my things last night," he assured her. "I cannot find anything that I'd think would be of interest to the shadows of the Crown."

She tilted her head thoughtfully, a brush of white-gold ringlets slipping over the arm of his coat. "Perhaps you need a fresh pair of eyes to assist in your search," she said. "Perhaps you are blinded by familiarity."

Perhaps so, he thought silently as they made their way down the autumnal drive. Perhaps inviting Gloriana Blakely into his bedchambers would present an array of very, very interesting possibilities.

CHAPTER 12

*I*f ever Gloriana had occasion to doubt her skill as a woman of talent in the arts of social grace, she told herself she must refer to this evening's recital as proof of her abilities. Her time at Mrs. Arlington's had served her well, just as she'd told Papa they would all those years ago. How else could she have executed such a spectacularly normal affair, smiling and calm, with all that was brewing just behind her mask of placidity?

They gathered in the music room for an evening of guest-provided entertainment as the sun sank low in the sky, brightening the room with shafts of orange-gold light that set off the ornaments the ladies wore in a spectacular shimmer.

As the de facto hostess, Rose presented her talent as one that could be enjoyed after the recital, when the guests would mingle with their drinks. She had brought down her trusty sketch pad and an array of charcoals with the promise to sketch anyone who dared be rendered into eternity by her hand. Gloriana had always found Rose's talent for capturing faces rather fearsome, and always avoided looking at depictions of herself for fear that Rose had caught some flaw that the mirror had not.

Gloriana and Tia took up the first of the active performances, with Tia at the pianoforte and Gloriana providing her voice. It was an ensemble they had performed many times this year in various townhouses around London, and while the performance felt baked into her bones by this stage, there was still a tremor of fear that her distractibility tonight would somehow taint her delivery.

Alas, her voice was as clear and sweet as it had ever been. She took note of the fixated admiration of Mr. Atlas as she performed and did her best to not seek out a head of shocking red hair in the crowd. What did it matter to her what Alex Somers thought of her voice, after all? It was secondary to the needs of the evening.

Lord Benton's daughters gave an amusing recital of a scene from *The Twelfth Night*, winning several laughs from those in attendance. Nell's true musical prowess lay in the harp, but without one in the manor, she made due with the pianoforte, delivering a somber, low-register requiem that shifted the mood markedly from the amusement of the comedic scene preceding it.

Unsurprisingly, Heloise Somers declined to participate in any sort of performance.

Many of the gentlemen were musically inclined as well, though their performances were more reserved, as men tended to be. The only spark of something unexpected was Alex himself, who performed an illusion trick he claimed to have learned from an Iberian magician, in which the room was dimmed save for one lantern. Using it, he created the most amusing shadows on the opposite wall with his hands, retelling the fable of the scorpion and the frog.

It was the perfect ending for the audience-based performances, as the lights came up and hors d'oeuvres were brought out, with everyone blinking away the impression of his story and finding cause to move about the room.

Tatiana was arranging a blanket on the floor in the corner of the room farthest from the commotion and placing her divination items upon it. She had not announced that she would be telling fortunes tonight, but anyone who took the time to glance in her direction would quickly glean what she was about.

Gloriana pressed her lips together, unsure if she approved of the inclusion of superstition bordering on light paganism at her gathering, but ultimately, perhaps a good look into the future would be beneficial just now, in the grand scheme of things.

Hopefully the vicar and curate in attendance would choose to look the other way.

"You sing beautifully," a deep voice said at her ear, sending a shiver of pure molten pleasure through her body. She turned, ready to thank Mr. Atlas for his admiration, only to find it was Alex Somers at her elbow instead, those green eyes glittering down at her with a most inappropriate intensity. "I did not know music was amongst your talents, though I suppose I should not be surprised that such a lovely mouth can produce beautiful song."

She hesitated in her response, her steady facade of calm flickering dangerously for the first time that evening. Her heart felt it necessary to speed as she resisted the overpowering urge to lean into the warm aura about his body. It did not help that his eyes were fixed with a predator's glimmer on her lips. His memory of their stolen kiss the night before might as well be shouted directly for how loud that look of hunger was.

Over his shoulder, shrouded somehow in the shadows of the lamplight, Mr. Atlas seemed nothing but a glossy phantom, whose shape could never quite take form alongside the vibrant presence of Alex Somers.

"It occurred to me," another voice boomed, as the Marquis of Moorvale squeezed his formidable frame into the space of the conversation, "that I might have brought Echo down and had her perform some tricks. She's a sight more talented than you, Somers, I daresay."

Alex grinned, that seductive demeanor shrugged away in less than the blink of an eye, and scratched the back of his neck as he peered up at his friend. "Bring your girl down, and she'll be leaving on my arm, Moorvale. You know how she fancies me."

"Ah, you wee cad. Don't start duels during your party. It's bad form, isn't it, Miss Blakely?"

"It certainly is," she replied, bemused that the men were bantering this way about a dog. "Lord Moorvale, your bond with your pet is quite remarkable. There is a cat here in the manor that I have become very fond of myself, but I cannot imagine having a shadow at my side to the degree of intimacy that you share with your hound."

Moorvale sighed, tipping the remains of his drink into his mouth. "You didn't grow up with dogs, did you, lass?

Perhaps I'll gift you a puppy one of these days and you'll learn just how superior one creature is to the other."

"Oh, I rather like cats," she protested, surprised at the feeling behind the statement.

"Sheldon doesn't appreciate their refinement," said Heloise, taking her brother's arm as she joined their little clutch. "I admit, Glory, I am not surprised that you are a woman of taste in this regard, though I can't say I sanction decorating my Nero with velvet bows."

Gloriana narrowed her eyes at the use of her pet name coming from the lips of Heloise Somers. She looked almost a lady tonight, her hair arranged conservatively, though she could never hide its brazen color nor the generous smattering of freckles that covered her face and arms.

It was truly strange how these features were so appealing on her brother and so infuriating on her. Still, she was clearly making a point of politeness, though such behavior always came with a whiff of a hidden trick just below the surface.

"I thought he looked quite handsome," Gloriana replied with what she hoped was not a stiff smile. "In Devon, we always collar our cats so that they are not mistaken for strays by the villagers. I thought perhaps such a precaution would suit Nero himself, as he likes to vanish into the wilderness on his own."

Heloise paused, her eyes widening a little with surprise. "I had not considered that," she confessed, albeit a little begrudgingly. "Perhaps it suits him after all."

"Where's that cheeky physician chap?" Alex wondered,

glancing around the room. "I'm surprised he's let you out of his sight for even a moment."

"Stop it," she whispered with a quick elbow to her brother's ribs. "He is simply a colleague."

Both Lord Moorvale and Alex made grunts of disbelief at that assertion.

Gloriana couldn't help but look around herself. She'd taken next to no interest in the doctor from the township, aside from a precursory greeting, but if he was courting Heloise, that would explain Gideon's insistence that he be included on the invitation list.

"Oh, look what you've done," Heloise sighed, immediately keen to Gloriana's curiosity. "Stop that, Miss Blakely, it is just my brother's ever-present foolishness. Come, let's see what fair Tia is about, shall we?"

Before she could resist or truly react at all, she found her arm taken by her nemesis and her body tugged away from the confusing electricity she felt in the wake of Alex Somers. Over her shoulder, he gave her only the slightest nod, his eyes locked upon hers, and then returned to his conversation with Lord Moorvale, presumably on the merits of cats and dogs.

"Do you ever pause, Gloriana, and thank God that you have no brothers?" Heloise muttered, in perhaps the first ever private address she'd ever given that was not a barb.

It took only a moment for Gloriana to gain control of her surprise, the niggling thought that perhaps this was an elaborate trap set to spring at a later moment still twisting at the base of her thoughts.

"Why, no," she confessed, "I've often thought rather wistfully of what it might be like to have strapping brothers to protect my honor and dote upon me."

Heloise made a rather unladylike snort as they approached Tia's blanket. "Of course you have. Hello there, Tatiana."

Tatiana startled visibly, gazing up at Heloise and Gloriana arm-in-arm with naked disbelief. "Lady Heloise!" she said, pushing herself to her feet and leaning forward to apply the merest ghost of an air kiss to Heloise's cheek. "I did not think we would have the opportunity to ... erm, converse! Please, sit."

"All right." Heloise grinned, sending all of the warning signals in Glory's head to a frantic buzzing. The wretch was clearly enjoying their discomfort.

All the same, the two of them settled onto Tia's blanket, Gloriana's puddle of sky-blue satin blending with the jagged lace of Heloise's gray and red. Heloise seemed as comfortable as could be, as though she were conspiring with old friends, while Gloriana was certain all of her bones had turned to oak and her posture was the most correct it would ever be in her life.

"Well, what's this?" Nell piped as she crumpled to the floor next to them, taking no time to settle to the ground in a careful fashion. "Am I to witness an armistice?"

Heloise grinned, but Tia drew her mouth into a humorless line and grabbed her deck of dusty old cards. She'd brandished these cards many a night at Mrs. Arlington's, entertaining the girls with tales of cartomancy and her mysterious grandmother, who acquired the deck in Marseilles before the war.

Her pale fingers slid over the peeling edges of the painted cards, flipping and shuffling them quickly before dropping them into the lap of her skirt.

"We've three of you," she declared, "and all women here, young and unmarried. Shall we ask the spirits the wisdom of the goddess?"

"Ooh, heresy," Heloise said with a little clap, winning a giggle from Nell and a roll of the eyes from Gloriana. "Yes, let's."

"Mm," Tatiana nodded, lifting the deck and tapping it to her chin. "Wise women say that there are three stages of womanhood, and three fonts of wisdom that we all must draw upon at different points in our lifetimes, in order to be true to the goddess within. These are the three faces of Hecate, and every woman shares the lot."

"Blimey," Nell muttered, folding her hands in her lap.

"Tonight the three are with us through the three of you," Tia said mysteriously, flipping one card face down in front of each of them. To Nell, she said "Maiden," as the card flicked from her fingers to the carpet. To Heloise, she said "Mother," repeating the same motion, and to Gloriana, "Crone."

"Crone!" Gloriana repeated in horror. "Why am I the crone?"

"Hush," Nell giggled. "Heloise is the Mother and she's not complaining."

"The Crone is my favorite anyhow." Tia sighed, shaking her head as though it were her most solemn burden to educate her friends in the arcane. "She speaks of learning from the path you've already walked, and remembering how to avoid the dangers along the way."

"Hmm," Glory managed, sparing a not-so-subtle glance at the historical hazard sitting to her right.

"The Maiden," Tia continued, "is a symbol of innocence and intuition, of curiosity and self-discovery. It speaks to trusting the instinct over the mind."

"Then why on Earth is it in front of me?" Nell scoffed. "Other than to remind me that a maiden I shall be until my dying day."

"The Mother," Tia gritted out, a little louder than strictly necessary, "is a spirit of abundance and nurturing growth. It is a reminder to be thankful for what we have, kind to those we see, and patient above all else."

Heloise only nodded, accepting her assignation with a quiet grace that immediately made Glory resent herself for her own outburst. Surely the Crone was better than the Mother anyhow!

"Now, if you flip over your cards, you will find the advice each of these spirits has for you tonight," Tia said, glancing up as Lord Benton's daughters approached to observe the telling of fortunes. "For the Maiden?"

Nell flipped her card over with a marked lack of enthusiasm, perhaps a little more stung by her own commentary on her status as a maiden than she had intended.

"The Devil," Tia said, with what sounded like genuine surprise. "Have you vices, Nell, you secretive girl?"

Nell shrugged. "Perhaps a bit? I am more fond of sweets than I ought to be."

"No," Tia said with a shake of her glossy black ringlets. "This is true vice. Lust, lies, and luxury. Think secret lovers or opium dens. A card far more salacious than I would wager for you, Miss Applegate."

"Pishposh," Nell scoffed. "And what, the goddess maiden thinks I ought behave myself, then?"

"No." Tia laughed. "She thinks you ought to indulge."

"My, my," Heloise murmured with a raise of her eyebrows. "Here's hoping my card is half as exciting."

She flipped it over without prompting, revealing a woman in the nude, kneeling at a riverbank, with loose hair flowing over her shoulders. Her bosoms were rendered in shockingly ribald detail. "Wonderful," she tittered.

"The Star," Tatiana said softly, her brow furrowing as she turned her large, glistening eyes onto Heloise. "You've recently been through an upending. Something that shattered the entire world in which you live."

Heloise lifted her chin, almost in challenge. "I can't think what you mean."

"You do not have to tell me," Tia replied, her tone soft, almost conciliatory. "The Mother advises you to rest and reflect, to be still and calm in the peace after the battle. To look within and decide what you want for when the storm returns."

"It storms here every summer," Heloise said easily, pushing the card back toward the dealer.

Gloriana put two fingers on her own card, impatience roiling in her chest. It was almost too much to hear her most trusted friend speak to Heloise with such a sweetness and concern. She must not be jealous. It was only an act, after all.

She flipped the card over and bottled up the urge to utter a curse of frustration as the other three girls said in chorus, "The Fool."

"It is only my brother Alex," Heloise laughed, "here to tell you what a spectacular waste your efforts were on launching his future."

"Or it's me," Glory muttered. "A fool and a crone."

"It is an unexpected card for the Crone to choose," Tia allowed, tilting her head thoughtfully. "The Fool walks his path blindly, on dumb intuition and impulse. You see, he is about ready to step off the ledge of a cliff while he looks over his shoulder at the things he's already left behind."

"It's because a cat is scratching his bollocks," Heloise said placidly. "I'd be looking behind me too."

Lord Benton's daughters erupted in startled giggles. Even Tatiana smiled with a little shrug. The card was old and faded, but it did appear that the cat following the Fool was attacking a rather tender spot.

"So what does it mean?" Glory snipped impatiently. "Follow the Fool? Be the Fool? Avoid the Fool?"

"I ... don't rightly know," Tatiana confessed, frowning. "The Crone espouses remembering what you've learned on your travels as you plot the course ahead. The Fool says follow your heart and damn the consequences. I suppose there must be a way in which you could do both."

"Naturally," Gloriana sighed, the thrum of the clocks throughout the manor echoing in the lift in her pulse. "How else is one to be a woman in Society without looking ahead and behind all at once?"

"How indeed?" Heloise replied, giving her a sidelong glance that hours later, she still could not interpret.

CHAPTER 13

*I*t wasn't until she was back in her chambers, supposedly retired for the evening, that Gloriana felt she could breathe again. This was an irony, she supposed, as the dangerous part of her evening was only beginning.

Still, she'd readily take unraveling murderous mysteries and the seductive gazes of dangerous men over sitting next to Heloise Somers for the better part of an hour, having an unsettling future told for all to hear, while maintaining polite decorum.

Really, it had been too much. The instinct she'd had to pick up that wretched Fool card and rip it into a thousand psychic pieces had been a strong one. Again, she congratulated herself on an education well learned, and the true control of a lady born and bred.

Now, all she had to do was change into something modest but comfortable and ... well, and steal away into a man's room in the dead of night. It was for a pure cause, she told herself. It wasn't nearly as salacious as it sounded.

Still, a little part of her wished she'd drawn that Devil card herself. A sign from the beyond to indulge in one's most wicked urges would be a most welcome thing just about now.

She sighed, giving the dresses hanging in her wardrobe an irritated flick. How was it possible that she didn't own a single simple, serviceable frock? Surely she'd needed one at some point before tonight. At this stage, she almost thought her night rail was going to be more sensible than anything she'd brought with her from London, but of course, that was entirely inappropriate, wasn't it?

She was going to Alex's bedchambers to assist in saving his life and his reputation, *not* for a tryst or seduction. Of course she knew that. He knew it too. He must. Goodness knew he couldn't possibly still be harping on about their kiss in the linen closet with such dread hanging over his head!

She sighed, drawing out a frothy, cream-colored walking gown that had been shoved to the back of her things since she'd arrived. It was much better suited for flitting through the warm summer gardens surrounding their townhouse in Mayfair than the brisk autumn winds of Yorkshire. In fact, it was cut so high on the calf that it was meant to be worn with a pair of lace pantalettes, a daring fashion that she was surprised her mother had allowed, but not so half as daring as *n*ot wearing them and leaving such a large amount of leg bare.

She gave an ironic chuckle, spreading the dress out on her

bedsheets. Her mother must never know the first thing about her interactions with Alexander Somers. If she were aware of half of the misadventures Gloriana had gotten up to since arriving at Somerton, she'd no doubt faint clean to the floor, the way Rose's mother had after she'd learned of the elopement.

After all, she had invited Nathaniel Atlas into this home in the hopes of bringing him up to scratch before he could return to London. An *accepted* proposal would surely soothe the rift her parents had scorched between them after the last debacle. She knew they couldn't really understand the importance of making the right choice, for neither of them had ever involved themselves in the grand game of London Society like their daughter had. That corpulent, flatulent suitor that had been so unpleasantly thrust upon her would never, ever do. Especially when there were men like Atlas out there, whose position on the playing board offered a limitless future of strategy, intrigue, and excitement.

She knew, of course, that she should have been snogging Mr. Atlas in linen closets, laying the groundwork for the rest of her life. Yet here she was, still replaying the memory of such a short-lived kiss with a man who cheerfully described himself as without prospects over and over in her head like a ninny.

She pulled the dress on over a clean shift, not bothering with stays or any other formalities, other than securing the ribbon below her bust that made the dress baseline presentable. She had allowed a maid to take her hair down after the evening's entertainments and so had no recourse other than to bundle the lot of it into a ribbon at the nape of her neck and hope such a thing passed as presentable.

She frowned at her reflection, flickering in the low light of the lantern. She looked like a country maid off to milk a cow, she thought. The curls in her hair, so carefully coiled by the heated wand, had become uneven and messy while pinned and arranged along her scalp, so instead of a fall of perfect ringlets, she had a mess of white-blonde waves and springs about her face.

Without the stays, there was no illusion of womanly curves, with her skin pressed so directly into the bodice of the gown, and she feared she might have circles beneath her eyes so late into the evening. She started to pinch at her cheeks to raise the color, but stopped with her fingers halfway through the process, huffing at the absurdity of such a thing. What did it matter if she looked curvaceous or well groomed or rosy-cheeked? This was serious business, not a social visit!

She spun on her heel, whipping the lantern up from its place on her nightstand and sliding her feet into a pair of well-worn slippers.

This morning, as they'd walked the perimeter of the grounds, she had suggested Alex meet her in the little library and guide her to his chambers. He had pointed out that this was far too dangerous a plan, as they could not explain away being seen stealing about the hallways together in the dead of night, whereas Gloriana on her own could fabricate any number of plausible explanations.

"Surely you are more practiced at trysting than you let on," he had teased, those mischievous green eyes roaming over her body, bold as you please.

She had not responded, choosing instead a cryptic lift of her brow and a demand for his own stratagem, if it be so far superior. She had not yet decided what impression she wished Alex Somers to have of her, after their kiss in the dark. Clearly he thought her an accomplished seductress, well-honed toward subterfuge and passion.

On one hand, she rather liked the idea of seeming confident and experienced to a man like Alex, who certainly found much more to respect in an adventurous woman than a chaste one. On the other, the reality of her own chastity bristled at the implication that she might be anything less than pure. Besides, it would be an absolute disaster if her reputation took on the taint of a girl known for whisking off into hidden alcoves with roguish men.

Men like Alex Somers, she reminded herself. Nell had said he had quite the reputation of his own, after all.

She counted the doors down from her own the way he had instructed her, keeping a keen eye out for the one that was left ajar. Her pulse raced at the risk of it all, her instincts telling her to flee back to the safety of her own chambers at every creak of the old wood that made up the walls of Somerton.

Strangely, catching sight of the door she was looking for did absolutely nothing to calm her nerves. Instead, a flurry of butterflies erupted in her chest at the knowledge that once she pushed the door open, she'd be alone in the bedchambers of a man who looked at her the way a wolf looked at a rabbit.

She doubted, however, that any rabbit had ever been quite so silly about wandering into a wolf's den.

She put her hand to the oaken grain of the door, just above the knob, steeling herself to push it open. She bit down on her lip and edged forward, attempting to glance through the crack where the door was left ajar, just to ensure beyond any possible doubt that she had the right place.

Her breath caught in her throat. There, just beyond the entryway, was Alex Somers, standing with his back to her, naked from the waist up.

She froze, her fingers settling onto the cool brass of the door-knob. She found herself quite unable to tear her eyes away as he snatched a shirt from an open chest of drawers and shook it out before him.

He turned to the side, ruffling his hand through his short, red hair, revealing a stunning profile full of lithe, lean muscle. Exposed like this, he truly was a thing of beauty, with a generous sprinkle of freckling down the toned lines of his back and shoulders, over the broad expanse of his chest, and she noted as he turned toward the door, trailing down over his navel and vanishing beneath the band of his trousers.

She hoped sincerely that he could not see her, struck as she was in place with the shaft of light from his room slanting over her wide blue eyes and parted lips. Even if he discovered her in that moment, she was not entirely certain she'd have the presence of mind to react or flee.

She couldn't be certain that she'd never seen a man so unclothed before. After all, there were all manner of beggars and workers between London and Devon who spent their days in all manner of disarray. She was certain that she'd never seen so much of a man of breeding before, however, much less one so beautifully wrought. She wondered idly, as her eyes skimmed over the planes of lovely, bare flesh, what sort of activity a gentleman did that resulted in such a strong physique. It was nigh unfashionable how muscled he was, and yet that knowledge did very little to cool her blood as she beheld him.

He sighed, appearing lost in thought, and dragged the billowy white shirt over his head, the fabric slinking down to hide the incredible revelation of his exposed body beneath the modesty of vestments. He nudged the drawer closed and turned to consider his bed, reaching out to adjust the alignment of one of the throw pillows against the headboard.

It was such an absurd thing for him to do, so completely unaware of the way he'd knocked the wind completely from her lungs, that it had the most welcome effect of startling her back to the present.

She spun quickly out of the slat of light that streamed through the door, bracing her back against the cool wall just outside of the doorframe as she gathered her breath. She placed a hand over her heart, willing her breathing to slow and her heart to ease.

She reminded herself, for perhaps the hundredth time in the last hour, that she was here to assist a man who feared for his life, *not* to become embroiled in a passionate affair. She further reminded herself that a lady of her bearing and reputation need not fantasize about such ridiculous things when so many men would leap at the opportunity to make them a reality, even if this particular one was currently preoccupied with thrilling espionage and a dangerous mystery.

Right, then. She stepped away from the wall and approached the door again, giving it a light rap before pushing it open and stepping into the wolf's own den.

CHAPTER 14

*G*loriana had gone to work just as quickly as she'd appeared. Alex had barely had time to greet her before she was curled up at the foot of his bed, sorting through the last valise he had with things in it from Oxford. She was currently kneeling on the carpet, her dainty little toes curled against the soft fibers of his floor, as she flipped through a motley array of textbooks and note journals in search of secrets that might be hiding between their pages.

For Alex's part, he was frozen in place, afraid to take even the first step toward her, perhaps still in shock that she'd actually shown up as they'd planned.

Just what in the devil's name was she playing at dressed that way? Especially if her true mission here was simply to help him go over his things from Oxford once again?

It wasn't as though Alex was some green lad who'd never seen a woman in her particulars before. In fact, he'd seen some truly eye-popping bridal negligee in his day, courtesy of his penchant for ladies who'd already hooked a man and bankrolled a tragically neglected trousseau.

He'd never seen anything like Gloriana Blakely, half dressed in that thin, short little gown that clung so tightly to her skin that he'd immediately caught notice of her pebbled nipples straining against the fabric. She'd come here with her hair mussed and loose, tied pointlessly at the nape with a bit of velvet ribbon, as those otherworldly platinum curls sprang free around her arms and face, twining their way down to her hips.

His mouth had gone completely dry as she'd entered his rooms, and to make matters worse, she'd kicked off her shoes right away, bringing him right back to that night in the library when he'd reflected on how intimate it was to be around a woman without shoes on. The chit wasn't wearing stockings either, and the hemline of the dress she wore went well above the ankle, leaving her shapely little calves completely bare to his lecherous gaze.

He had been pacing around for the better part of an hour, convincing himself that she'd realized how ridiculous their plan for the evening had been. Yes, he'd dragged out the valise, and he'd changed from his formal tails into something casual, rather than simply stripping naked and falling into bed. Some part of him had obviously hoped he was wrong, had pushed him to leave his bedroom door slightly ajar. But whatever that part of him was, it had not prepared him for Gloriana Blakely to appear dressed as she was and tousled as though she'd just been rolled around a bit, the way a girl like her ought to be, if the world were a just place.

Even that night she'd walloped him with the ledger book, she'd been pinned and prim. No matter how well she kissed,

Gloriana Blakely was ever the debutante. Perhaps it was wrong, but the status of a Society miss, unclaimed and doe-eyed, somehow elevated her to a place above the serving wenches and naughty matrons he'd taken to bed over the years. The utter wrongness of being able to make out, so clearly, the shape of her pert little breasts clashed with who she was so thoroughly that it seemed as though there was no sense in the world.

And so he stood stock-still, afraid to take even a step toward her lest he be overcome by his ever-dominant instinct of raw stupidity.

"Are you going to help me or just stand and watch?" she asked without looking over her shoulder. There was a coolness in her tone that made the answer less of an option and more of a command.

He was unable to tear his eyes away from the downy curls at the nape of her slender neck, at the way the neckline of the dress sagged just a little, revealing the creamy expanse of her shoulders. He shook himself, forcing his gaze to the ceiling.

"I told you, I've already looked through everything," he replied, irritated by the insolence that always seemed to lurk in his tone. "Didn't you say what I needed was a fresh set of eyes?"

She sighed. "Perhaps so, but it would make me feel better if you participated, or at least made some conversation, instead of looming behind me like a haunted statue."

He chuckled, blinking away the burning in his eyes as he felt his shoulders relax. "Are statues often haunted, then?" he teased, pacing over to the opposite side of his valise to look down upon her. "A particular fear of the fearless Miss Blakely?"

She gave a begrudging smile, motioning for him to sit, and waited to respond until he was cross-legged opposite her, with only the valise between them. "The statues at our church in Devon used to scare the daylights out of me as a child," she confessed. "I was convinced that once you turned your back on them, their heads would turn and follow your movements."

"Well, I confess, that is a properly terrifying thought." He laughed. "Church must have been an agony for you."

She shook her head a little, that wry smile expanding into something more heartfelt. "I confided to Rosie about my fears, and she first offered to watch the statues for me when I walked away. She was always the brave one, even when we were little. I told her that *obviously* they wouldn't move if she was watching, which I maintain was a valid point. That Sunday, after the service, she scampered ahead of the family, climbed up onto the marble platform of Saint Sebastian, wedged herself between all the arrows, and kissed him full on the mouth!"

"Perhaps your cousin is simply attracted to very stony men," Alex suggested. "It would follow her current choices, after all."

She giggled, dropping the book she was inspecting into her lap and leaning back against the foot of the bed with a sigh. "Her mother scolded her so for doing that, but it became our little joke. We'd peck the saints on the cheek or give them a little swat on the bum on the way into service. When my father noticed, I thought he'd be furious, but instead he only wished to know what on earth we were about."

"And did you tell him?"

She nodded, sighing wistfully. "Yes, and the next Sunday he bowed to St. Catherine and kissed her hand!"

Her joy at this memory was infectious. Though he couldn't help smiling, Alex couldn't help but try to imagine his own father doing such a thing. Perhaps he would have, if he hadn't been such a tortured fellow and prone to drink. The way Gloriana softened when she remembered this little act of foolishness made his chest tighten with envy.

"You are very fortunate," he told her, "to have such a family."

"I am," she agreed, though in doing so, her smile faded into a frown. She bit her lip, lowering her gaze into the book in her lap and sighing. "I should be amazed if my papa ever treats me so sweetly again. He is very cross with me, you know. That's why I'm in Yorkshire instead of at home in Devon. I was banished."

Alex lifted his brows, resisting the urge to suggest in jest what wickedness could sour a doting father on such a delightful young miss. She appeared to be everything Society would want from a debutante. She was beautiful and talented, exceptionally skilled at social graces, and surprisingly well-connected for an unmarried maiden. The curiosity burned at him, but he didn't dare ask what sin she had committed to be banished to the North as the winds turned cold.

Instead, he took a deep, bracing breath and waited until her cool blue eyes fell to meet his own. "I should explain," he said softly, "what happened last night at the ball, and why I behaved the way I did. I do not know what has happened to create a rift between your parents and yourself, but perhaps hearing about the snarls that tangle up House Somers will ease your concern."

"You don't have to do that," she murmured. "I am sorry I chased you and scolded you. It was not my place."

He gave her a wry smile, shaking his head. "You were completely within your rights. You've spent weeks planning this gathering and I embarrassed both of us acting as I did. I have been avoiding my mother for three years now, you know. She returned from Philadelphia around the time that Gideon ran off with Rose, and I've managed to never have to come face-to-face with her in all the time since. I can't tell you how relieved I am that she skipped the festivities tonight."

"Is she very cruel?" Gloriana whispered, clutching her hands together in concern. "What has she done to you?"

"She left." He sighed. "She abandoned us here with our drunkard of a father and I've never forgiven her for it. She didn't even come back when he died. Do you know how my father died?"

She shook her head, the candlelight sparkling on the fringe of her eyelashes as she stared at him in rapt attention.

"He froze to death on a park bench outside of a copper hell in Clapham Common. His pockets were empty when they retrieved his corpse, though we do not know whether he lost his coin at cards or if he was robbed as he succumbed to the elements. It was a massive scandal. Humiliating."

"Oh, Alex," she gasped, lunging forward to place her hand over his across the open valise. "Oh, that's terrible. I am so sorry."

"Thank you," he said, glancing down at that pale white hand covering his own, both of them resting upon his knee. He turned his palm upward, lacing his fingers through hers, marveling at how well the two suited each other.

She did not pull away, despite leaning awkwardly over the valise. She seemed concerned only with the expression on his face and the confession of his pain.

"It was a relief," he said thinly, his eyes fixed on their clasped hands. "No more drunken rants or surprise debts. No more late-night eruptions dragging us from our beds. Gideon is a right prig, but he's good and patient. He's just, albeit irritating. Gideon as Viscount Somers meant peace, and I have always wondered if it was an evil thing to feel a spark of happiness at the death of my sire."

She was silent, allowing the weight of what he'd said to settle down around them. He didn't know if he'd expected her to immediately assure him that he was not evil and that anyone would have felt relief, or to whisper meaningless platitudes about God's plan for us all. He hadn't anticipated silence.

If she were disgusted, surely she would pull her hand away. Perhaps she'd leave the room altogether, leaving him to his conundrum on his own.

She did neither of these things, instead taking a moment to absorb the story and consider it. Finally, she took a little breath and said with a voice that trembled with emotion,

"Your mother fled a dangerous and volatile husband. For that, I cannot blame her."

She lifted her eyes to meet his, her forehead wrinkled in thought. "How, though, could she leave her children behind? What sort of mother does that?"

"She offered to bring us with her. She gave us very little time to decide and told us she would not be coming back. We were all but young. The idea of leaving Somerton was unfathomable, much less abandoning England itself for some strange and unknown shore."

Her hand flexed within his own, as though this information had shaken her. Her eyes narrowed as she leaned closer, almost inspecting his face. "Did she write to you?"

He shrugged. "I had no interest in letters from a mother who'd abandoned us. Hel is the only one who kept up a correspondence."

"And your brother?" she pressed. "Lord Somers?"

"Gideon does what is appropriate and rational," Alex said with a roll of his eyes. "Who knows how he really feels about her return? If she had come back when Father died, that would have been one thing, but she waited until—" He stopped abruptly, pressing his lips together.

How close had he just come to betraying his sister?

"Until years later," he finished awkwardly, shifting his gaze away from the intent blue of her eyes. *Shit.*

"It is difficult," she decided, "when you understand your parents' reasoning, but still feel wronged by their actions."

He nodded in agreement, a strange ripple of emotion

passing through his chest. In truth, his parents' reasoning had never seemed important. He had never spent much time at all wondering about how Ruthie Somers felt or why she'd done what she did. He hadn't cared. All he had been concerned with was what she'd left behind at Somerton.

He sighed heavily, releasing Glory's hand as gently as he could, accompanied by what he hoped was a convincing smile of nonchalance. "I should have brought a bottle of wine up," he said, "it might have kept the mood in here a bit more jolly."

She sniffed, pulling back and wiping at her cheeks with the palms of her hands. Good Lord, had she been crying while he spoke? Had he made this lovely creature cry? The thought horrified him.

She smiled at him weakly and shook her head with a little laugh. "Do not fret, Lord Alex," she said. "I am only being a silly girl."

"You are sweet," he replied softly, regretting that he did not still hold her hand in his own. "Sincerity can never be silly. I do not deserve such gentle regard."

"Perhaps that wine would not have been a bad idea." She sighed, leaning back against the foot of his bed once again, her cheeks pink and eyes bright from emotion. "Though you'd have much regretted it on the hunt tomorrow."

"Oh, the damned hunt," he grumbled. "Must I really go?"

"Yes," she said with a lazy flip of her hand. "You know why."

"I don't suppose you've found the hidden parcel in my schoolbooks?" he said hopefully, reaching out to take one and shake the pages out. "Perhaps a map to the crown jewels or a secret alliance with a foreign general?"

"Unless the Crown places a particular value on doodles of nude women in the margins of a philosophy text, I'm afraid not," she said with a little grin. "You must have been a terror of a student."

"Oh, Christ and damnation," he hissed, heat flooding to his face. "I had completely forgotten about that."

She laughed, the apples of her cheeks rounding in such a lovely way, framed by her wealth of hair. "I confess, I find your depictions most charming. Would that I had such a frame as the ladies who grace the words of David Hume."

He could feel the heat in his cheeks creep right up to the tops of his ears. He had indeed once been fond of absently sketching women with *very* generous proportions.

Gloriana must think he fancied only women with over-flowing busts, dimpled bellies, and round hips. To be fair, that particular type of woman had always been what caught his eye. Bountiful flesh and a healthy jiggle got the blood flowing in any man, didn't it? Still, he knew that the exquisite woman sitting opposite him did not fit that description at all, and yet her body had haunted his dreams for weeks.

She watched him in amusement, likely enjoying having caught him so completely off guard. This was somehow even more embarrassing than their first encounter, when she'd nearly knocked him unconscious with ... well, with yet another book.

There was a concerning pattern developing here.

"Perhaps," she said, stifling a little yawn behind her fingers. "Perhaps tomorrow I can find an excuse to remain in my rooms. If I am upstairs for the day, perhaps I can catch whomever it is that plans to come search your chambers."

"How would you manage that, short of squatting in the hallway for several hours?" he wondered, doing his damn best not to compare the breasts of his adolescent drawings to the pair directly across from him, melded into tight relief by gauzy fabric.

She arched her back, stretching her arms over her head, her body on wondrous display in the slip of a dress she wore. She stretched with her eyes closed, which allowed him a moment of abject admiration of her form. The tension that had frozen him in place as she entered the room had fled for a time, replaced with a surprising series of confounding emotions as they'd sat across from one another, but here it was again, rooting him to the spot and awakening all sorts of baser instincts that he knew he'd damn well better keep under control.

His illustrations of bawdy fantasies paled in comparison to the sleek and elegant figure of the woman across from him. He couldn't help but remember the way she'd clung to him as he'd plundered the sweetness of her lips, the way her body had felt in his hands, their bodies pressed so tightly together in that closet.

"It is unfortunate business," he heard himself saying, "that intrigue and danger interrupted such a singular first kiss, wouldn't you say?"

Her eyes popped open, lashes fluttering as she focused on him in surprise. She drew her arms down from over her head and into her lap, tilting her head to examine him. "You found it singular in quality?" she inquired in that cool, practiced tone she'd learned at finishing school.

He grinned. "Am I to posit that you did not?"

"I said no such thing," she replied. "All in all, it is rather difficult to remember, what with all the dreadful things that came next."

"Difficult to remember?" he repeated, mock outrage in his tone. "Madam, you wound me."

"I've rather made a habit of wounding you, it seems." She smirked. "Perhaps you are not my equal on the battlefield."

"Oh, such hubris! All this from a girl who has come, unaccompanied, into my lair." He tsked, sliding the valise that separated them off to the side as though he were dismantling a shield before a warrior maiden. "Did you not think I might demand satisfaction?"

"You may demand all you wish," she replied loftily, lifting her nose and squaring her shoulders like a queen on her throne. "I have flouted many a man."

He resisted the urge to laugh, delighted at her ability to match the absurdity of his jests. Instead, he tilted himself forward onto his hands and knees and took a crawling step toward her, hoping the effect was more that of a lion than a beggar.

She giggled, keeping her chin high, but did not otherwise move nor make an attempt to escape as he paced nearer.

"Are you meant to be a beast, rather than a man?" she teased. "So that I might be unable to flout you?"

He drew a breath away from her, leaning back on his heels and reaching forward to coil one of the escaped strands of her ashen hair around his finger. "Do you find me beastly?" he whispered, drawing the pad of his thumb along the curve of her cheek.

She shivered, the points of her little nipples hardening beneath the fabric of her dress, draped so temptingly in soft wrapping, like Yuletide sweets begging to be sampled. "I find you all manner of things, Alex Somers."

"Mhm." He nodded, his body ringing with desire as his fingers dug into her loose hair, reveling in the silken texture of it he'd dared not explore the night of the party. "And yet I still must spark your memory about the quality of our stolen kiss."

"Yes," she breathed, reaching out to brush her fingers against the collar of his shirt. "I'm afraid you must. I am so very, very forgetful."

"Well, then, I haven't a choice," he whispered, cupping her face with his other hand as he descended upon those lovely, pouty lips, satisfying a craving he'd been unable to shake for what seemed like a hundred years.

The pure decadence of it flooded him to his fingertips, as though he had been starving, gasping for this very thing and suffering in its absence. She tasted of mint and flowers, the scent of her skin a delicious bouquet of feminine perfume. He raked his hands into her hair, tugging loose that silly, futile ribbon from the base of her neck. He nipped at the abundance of her bottom lip, spreading her unbound hair around her shoulders like a cloak.

He leaned back only to take in the effect, to see her without any of her Society armor, wild and natural, sprawled on his floor.

She did not care to be observed in this moment, however, and pushed herself forward, looping her arms around his neck as she brought her pretty pink lips crashing back down over his. The full length of that lithe, feline little body melded into his chest. He reacted on instinct, pulling her into his lap with a firm grip on her thighs and answering the intensity of her kiss with a passion that confirmed it was mutual.

He released a light groan, all too aware of how easy it would be just now to take her maidenhead, with her sitting astride him as she was in that flimsy little dress. He couldn't resist twisting his hands in her hair, wrapping the long, ashen strands around his fist possessively as he tasted her. Running his free hand down the length of her spine revealed that she was not wearing stays beneath the provocative little frock, which meant one or two strategic tugs would bare her completely to him. God, how he wanted to see her naked, to lay her down on his bed and commit every inch of her soft flesh to memory.

She mirrored his motions, sliding her fingers along the length of his neck, into the short strands of his own hair. She tugged at it gently, as though she were declaring ownership, and flicked her tongue against his in satisfaction as she did so.

He knew she must be aware of his arousal, straining against the doeskin breeches he wore, throbbing against the soft flesh of her thigh as she clung to him from above.

She left his mouth, kissing along the line of his jaw, her

fingertips trailing down over his cheeks and throat, dipping into the collar of his shirt with a gentle rake of her fingernails. "I saw you," she whispered, her breath hot and sweet in his ear, "before I came in tonight. I saw you with your shirt off."

"Oh?" he said, his voice breathy and dark. He allowed himself to trace his own fingers along the sides of her body, enjoying the dip of her waist and the elegant lines of her ribs. He wanted nothing more than to cup her breasts, but held himself off, not willing to risk breaking the spell that currently held them. "Do you wish for me to take it off again?"

She nodded, catching her bottom lip between her teeth, eyes glossy with desire.

He did not hesitate, dragging the shirt up over the planes of his stomach and chest and over his head, and tossing it carelessly away.

She sighed contentedly, reaching out to touch him, chewing on that lip as she drank him in. Her fingers slid over his bare arms, following the dips of muscle tone down to his hands, and then trailed back up over his stomach, hands spreading wide over his chest with a sudden push.

He fell back onto the carpet with a laugh, reaching up to catch her as she descended for another kiss, her hair blanketing the light from the room around them. It was too much to resist rolling her over, pinning her to the ground and taking more sweet affection from that beautiful mouth.

"Do you remember saying I could have overpowered you?" he breathed into her ear, gently tracing the length of her arms as he pulled them over her head, wrapping his fingers around her wrists. "It sounded like you wanted me to."

"I ... oh," she gasped, arching her back against him as he held her in his grip. "Oh, yes. Perhaps I do."

"I would enjoy that very, very much," he replied darkly, tasting the slim column of her throat, kissing his way down to where those sweet little breasts were so well displayed under her gown. He released her arms, dragging his hands along the same path. His kisses made their way farther south, over the swell of her ribs and the dip of her waist, his warm breath sinking into the fabric.

When he touched her breasts, he braced for protest, fearing his inability to resist their temptation would ruin their interlude. However, far from crying out in outrage, she released the sweetest little moan, wriggling under his grip like a purring, well-tamed kitten who was enjoying the attentions of her master.

It was enough to blur his vision, to take total control over his impulses. He dragged himself up over her again, sinking onto her mouth, knowing that his kiss was rough and demanding. He slid his fingers over her hardening nipples, teased them through the fabric as he filled his palms with the modest but delicious swell of her bust.

He pressed his arousal into her, wanting her to know how she maddened him, how she affected his body. He did not know just how much until they were entwined like this, half naked and panting on the floor of his bedchambers.

"I want you," he said to her, his lips moving against her own. "Badly."

"Oh, God," she gasped, one little bare foot grazing along the length of his calves. "Oh, we can't. We can't. Oh, Alex, don't stop."

He forced himself to breathe, to pause, though it was the last thing on earth he wanted to do. "You are a maid?" he asked, lifting himself to gaze down at her, his hands still cupping those delicious little breasts.

She nodded, somehow managing to blush at this confession despite all they'd just done.

He sighed. No matter how much he wanted to, he couldn't take her maidenhood, especially when she was so addled with desire that her judgement was suspect. This was why he avoided debutantes in the first place, after all. Ruining a girl was simply a line he did not cross. Hadn't crossed. Yet.

Damn it all.

"I'm sorry," she breathed, reaching up to touch his face, to gently brush her fingers along his cheeks. "Are you very disappointed?"

"With you?" He smiled. "Never. But we had better stop here, before we cross into a place from which there's no return."

She echoed his sigh as he rolled off her. She stayed flat on her back, staring at the ceiling. It wasn't until he pushed himself to his feet and offered her his hand that she moved, accepting it and coming to stand, tilting her head up to meet his eyes, their noses nearly brushing.

"We've done a very poor job of searching your things," she said gently, her eyes flicking down to his lips.

"That's all right," he said, unable to resist stealing one more kiss, this one soft and gentle as he wrapped his arms around her. "Someone else is going to do it for us tomorrow, after all."

She sighed, resting her head on his bare shoulder. "I wish I could stay, but I must return to my rooms before the men begin to rise for the hunt. I'm afraid you will have gotten no sleep at all!"

He rested his chin on her head, inhaling the sweet lavender scent of those wild, blonde curls. "It's all right," he assured her, "my dreams would only have been of you anyhow."

CHAPTER 15

*I*t was well past midday when Gloriana was finally pulled from her bed.

If it had been up to her, she would have stayed wrapped in her sheets, reliving the hours from the night before over and over until the end of time. Evidently, her excuses of feeling unwell only gave her reprieve from the festivities until luncheon.

At the very least, she was able to feel a smug sense of victory that Nero had chosen her bed tonight rather than attending Heloise. He was curled at her feet, his pale stomach facing the air, as his little paws flicked in time with whatever he was dreaming about so late in the day.

She thought that seemed like a rather fine way to spend a dreary afternoon, especially with clouds hanging misty and low to the grass outside in the ever-darkening chill of the season. Nell, however, had other ideas.

She'd burst into the room without knocking, which Gloriana supposed was at least well timed, as she had emerged from her most recent fantasy regarding Alex Somers with his shirt off. She was carrying a tray and bustled about as though she hadn't just committed the most grievous intrusion on a woman who was—or rather claimed to be—feeling ill.

"Go away," she'd moaned, pulling the pillow down over her face. "I'm dying."

"Well, then we'd best make proper use of the time you've got left," Nell chirped, clapping the tray onto the bedside table and setting about preparing two cups of tea. "I'm bored silly. I can't believe Peter went on that blasted grouse hunt. Does anyone truly enjoy eating grouse, Gloriana? Much less huddling down in heavy tweeds in cold rain and murdering them in a line from the hedgerows? I tell you, it's repugnant."

Gloriana opened her pillow-shield a crack, squinting at her friend as she finished her rant. "Why don't you go bother Heloise, since you love her so much?" she asked, well aware of how childish she sounded.

"Because," Nell said, plopping herself on the corner of Glory's bed, bold as you please. She used her knee to push Gloriana's stubborn form farther back on the mattress. "She is in the village today with that handsome doctor, attending to her clinic. Sit up! The tea is just as you like it."

"Oh, very well." She pouted, shoving herself up and tossing the pillow away.

This had the effect of deeply offending Nero, who had managed to snooze comfortably through Nell's intrusion, but now yowled and leapt from the bed as though he'd been burnt.

Of course, the cat was out of the bag now, so to speak. He had only chosen to lounge away his day in here with Glory because Heloise was otherwise occupied. The little traitor. She did not feel badly for rousing him!

Nell was staring at her, paused with her cup of tea halfway to her lips.

"What?" Glory snapped, leaning over to retrieve her own cup of tea from the tray. A tiny sip told her that it was indeed just as she liked it. Oh, bless Nell.

"Nothing, you just ... you look quite unkempt, Glory! I don't think I've ever seen you thus before."

"Nonsense," Gloriana sniffed, sipping at the glorious liquid in front of her. "You saw me many an early morn, before we were dressed, at school."

"Yes, quite," Nell replied earnestly, "and you always seemed somehow pre-coiffed, even then. You look a right fright this morning!"

Gloriana narrowed her eyes. "Did you not hear me earlier when I told you to go away?"

Nell ignored her, looking around the room curiously. It was a fair deal grander than the one she was sharing with Tatiana, but Gloriana doubted she was experiencing any manner of envy. Nell's interest was always some boring aspect of the construction or what have you rather than the simple act of appreciating a well-fitted room.

"This is such a big house," she said. "Do you wonder who stayed in this room before you? How many times it's been redecorated? I wonder how old this estate is, how many have walked these halls before us."

"Is Tia attempting to summon spirits in your quarters?" Gloriana replied. "Is that why you're bothering me instead of her?"

"Ugh," Nell said with a roll of her eyes. "I wish she would! She spends all her time complaining about that big Scottish fellow with the dog. I can't figure out what he's done to offend her so! Whatever it is has made her a right bore to be around. Do you remember Elizabeth Parrish and how she'd obsess and obsess and obsess about every boy she set her eyes on?"

"Unfortunately, yes." Glory laughed. "And then she married that nasty old barrister! What a tragedy. I bet she never mooned over a fine young man again."

"Well, I was going to say it was exactly like that," Nell answered, pulling a face, "but now you've made it sound so tragic, and I feel guilty for thinking it."

"Ah, thus explains your ominous fortune-telling last night," Gloriana announced, scooting back against the headboard as the warmth of the tea flooded to her fingers and toes. "The cards want you to embrace your inner gossip and say the most dreadful things about other girls!"

"Oh, heavens," Nell muttered, shaking her head as though to dispel the very thought. "That wouldn't be a very fun vice, now would it?"

"I heartily disagree, and so would Elizabeth Parrish, come to it." Gloriana watched Nero leap into the cushioned plat-form beneath her window, winding into a ball as though he hadn't just been evicted most rudely from the bed. "Say," she said, turning to her friend, "what did Heloise make of that book?"

"Oh." Nell blushed, averting her eyes. "I haven't given it to her yet. I've not found the right moment."

"You need a particular moment?" Gloriana scoffed, turning to inspect what other offerings were on the tray Nell had brought up. She snatched a particularly appealing croissant, realizing for the first time just how hungry she was. "Just say, 'Heloise, old friend, dear girl, sorry I waited several years to return this to you. Hope you haven't spurned the fellow already!' and dance away before she can hex you."

"How can you hate Heloise so very much while being so fond of the brother?" Nell demanded, her little face flushing with frustration.

"Who said I'm fond of the brother?" Gloriana returned, a cool flash of concern trickling through her veins. "I thought you didn't partake in gossip!"

"Why else would you go to such lengths to organize this event?" Nell said, throwing her hands up in exasperation. "Why else would you play sick when the men are gone, and avoid all the ladies?"

"There are more men here than Alex Somers," Gloriana huffed. "Who says I'm not simply awaiting the return of Mr. Atlas? Or have you forgotten so quickly that we are courting?"

"Are you?" Nell replied, something flashing in her eyes. "One couldn't know for sure, watching you these past days. Are you so certain Mr. Atlas is the right match for a girl like you anyway?"

"*A girl like me?*" Gloriana repeated, drawing her back up. "What exactly are you implying?"

"Only that you seem to lack the calculating, icy facet that makes Mr. Atlas such a practiced politician," Nell said, shrinking under the spark of rage in her friend's eyes. "Surely you would prefer someone whose blood runs a little hotter?"

"Nonsense." Gloriana sniffed. "Nathaniel is the perfect match for me. Together we will have the run of London during the Season and the most exciting adventures throughout the year. He has told me himself that I would have made a fine politician myself, had I been born a man."

"Oh," Nell said, glancing down at her hands. "Perhaps he knows better than I, then."

"Oh, Nell, stop it." Gloriana sighed, leaning forward to pat her friend's hands. "He's the one who actually is both a politician and a man, after all, isn't he? I promise you I've thought about the match much at length. I am confident that it is the right one."

"Then why ..." Nell furrowed her brow, taking a little breath of regret at speaking.

"Why what?"

She pressed her lips together, clearly wishing she'd never spoken. "Why," she finally said, "do you watch Lord Alex so keenly, and laugh with him, your heads bent together like conspirators?"

"Do I?" Gloriana said with genuine surprise. The thought was not displeasing. "Do you think Alex Somers is a better match for me than Nathaniel Atlas?"

Nell paused, the question seeming to momentarily stump her.

Gloriana found the hesitation somewhat disappointing. She wasn't sure what she wanted to hear. She knew very well that Mr. Atlas was a much better-suited match for her, after all. Besides, surely any man was hot to the touch and disruptive to the senses when half clothed and using his hands and mouth so brazenly?

She tried to imagine, for a moment, the cool and refined Mr. Atlas touching her that way, peeling his shirt off and rolling around with her on the carpet. The image would not come.

"For God's sake, Nell," she snapped in irritation, throwing back her bed covers and pushing herself to stand. "One would think you believe me unsuited for any man at all! Perhaps you think I should have accepted that last proposal."

"Certainly not!" Nell gasped, surprise affirming her sincerity. "I would have been horrified if you had done so."

"Well, perhaps I'm just another Elizabeth Parrish, then?" She stalked to her wardrobe, not bothering to turn around, and flung it open with the force of her snit. "I'm just silly and hopeful, but doomed for a vile old man. So, I might as well put a frock on and comb my hair and get back to it before I'm sold off to the next repulsive lecher who sets his sights on me! Clearly, I ought to be grateful for the privilege!"

"Glory, I said no such thing!" Nell huffed. The china clinking together suggested that she had begun to tidy up in the wake of Gloriana's departure. "I simply don't see why I must choose between a dishonorable rakehell and a man in a mask."

"You say that as though we do not ourselves wear masks

every time we venture into Society," Gloriana muttered. "My visage only shocks you because my own mask slipped away in the leisure hours this morn. Who knows what truly hides between the cool and composed diplomat that Mr. Atlas wears?"

"Yes, Glory," Nell said with a frown. "That is exactly my concern."

CHAPTER 16

*T*here was a horrible sort of irony in catching the grippe because you'd decided against pretending to have it in the first place. After ten miserable hours in the cold, wet moors, watching as the others killed a truly unseemly amount of grouse, Alex rather thought his suffering should have come to an end.

Of course, the actual physician in their party had chosen this day to excuse himself from the festivities. So, instead, Gideon shuffled him up to his bedroom and called in Rose and Mrs. Laughlin to observe his misery and discuss it casually betwixt them.

"There must be something catching," Rose had said with a frown, feeling his forehead with the coolness of her fingers. "Gloriana was abed for most of the day as well."

"Was she?" Alex had said with a wry smile followed by a sneeze. "Perhaps I caught it from her rather than the hunt."

"Hm," Gideon had given a frown bordering on a glower.

"And how would you be contracting anything from Miss Blakely, Alex?"

"We're all at the same party, aren't we?" he'd snapped back, perhaps devolving into a slightly more dramatic coughing fit than was strictly necessary while quickly glancing at the carpet at the foot of his bed to ensure there were no damning imprints of their entwined bodies left behind from the night prior.

"He's right," Rose had sighed. "Which means it's best if he stays apart from the others until this has passed, lest we all take a turn on the misery wheel. I especially shouldn't want Reggie or Caroline catching anything at their delicate age."

"The true misery was the grouse hunt. Keep the children from ever experiencing one, and all shall be well," Alex had informed them, before rolling onto his side and passing into oblivion until well into the following day.

The only truly positive outcome, as far as he was concerned, was that he didn't have to eat any of the grouse he'd watched mercilessly shot from the sky and heaped into blood-soaked burlap. He'd never be able to eat it again without thinking of tragedy and feathers.

He supposed the hunt was supposed to be some sort of opportunity for him to bond with the powerful gentlemen Gloriana had assembled for this outing, in the hopes of leveraging those relationships to build a future. Even the vicar had a truly shocking bloodlust when it came to the unfortunate birds of the moor, and despite the miserable weather, they had all been in markedly better spirits than he.

Mrs. Laughlin had pressed a variety of foul folk remedies

upon him, but he was reasonably certain that it was the ability to spend three days half asleep amidst a collection of kerchiefs that healed him in the end. It wasn't even until the third day that he had the wherewithal to glance around his room in curiosity, wondering if anything had indeed gone missing while he was out at the hunt.

Perhaps he wasn't taking the threat to his person seriously enough, he thought. On the other hand, taking it more seriously would only serve up the same experiences with a heaping of additional discomfort, so why bother?

He had intended, sincerely, to gauge the other men whilst they were out and armed in the blasted wilderness. Surely if one of them were the particularly violent fellow from the library, he'd be constantly grimacing and struggling to not just shoot Alex directly where he stood. Alas, damp tweed and a cold breeze were all it took for him to forget that endeavor completely and simply take up the business of repeatedly wishing either the day or his life would end quickly, as to not prolong his suffering.

Of course, amongst the various unpleasant features of any grippe worth its salt were the feverish, nonsensical dreams that ensured one could not even enjoy the escape of sleep for a few hours.

It started out all right, mostly with a few creative recreations and embellishments of Gloriana on his floor with her hair wild around her shoulders and all the delicious ways that evening might have unfolded in a kinder world. But, of course, the latent dismay at having to spend three days abed rather than continuing to flirt with that glorious creature wove its way into his subconscious, providing less-than-amusing scenarios in which the missed time had dumped her directly into the bed of that suspiciously well-groomed Nathaniel Atlas.

He had heard the name, of course, prior to leaving Oxford. He was a model alumnus and had made considerable waves amidst the *ton* a few years prior when he'd returned from the West Indies having accomplished some sort of particularly troublesome trade dealings. Alex did not particularly find trade dealings worth their necessary details, and so that was all he knew of the man.

Well. Now he knew that Gloriana Blakely considered him her future husband, and that they were evidently *courting*. He also knew that despite the man's impressive inability to do anything anyone might find objectionable, he was also attractive enough that even Alex might have been tempted after enough drink and on a dark enough night.

Damn the man.

"Do you think that Atlas bloke is going to propose to your cousin?" he'd asked Rosie during one of her visits to his rooms with hot broth and fresh kerchiefs.

"I do," she'd responded with a lift of one flaxen eyebrow. "Why? Are you jealous, Alex?"

"Naturally," he'd replied with a wink. "The man's quite a catch."

She had rolled her eyes and shaken her head. "If you like him so much, you ought to spend more time in his company once you've recovered. I don't think I've seen you even have a passing conversation with most of our guests. Aside from Lord Benton, Mr. Atlas is the most well-connected man in attendance. Have you an interest in a life like his?"

"Sailing to the Caribbean and being fawned over? Having preternaturally glossy hair? Yes, I rather think I do."

She'd studied him for a moment, a strange sort of smile on her face. "You *are* jealous, aren't you?"

"Why shouldn't I be?" He'd sniffed, making a show of reaching for his broth with a shaking hand. "He's got it all figured out, hasn't he?"

"I wouldn't know," Rose had replied, still looking as though she had caught onto some secret jest. "I will say, Alex, if you covet something Atlas has in his sights, you had best act quickly to secure it. I've arranged for a surprise in the next few days that will likely throw a bit of a wrench in Glory's vision for this party."

"A wrench, you say? Well, I love a good secret."

"Isn't that funny?' she'd said fondly. "So do I."

IT WASN'T PRECISELY that Alex was *nervous* about rejoining the party. It was simply that he couldn't account for what might have changed while he was abed. He'd checked his appearance far too many times before venturing out of his rooms, frowning at the cowlicks in his hair and the way the cravat refused to lie as well as Gideon's against his throat

It was only dinner, in his own damn childhood home, but somehow he found himself falling short of new and exacting standards for personal appearance.

He'd finally steeled his resolve and made his way out into

the hall, toward the staircase, only to be frightened nearly out of his own skin by a hand shooting out of a dark corner and gripping his arm, tugging him insistently into the little library that had once been so easy to ignore.

If he'd had his wits about him, surely he would've noticed that the assailant had delicate hands belonging to the fairer sex, wrapped in satin gloves that practically shone with honest intentions. He didn't have time to make these observations, however, for as soon as he was within the dark library, she had already begun to rant.

"How dare you not send word to me that you were not poisoned or otherwise injured by one of the three villains!" Glory cried, giving him a gentle shove on the shoulder. "I have been out of my mind with worry, and no one would tell me anything!"

He held his hands up in a defensive apology. "It was but the grippe!" he said. "Surely Rosie told you that!"

"Oh, it's never truly the grippe," Gloriana scoffed with a flip of her hand. "I said I had it just a few hours prior to you. It is the thinnest excuse in the world."

"Alas, my dear," he chuckled, "occasionally the grippe does make itself known. Quite violently in my case."

"And you couldn't pen a quick note?" she demanded, stomping her little foot on the carpet.

He couldn't help but chuckle again. Here in the dark, her hair shone like silver, her eyes flashing against the shadows from without. He'd never be able to stand in this room again without thinking of Gloriana Blakely.

"I'm not sure how I would have gone about that without

raising a few inconvenient questions via the delivery method," he pointed out. "Besides, you could have always checked upon my room, couldn't you? You know well enough where it is."

"Oh, I didn't dare." She sighed, her frustrations seeming to gust out of her like a sudden changing of the winds. She took a step backward, raising one of her gloved hands to her brow. "I never knew when you were being attended upon, nor what state you were in. I have been dying to know if anything went missing while you were on the hunt! Oh, Alex, I was ever so worried!"

"Were you really?" he asked softly, reaching out to pull her closer and taking the hand she held to her brow into his own. "Did you watch for me on the horizons, mourning my absence like mythical Penelope?"

"Humph," she pouted, though the corners of her lips twitched in amusement. "Isn't Penelope the one who never even *thought* about any man but her husband?"

"You haven't a husband," Alex said, perhaps a little harsher than necessary. Atlas hadn't claimed her yet, after all. If anyone had a right to be jealous of the other, it was the one who'd held her in his arms properly.

"Much to the dismay of my parents." She laughed, blissfully unaware of his little spark of envy. "So tell me, please. Was aught missing from the room when you returned?"

"Not that I've noticed. Though to be completely frank, I haven't had much will to search. What are the odds the spy found her item and has absconded peacefully, never to be heard from again?"

"Hm," she considered, stroking the side of his hand with her gloved thumb. "If they truly were serving staff, it is possible. Mrs. Laughlin has reported a turnover of about a dozen of the temporary servants, including one or two who had been caught stealing."

"Then perhaps I am safe and clear," he suggested, leaning down to catch her lips in a quick, sweet kiss, then placing another on the tip of her nose. "Though I shan't abide you conducting intrigue without me. I cannot entertain the thought that you've drifted from my spell so quickly."

"One must be caught in a spell if she is to escape," she replied playfully, twining her arms around his neck. "You are no sorcerer, my Lord."

"Well, now, you can't prove that I'm not." He laughed. "I believe I just rose from the dead *and* executed a perfect vanishing trick from the hallway just now."

"Oh, drat," she said, biting her lip. "You are right. We had best go down before anyone notices that we've both gone missing. I apologize for my impetuousness, but I just couldn't stand knowing you'd be joining us for dinner and not intercepting you beforehand. I so hate being left out of the know!"

"Oh?" he asked, slipping his hand from the curve of her waist over her backside and pulling her into the line of his body. He stole another kiss, this one long and lingering in answer to the feel of her elegant shape against his own.

He would have to get a grip on his arousal before he could traipse down the stairs and into polite company, but having her here in his arms again was absolutely worth any inconvenience.

"There are many things I'd like to educate you about, truth be told," he confided against the sweetness of her lips, "to bring you truly into the know."

"Perhaps you should leave your door open for me again," she replied, her voice thin and hot. "So that I know I am welcome."

"Gloriana ..." he groaned, his body reacting to those words with a surge of heat and desire. "You know not what you are suggesting."

She licked her lips, taking a step back from him and turning those big, shining eyes up to meet his. "Many a rogue has tried to seduce me, you know. I am not completely innocent."

"I have never implied you were any such thing," he returned, crossing his arms over his chest. "In fact, it is quite clear that I am not the first man you've kissed with those siren's lips."

The lips in question curled up into a grin, her little white teeth gleaming in the dark. "No," she agreed, "you certainly are not."

"But you are a maid," he replied. "You said so yourself."

"I am," she confirmed, her smile unwavering. "Just listen to me, you insufferable man. What I was going to say is that in my encounters in London, many men who are known for their seductions have attempted to proposition me. When rejected, several of them recited the same cryptic thing."

"Oh?" he asked with a raise of his brows. "Are men all so similar?"

She carelessly lifted one pale shoulder. "I used to think so."

"Well, what was this reaction to being turned down by the exquisite Miss Blakely, then?" he teased, his arms loosening and his feet itching to close the space between them. "Lamentations of sorrow and defeat? A lack of passion for ongoing life?"

"Mm, eventually." She giggled. "But first, they'd all insist that there were many pleasures we could take in one another without compromising my virtue. That ecstasy could be reached by clever means that would leave me fully intact. While I always declined, as any girl who safeguards her reputation must, I confess, I have always found the implications of such things intriguing. Is it true?"

He gaped at her, certain that all of the blood had just drained from his face. If she was suggesting what he thought she was suggesting ... well, she didn't even know what she was suggesting, did she? He cleared his throat, reaching up to rub the back of his neck, "Erm ... yes," he managed to eke out. "Yes, there are ... other things ... that can be done between men and women."

Not things a girl of breeding gets up to, though, his mind chided him, to which the less sophisticated part of his brain returned a quick and profane command to be silent.

"So perhaps, then," she said, holding his gaze as though she were proposing a turn about the gardens, "perhaps I might call upon you tonight? If you are well enough. Perhaps you might bring me into the know?"

He didn't trust himself to speak. Instead he simply gave a wordless nod and then remained frozen in place for several minutes. She had brushed past him and exited the little library with a pleasant kiss on his cheek at some point, though he hardly could say how quickly it happened or how long it had been since.

He stood in the dark, gazing out the faulty window, blood ringing in his ears, and didn't think about much of anything at all that would pass for coherence for quite some time.

CHAPTER 17

$\mathcal{D}$espite a heart racing so fast she thought it might audibly hum, Gloriana executed her entrance into the dining hall with the coolness and composure of a lady whose worries were so insubstantial that they could never interrupt her social graces.

Rose was the only person who seemed to notice anything amiss, and seemed to be avoiding her eye in a way that was most strange. Not to mention she had been seated rather far away from the head of the table tonight. It was not the first time she had suspected her cousin to be a mind reader.

She couldn't believe she'd actually managed to deliver that proposition to Alex Somers so smoothly. She had been stewing upon it for days, remembering those cryptic offers of a consequence-free seduction from the rogues and rake-hells of the *ton*. Nell had described Alex himself as "a bit of a cad," so surely he'd know to what they were referencing, she'd reasoned.

All she knew was that she could barely move from one task

to the next for the last several days without finding her mind tumbling backward and landing on the soft carpet at the base of his bed. The impression of his lithe body, bare and under her hands, haunted her as she took the motions of tea with the ladies and entertainment in the evening.

She allowed Mr. Atlas to hold her hand on an excursion to the township to enjoy the fresh apple cider, but his fingers felt cold against her palm and her heart did not speed the way it did when Alex Somers was merely in the same room. If she must be destined to marry sensibly, then why not experience a hint of the forbidden before she was tethered to another?

She hadn't been lying when she told him she'd suspected a bout of foul play as explanation for his sudden illness. He did not seem to take the threats they'd overheard very seriously, though to his credit, there had been no hint of intrigue regarding his suspected status as a foreign agent in the week following the incident in the library.

Still, they were never meant to know about it. It had only happened in the shadows. And at least one of the players of this secret game would take no qualms in cold-blooded murder on the basis of nothing but a misplaced suspicion! Truly, Gloriana knew she should have been the voice of reason, putting a stop to the kissing in favor of more mystery solving, but it was so very difficult in the haze of pleasure that seemed to descend upon her so quickly when he touched her.

It had not been hysterical or unreasonable to suspect something had befallen Alex these last days, especially considering the timing. What were the odds that he'd fall ill on the very day when they knew his room was to be searched? The fact that he truly had contracted the grippe was almost funny in its absurdity.

Why was it that when fear turned to relief, one always had the urge to laugh?

She smiled prettily, settling into her spot at the table and sipping at her wine. She asked the right questions to spark a lively conversation amongst those around her as they awaited their first course, none of them any the wiser of the way her little heart thundered beneath the pressed silk of her bodice.

She did not know the specifics of what she had proposed, truly, only that it would give her more of what she'd felt during that heady and delicious encounter some nights past. It was as though she'd eaten nothing but porridge for her entire life and had suddenly tasted cake. What girl wouldn't want more?

She thought again of the coolness of Mr. Atlas's hand holding her own. It was a silly thing to judge him about, considering the temperature had dropped rather steeply over the last few weeks and they had been out of doors. Still, she could not imagine those polite and proper fingers stroking her hair and exploring her skin, could not truly believe they'd awaken the same electric surge of heat and pleasure upon her. She could not imagine they were ever anything but cold.

Alex was the last to arrive, which did not arouse any suspicion. After all, he was just now recovered from an illness. Many of the guests stood to welcome him, shaking his hand and congratulating him on his restored vitality.

He did seem to glow with health, she thought as the candlelight created threads of gold in his hair and his strong hand clasped the others who welcomed him. When he smiled, his face lit. He smiled with his teeth showing, completely unconcerned with maintaining a guise of mystery, and when he sat to enjoy dinner, he made the time to address everyone around the table, considering no one too far above nor beneath him.

It was dumb luck that Ruthie Somers had chosen not to attend tonight's dinner. She had appeared twice in the past days to join the festivities, seemingly unconcerned with both her initial reception to the events and the overt absence of her middle child. Like Heloise, she seemed to have quite a lot of vocation that kept her occupied day by day, and only appeared here and there when time permitted.

If Alex was to rejoin the party in earnest, he would not be able to avoid his mother forever.

He caught her eye as his wine was poured, a secretive glint in his gaze and the ghost of a knowing smile on his lips. She could not resist smiling back, dipping her head to hide the blush rising on her cheeks as her heart gave another surging thump.

He had been seated between the dour Lady Benton and bookish Peter Applegate. It truly was incredible to Gloriana how quickly he got them to smile, to engage with one another at his end of the table. How unlikely it was that laughter should arise from those two particular guests over dinner banter!

She had her own gifts for socialization, but she approached people from a position of flattery and (often feigned) shared interests. Alex seemed to simply weave a web about whomever was near him and draw them directly into his own world of humor and ease. It was truly impressive, she thought, even without her notable bias in his favor.

She blinked away her reverie, returning to her own end of the table and the demands of the socialite on keeping an entertaining discourse flowing. Though it was impossible to resist exchanging the occasional glance or secret smile with Alex Somers, they both played their parts, she believed, to perfection, well past dessert.

SHE HAD WONDERED if she should change into something more formal than her night rail and dressing gown to go about her secret business tonight. Somehow, despite the salacious nature of the thing she was about to do, and despite the fact that she, herself, had suggested it, Gloriana felt extremely self-conscious about appearing in mixed company wearing so very little.

She'd had to firmly remind herself that this was not polite socialization, not even a little bit! Wearing a gown would only delay the progress of this experience, and the cover of night was not infinite, after all.

She hadn't bothered to braid her hair, nor to tie it back as she had done last time. Goodness knew he'd only wish to pull any coif apart at the first opportunity. She so rarely wore her hair completely unbound around her shoulders like this, even when back in her childhood home. The combined effect of her scant clothing and her undressed hair was enough to make her feel both daring and doubtful, all at once. It was an alien sensation and not in the least bit unpleasant.

She made her way down the halls slowly, taking care that each step should be silent and that her senses be keenly honed on any disturbance in the halls. It would not do to be caught, but so long as she spotted another midnight wanderer first, she could always fabricate a defensible reason for wandering about in the dead of night.

The instant that the faint glow of light emitted by Alex's cracked bedroom door fell into view, she lost her breath. She urged herself forward, determined to experience this evening, to cherish it in her memories forever. She had been wooed and pursued by all manner of men in London, had been spun around the most exquisitely outfitted ballrooms in the world, but somehow this absurd, endearing man, in a chilly estate in the wilderness, was the first one she had ever desired, the only one who had ever made her feel a temptation to toss caution and planning to the wind and give in to the demands of the flesh.

Just thinking about her own desire sent gooseflesh prickling across her body, awakening a hyper-awareness of the way the smooth fabric of her dressing gown swished against her bare calves and brushed so sweetly at her wrists.

She could not resist peeking into the room before making herself known, curious as to whether she'd catch him in a moment of unexpected vulnerability again. Sadly, she couldn't make out anything but his shadow just outside of her window of visibility. Not quite the preview she had hoped for, though pleasing nonetheless.

She pressed the door wider, wincing at the way the hinges

creaked, the sound seeming to scream down the empty hallway. She slipped into the room as quickly as she was able, pushing the traitorous door shut behind her with the weight of her body, relieved to hear the doorknob click into place.

The suddenness of her appearance seemed to startle him, from the way he whipped around to see who had upset the motion of his door.

Her breath caught in her throat at the sight of him, as though he'd manifested in the flesh at the behest of her girlish fantasies.

He wore nothing above the waist, just as she'd imagined, his bare upper body lean and lithe in the candlelight. He did not hesitate nor spare a moment to greet her, opting instead to take three long strides across the length of the room and dig his fingers into her hair, descending onto her lips in a ravenous kiss of greeting. The warmth of his body seared through the thin garments she wore, sending a ripple of heat through her that rose to her cheeks and sank directly down to the tips of her toes.

She had expected that they would awkwardly circle each other when she arrived here, perhaps discussing what they were about before beginning. She couldn't have imagined skipping the formalities so completely and immediately. It was simply not something she had ever encountered, even amongst intimates and family.

Admittedly, she found this to be significantly more enjoyable than the process she'd envisioned, or rather assumed.

He pulled back before she felt that she'd had enough of an opportunity to properly react. Her hands had come to rest on his shoulders, but otherwise she was pinned quite firmly against his door, once again at his mercy.

"I could not actually convince myself that you would come," he whispered, his eyes drinking in the details of her face. "I actually had begun to think I'd fantasized it all, and perhaps was still sick and asleep in my bed and the lascivious Gloriana Blakely who had proposed this tryst was naught but a hopeless man's fever dream."

"If this were a dream," she whispered back, trailing her fingernails up over the lines of his throat and circling them back around his neck, "your door hinges would not make quite so much noise when moved."

His surprised burst of laughter was infectious, and she couldn't help but smile in return, even as she shushed him.

"It might be best if you lock the thing," she added, chewing on her bottom lip as she met his eyes. How was it possible that looking at a man who held her this way, and not for the first time, was still making her blush so deeply? She could feel the warmth in her cheeks and the giddy flush of excitement fluttering beneath her ribs.

He raised his eyebrows, a teasing smirk finding its way onto his well-sculpted lips. "You want me to lock you in my bedchambers, Miss Blakely?"

"Well, not in so many words." She laughed, rising on her toes to taste his lips again, to indulge in the thing she'd wanted for so many days on end and had been unable to take.

There was something unbelievably indulgent about kissing him this way. It was not a stolen moment in a dark corner, where the looming threat of being caught rushed the encounter, nor was it a flash of mind-addling heat, where the kisses, though delicious, seem to meld together in a manic flash of primal instinct. This was a present kiss. A kiss of decision, that could last just as long as she wanted it to, and cement itself in a mind that was still—mostly—clear.

She could be playful like this, she realized. She could take her time and try different things and see what happened. With a giggle sprung from that realization of freedom, she nipped lightly at his lip and pulled back, ducking under his arms with a little spin, her lacy nightclothes belling out around her slender body as she backed away from the door, leaving him without his captive prize.

He could not suppress a grin watching her prance away from him, making her way to the bed like a nymph enjoying a forest glade. "I suppose I should find the key, then," he sighed, "so that you cannot escape me again."

"I daresay, Lord Alex," she replied lightly, tossing her head as though she were making conversation in the stuffiest of tea rooms. "A captor who did not even plan so far ahead as to know where the key to the escape is kept does not seem like a very formidable villain."

"Just so." He nodded, pushing himself away from the door. He made his way over to a large wardrobe that sat in a nook away from his bed. When he threw it open, she noted that *those* hinges didn't squeak at all.

So the serving staff knew how to oil hinges, they simply chose to make it more difficult for Alex Somers to sneak about undiscovered. She admitted silently to herself that this had probably been a wise precaution, especially when he was a young scamp, though he clearly was not above making his exit via a window if necessary. Somehow, knowing he had sneaked out of this manor countless times, many of them likely in pursuit of nubile village maidens, did not fill Gloriana with jealousy. Instead it was a glow of something like fondness and perhaps even a little excitement.

Alex Somers was the most authentically sincere person she'd ever met in her life. He was comfortable in his skin, unconcerned with his status, and seemed to live ever in the moment, even as he mumbled Italian curse words to himself while searching for his room key in an old hat box. It was utterly charming in such an unexpected way. She had watched it dismantle and endear even the staunchest of the guests in the manor these past weeks.

That fond glow in her chest, interlaced with admiration, exasperation, and amusement, was a strange thing. She had felt that kind of warmth toward friends and family before, she supposed, but not with the flame of desire burning at its center. Was it simply that she had come to love him that was making her feel this way? Was this what love felt like?

"Aha!" he cried, flinging the hat box to the carpet and holding a tarnished silver key to the light. "I knew it was in here somewhere!"

"If you have this much trouble locating your own belongings, it does not fill me with confidence that our lady spy was successful in her endeavor," Gloriana said, her eyes following him as he returned to his door and fumbled with the key, forcing the mechanism past its flakes of rust and long bout of being unused. It took some doing, but finally the sound of the lock clicked into place.

"Nonsense." He grinned, leaving the silver key in the lock as he made his way quickly to where she stood at the side of his bed. "It was a servant. The thief, probably, and she is gone now with both of her cohorts, and I am perfectly safe. There is nothing to worry about tonight save for how best to enjoy one another."

She nodded, stifling the tugging uncertainty in her chest, at least for now. It seemed that her premonition of awkward discourse might indeed come to pass if she allowed herself to continue making such comments and observations.

"Shall I sit?" she began to ask, but the words were barely out of her mouth before he had scooped her up, catching her surprised squeal in a kiss, and climbed into the bed with her body nestled in his strong arms.

He set her down in the feathered luxury of his bed, cupping her cheek with his hand as he knelt over her, kissing her slowly, the same way she had done when they kissed at the doorway. She thought, somewhere amongst thoughts muddled by pleasure, that perhaps he too had realized that this was the first time they were not compelled to rush nor frenzied by unexpected passion.

His lips lifted from hers as he looked down upon her, sliding the backs of his knuckles down the crevice of her shoulder and down along the dip of her waist. "Glory," he said, his voice somehow deeper, more serious, "you must tell me if you wish to stop or if we've gone too far. I want only to share a night with you that will bring a smile to your face in remembrance, and never a pang of regret."

"I confess," she replied, shivering with pleasure as his hands warmed her through the thin layers of her clothes, "I haven't a single idea what tonight will entail. However, if all I must do is alert you if I wish you to stop, I believe I can manage that."

His eyes glittered, the flames of the candles on the walls reflected in their emerald-green expanse. "Very well," he said softly, easing himself down to lie next to her and pulling her to her side so that they were facing one another. He continued to stroke the side of her body, his eyes wandering over the frothy material she wore. "To preserve your virtue," he said, his voice barely above a whisper, "we may touch one another as much as we like and kiss to our hearts' content. The true pleasure is in experiencing our bodies as one, and while the final act of love is perhaps the most satisfying way to do that, it is not the only way. Do you want me to touch you, Gloriana?"

She nodded, swallowing hard on the way her insides heated at that question.

His eyes roamed down to the sash at her waist as his skimming fingers made their way to its knot. He unwound the satin and pushed the robe open, revealing her bare shoulders and the thin fabric of her night rail , which floated against her porcelain flesh in the absence of its wrapping.

The cool night air renewed her gooseflesh, her nipples hardening against the wispy fabric of her night rail as he gently peeled the robe away from her arms, one at a time. His eyes drank her in, intent upon the revelations of so little clothing, but did not yet move to strip her entirely bare.

He leaned forward to taste the hollow of her throat, using one of his heavy thighs to urge her onto her back as he rolled above her.

She gasped at the sudden weight, at the heat that sparked where his tongue dipped into the delicate plane of her skin. His muscled thigh pressed her legs apart, resting against the core of her desire, her most secret and tender place, with nothing but a bolt of thin muslin and the soft leather of his trousers separating flesh from flesh.

She couldn't resist reaching up to touch him, too, to stroke the hot skin at the back of his neck and trace the muscles of his arms as they held his body aloft above hers. She squirmed beneath him as he kissed his way from her throat to her collarbone, his tongue flicking and dragging against any skin he found particularly pleasing, his teeth nipping affectionately at places that he thought called for it.

His hands traced over her breasts, his fingers skimming over the hardened points of her nipples, lingering there after hearing the way this particular touch made her gasp.

"I have dreamed about these breasts," he murmured against her skin, "imagined them bare, exposed and begging for my touch."

"I haven't much of a bosom," she gasped, somehow still able to experience self-consciousness in a moment like this.

"You have a perfect bosom," he corrected, squeezing her breasts in his hands as his thumbs circled her nipples. "And I no longer have to dream about enjoying you this way."

She opened her mouth to quip back at him, to make some sort of clever retort, but his thigh pressing into her center while his hands plied her with these little jolts of lightning rendered her quite silent. She only watched in awe as he unlaced the top of her gown, pushing the muslin down until the swell of her breasts came into view, the rosy coronas that surrounded her nipples rising above the cream-white fabric.

He bit down on his lip, his eyes fixed on a reveal that went slowly by his own design, as though he wished to draw out the moment for his own pleasure as well as hers.

She could not stand it, could not wait and doubt and antici-pate like this. She arched her back, rolling her shoulders back into the mattress so that her breasts emerged without the assistance of those clever hands, naked to his view in the shadows of the night.

He blinked in surprise, drawing a deep breath at the sudden reveal of this part of her that he claimed to have dreamed about. "Naughty girl," he chided in a playful whisper, his hands returning to cup her breasts as his mouth once again descended on her own.

This time he was not patient and he did not linger. His tongue plunged between her lips, hot and demanding, and his hands took liberties upon her body that she had never thought to imagine. He repeated the path he'd taken earlier, kissing down her throat, trailing kisses, nips, and tastes down toward her chest. Only this time, he did not stop at her collar. This time, he used his hands to hold her breasts aloft like ripe fruit he wished to taste urgently.

Her hands flew to his shoulders, her fingernails scraping lightly against them, the pads of her fingers following the way the muscles moved beneath his warm flesh as he swirled his tongue around her nipples, drawing them into his mouth to suckle and lick to his heart's content.

She found herself instinctively drawing a leg up along that thigh that pinned her to the bed, using the bottom of her bare little foot to trace the lines of his legs, still covered in his trousers as he fondled her so brazenly, tasted her as though she belonged to him.

He made a sound, like a rumble in his throat, shifting his hips backward and pulling his thigh from where it had sat so firmly between her legs. She almost protested, the absence of his warmth and pressure there suddenly leaving her wanting.

Instead, he kissed the tip of each of her breasts, raising himself up to look down at her. His eyes had gone dark with whatever primal drive had gripped them both some nights prior, and his hands worked quickly, skimming down to her legs and bunching the fabric of her night rail up over her knees and onto her thighs.

"Oh," she managed, her voice thick and dazed, as she realized what he intended. He was going to touch her *there*, a place she'd scarcely ever touched herself!

He did not rush to do so, nor did he pull her clothing up all the way, revealing her to him in an instant. It seemed that Alex Somers enjoyed a slow reveal. He watched her face instead, stroking the insides of her thighs as he gently urged her knees apart.

One of her feet stayed resting against his leg, as though she were holding on to him as he put his hands on her. He was making his way up to touch her most forbidden place in an agonizingly patient fashion. The closer he got, the more she wanted it. The more he touched her, the less she could worry about that particular part of her and the impression it might make.

Despite his progress, he still appeared far more interested in her face than in watching his own ministrations. As his thumbs finally made their way to the very cusp, stroking the velvety smooth skin at the outer precipice of her lower lips, she thought she might faint straight away at the power of sensation that jolted through her.

She was fairly certain if he had gone to immediately touch her there, that it wouldn't have felt nearly so explosive. She was positive that doing it herself would have rendered no such results. So why had this slow ascent built the foundations of such a sensation? How had they?

She did not have time to ponder the answer, her breasts rising and falling in rapid time as he explored his way closer and closer to the center, treating every inch of flesh beneath his fingers as equally precious and desirable to touch.

She could feel a slickness, warm and silken, making its way onto his fingers, aiding him in his exploration. She could not force herself to keep her eyes open, no matter how much she wished to cement these sensations into her memory, and found her lashes fluttering onto her cheeks and her lips parting in a soundless gasp as he did the most wonderful things beneath her skirt.

"Do you like when I do this?" he breathed, testing his fingertip at her entrance, slipping just a bit inside of her in a way she had never even considered.

She nodded, not trusting herself to speak, her hips bucking up against his hand in a silent plea for more, for this to go on forever. She heard his breath catch and hoped it was a sign of approval at her enthusiasm. It certainly seemed to be as he made his way, again very slowly, inside her most intimate place, using his thumb to continue circling and teasing the lovely, lovely places on the outside as he did so.

He found a rhythm in this, a way of touching her that sent her breaths into a shallow desperation and her toes curling into the silk sheets. Rather than ease off her, he bent down, returning his mouth to her breasts, seemingly determined to layer every decadent pleasure he'd uncovered so far upon each other until she burst, leaving behind only a glittering shaft of light in her wake.

She realized, with some small wonder, that she was panting, that the rising urgency that seared its way through her body was somehow becoming louder, more insistent, and she hadn't the first idea how to answer it. If she *could* tame this sensation of building, this physical panic, she wasn't sure she'd have the willpower to do so, for it was as delicious as it was alarming, and seemed only to sharpen its edge as Alex's fingers and tongue, his scent and the weight of his body, all combined together in a concentrated effort to push her directly over the cliff of madness and into a place from which she'd never return.

"Alex," she gasped, her fingers digging into his shoulders, knees pressing into his legs. "Alex, oh, what is this?"

He did not answer, nor did he slow or change his movements. She suspected that she felt the curve of a smile at her breasts, a tensing in his muscled back as though he were satisfied with his own work. There was no time to consider it, nor to wonder what was happening to her.

The cresting wave broke in a sudden shock of sensation, ripping through her in a way that seemed to numb all of her senses, save touch, to nothing. For just that moment of perfect bliss, she was suspended in nothingness, blind, deaf, and dumb, and there was nothing in the world but her body interacting with Alex's body. There was nothing but a pleasure so powerful that it would knock any woman right off her feet.

It fell upon her once, twice, and again, each wave a little weaker than the one that came before, but no less miraculous. She hadn't noticed him moving, withdrawing his hand from within her, nor kissing his way back up her throat and pulling her into his side, her cheek resting against his bare shoulder as she rode the chaos of her body's reaction over each new peak of discovery.

When finally things seemed to still, as much as they could with the buzzing hum that seemed to sit in an aura around her body in the aftermath, she allowed her muscles to release, to relax into the warm embrace of the man who was holding her steady against him.

"All is well?" he asked softly, stroking damp hair from her brow.

She nodded, swallowing with some effort on a suddenly parched throat. "Alex," she breathed, her eyes wide with wonder. "Will you teach me how to do those things?"

"To yourself?" he asked with a raise of his eyebrows and a marked sound of interest in his voice.

"No," she replied, her breaths still shallow and weak, "to you."

He seemed to freeze, his breath stilling in his chest and the comforting stroke of his hand on her back coming to an abrupt halt. After a moment, he tilted her chin up to where her eyes could meet his own, his eyes hooded and dark. "You want to touch me like that?" he asked, the deepness of his voice resonating through his chest and into her own body, melded into his as it was.

"Of course," she said, licking the dryness from her lips and blinking the haze from her eyes. She gently placed her hand on the dip at the center of his chest, feeling his heartbeat beneath her fingertips. "Yes, I do."

He nodded, holding her gaze, and reached across his body to take that hand into his own, his thumb rubbing circles into the palm of her hand. He guided it downward, over the waistband of his breeches, to the place between his legs that distinguished him as a man.

She drew her breath in, her hand settling over the rigid bulge beneath the soft leather he wore, the heat of his skin palpable and sweet. He allowed her to explore him, to trace the shape of his manhood through the fabric as he worked at the laces that held his trousers together, his breath shallow in his chest.

"It will not take long," he said with a half smile that seemed almost apologetic. "I'm afraid you rather have that effect on me."

"Oh," she replied, wondering if perhaps she had taken a very long time. She hoped not. She hoped that he did not think he was anything but devastatingly attractive to her. Perhaps later she would ask him what the usual sort of timing for these encounters should be.

He lifted his hips, hitching his thumbs under his waistband and urging the trousers down over the two angled bones that marked his hips. She could not resist gazing down, leaving the otherworldly intoxication of his eyes to observe the primal curiosity of his body.

The copper hair that curled in a sparse spray over his chest, and reached downward into a thin line at his navel, did indeed continue past the hidden threshold of his clothing. It twined over the lean plane of his lower body, arriving in a thatch of rose-gold curls that framed his man's organ.

She had seen this body part in sculptures and paintings, and had thought herself prepared for the impression it made in person. However, rather than the modest appendage that could be sheltered 'neath a fig leaf, his organ was imposing, rigidly stiff, and appeared to throb of its own accord in want.

She didn't wait for him to reach for her hand again. Instead, she slid her fingers over the trailing of hair, coming down to twine around this strange and alluring part of him, which seemed to want her touch so desperately. Gripping him this way made his breath catch, gave his body the slightest spasm beneath her own that was immediately gratifying.

She thought the primordial remnants of the beast inside her knew instinctively that this part of him was meant to plunder the matching part of her, and it was only with great effort that her evolved, modern mind could quiet this overwhelming desire. Even after achieving such pleasure, she somehow wanted more. She wanted all of him.

"Like this," he breathed, wrapping his large hand around her smaller one, and guiding her along the length of his shaft. "Don't be afraid to squeeze."

She nodded, tightening her grip on him as he taught her a smooth, gliding motion that brought him pleasure. He had predicted that this would be a fast endeavor, and perhaps had foreseen that she would learn how to mimic this touch he enjoyed quickly, for his hand fell away swiftly, allowing her full control, his little gasps of pleasure filling her with a desire to send him into that oblivion she'd so recently returned from.

She understood, as she heard these sounds of pleasure escape his throat, why he'd wanted to watch her face. She pressed her face upward, moving to kiss the indent of his throat, to taste the salt on his skin and nip at the tender flesh there. This one night, she knew, would never be enough.

"Yes," he groaned, his fingers digging into the muscles along her spine. "Yes, my love, only a moment more. Just like that."

She did not answer, her kisses trailing up along his jaw, stopping only when he tilted his head down to capture her lips in a kiss, an anchor to the world as he toppled into bliss. He kissed her hard, everything in him seeming to blaze in a moment of heightened need.

She was held in thrall, gripped tightly to his body as his organ flexed within her hand, releasing a torrent of molten liquid as testament to its satisfaction. She released her grip, allowing him to rock his hips for a final decrescendo of thrusts into her fingers.

His body seemed to go slack, even his lips against her own becoming languid and sweet.

For some time after, the two of them remained still, twined around one another, his lips grazing her forehead and her body melded into his. It was only a moment, but within it, the world seemed to spin a little slower, preserving their breathless silence in a stolen moment of perfect calm.

CHAPTER 18

*A*lex had taken his time pulling himself off the bed, pouring two glasses of water from his bedside carafe and handing one to a dazed and beautifully tousled Gloriana before he went in search of a kerchief with which to tidy them up. He laced his trousers together with fingers that felt somewhat numb, his head still swimming with the intensity of his climax.

He had truly intended only to pleasure her tonight. In fact, he had thought that was all she had been suggesting earlier in the library. He hadn't realized, entirely, just how pent-up he was until this moment of reflection after release. He wasn't sure he'd ever wanted a single woman so badly, even as a green lad.

He returned to the bed and sat next to her, cleaning his seed from her fingers with gentle strokes of the kerchief in his hand. She was pliable like this. Trusting. She allowed him to do this unspeakably intimate thing without even a word of curiosity or protest, her gown still untied and wrinkled around her lounging form.

God, how he wished she could stay. It seemed like the most natural, correct thing in the world that he might crawl into bed, snuff the candles, and drift off into a contented sleep with her nestled in his arms.

Funny that it was usually his liaisons who spoke those words to him as he hastened to make his exit before an angry husband arrived home. Perhaps he'd never had the luxury of contemplating spending an entire night with a woman, or perhaps he'd simply never met one who made him want to before.

Despite all rationality in his head telling him he ought to hasten her back to her room while it was still quiet in the manor, he climbed back into the bed with her, pulling her back into his arms, and savoring the weight of her head resting so contentedly on his shoulder.

There were a thousand anxious impulses he had to quash. The desire to ask her to detail, in copious reassuring language, just how much she'd enjoyed this encounter was surprisingly powerful. He somehow resisted it, choosing instead to inhale the floral scent of her tangled hair, which wound its way around them both, like some maiden in an enchanted forest who'd deemed him worthy of a visit.

"I do not know if I should qualify this evening as a mark in the positive for my party or a sign that I've abandoned all original goals by now." She sighed happily, tracing a finger over his chest. "I was to snare a proposal for myself and an assortment of promising vocational prospects for you. Instead, we've gotten caught up in espionage, failed miserably at unraveling it, and ... well, this, I suppose."

"I'd call it a roaring success." He chuckled, planting an affectionate kiss on the crown of her head. "And at least both of us may strike spymaster off any list of potential future occupation."

She huffed. "Well, perhaps *you* can. I think I'd be rather adept with the right training and preparation."

"Perhaps you would at that," he agreed, warmed by the way he could feel her smile curve against the bare skin of his chest. "I'm not sure what I'd be adept at, myself."

She pulled away from his embrace, just enough to plant a hand on his chest and raise her head to meet his eye. "What do you mean? You've clearly made an impression on both of our bureaucrats in attendance. You'd be a plum pick for some political office or other."

"Me?" He laughed, shaking his head at the preposterousness of that suggestion. He pushed himself up against the headboard so that he could sit, facing this fascinating woman who believed such perplexing things. "I couldn't trust myself with the weight of it. One wrong move, and I've damned a bunch of unfortunate sods to poverty or accidentally sent explorers to their deaths because I didn't read the map correctly."

She shook her head, giving a little roll of those lovely blue eyes. "Not every assignment of government is quite so lofty," she said. "I know a man whose entire duty revolves around reading scripts for production in our local playhouses. He removes anything that might be objectionable, often attends a performance or two, and collects his stipend from the Crown and their thanks."

"How did he land that assignation?" Alex gaped. "What luck!"

She shook her head with a laugh. "You'd be shocked how many posts are that simple. You, I think, would make a very fine ambassador or delegate, Alex, particularly with those who are difficult to charm. It would hardly be work for someone who clearly enjoys dismantling the shields around others."

The thought had never occurred to him before. At the forefront, it immediately seemed ridiculous. Impossible. He couldn't be trusted with simple tasks, much less the success of government operations and their impact on the future of Britain. Surely not. But the way she put it made him wonder .... or perhaps what he was feeling was hope.

"That sounds like a task you would be particularly adept at yourself, my sweet Miss Blakely." He grinned. "A woman so beautiful need not be so utterly disarming in her social graces, and yet you've become so anyway. Perhaps you deserve the job more than I."

"Oh, without question." She grinned, a twinkle in her eye. "Alas, I can only hope to serve in the shadows, behind a powerful man, as a means to achieving that dream. It's why I've turned down so many proposals and driven my parents right to the point of forgetting why they ever thought of me so fondly, you know. I cannot saddle myself with a quiet life in the country, where there is no joy or revelry and never a new person to meet. Why is that always the fate of well-married wives?"

"And somehow you're certain that Mr. Atlas won't shunt you off to a country estate, never to be seen again?" he asked skeptically.

"He won't." She shook her head, averting her eyes from his

gaze at this question. When she spoke again, her voice was softer, almost apologetic. "A man in his position benefits from a wife in attendance to aid in diplomatic sway. Most of the governors he visits in the Indies have wives of their own, and during the London Season, many elite events are behind closed doors with only established families. I am not a perfect match for him, nor do I claim to be, as my father is only a knight and we have no great fortune nor titles to offer, but it would be a mutually beneficial arrangement and would not damn me to a lonely life, locked away from the world."

His chest clenched hearing her talk this way, listening to the way she'd had to bargain for a tolerable future. A woman like this should have her choice of kings and gods. He wasn't certain if knowing her reasoning for choosing Mr. Atlas made the intention she had to wed him hurt more or less. Perhaps some part of him would have been better able to cope with knowing she had a passion for them both, and simply wished to explore what one had to offer before committing to the other.

"I do not want to talk about marriage or other men," she said, leaning forward and into his side, resting her head on his shoulder. "I only want to be here with you until I must be banished back to my lonely room. I want the magic to last as long as it possibly can."

"Magic?" he teased, wrapping an arm around her. "So I am a sorcerer after all, Miss Blakely?"

She sighed in mock defeat. "Yes," she confessed, "the most dangerous sorcerer these lands have ever known, and I've walked willingly into your spell."

"Ah, don't fret," he said with a chuckle, resting his cheek on the top of her head, "your magic has trapped me as well."

ALEX DID NOT THINK he'd be able to sleep after seeing Gloriana back to her rooms before the first tendrils of dawn might spell discovery for them both.

He crawled back into his bed, which seemed suddenly far too large, and drew the covers up around himself, inhaling deeply for the last vestiges of her scent. He pulled the pillow she'd lain upon over to his own side of the bed and buried his nose in it, attempting to recall the finer details of the night they'd just shared.

Somehow, before he'd even recounted finding that silver key, the dark hours of the night slipped away from him, dragging him into a deep, satisfied slumber that must only be the result of the physical release he'd enjoyed earlier. He awoke feeling uncharacteristically refreshed, excited to start his day and to seek out another stolen moment or ten with the ever delightful Miss Blakely.

The dreary low mist that had descended upon the manor seemed to have scattered a bit, leaving behind a few shafts of sunlight to brighten the grounds. It wasn't exactly a beautiful day, but it was an improvement, and that was plenty enough to lift his spirits as he made his way to his wardrobe, pondering what options might be on offer at breakfast.

As he dressed, he glanced at the two glasses of water, sitting side-by-side next to the carafe. Chances were good that no servant would demand an explanation of such a curious thing, but all the same, he swiped one of the glasses, dumped its water into the other, and moved to hide it in his wardrobe until the next night. After all, any precaution taken to defend Gloriana's reputation was a prudent one, no matter how paranoid.

Satisfied that his wicked deeds were all concealed within the presentation of his room, he stepped out into the hall, eager to see what today might bring him. It wasn't until he reached the stairs that the sudden tense feeling that all was not well floated up from the ground floor.

"I didn't know we were expecting any other guests," a female voice said excitedly, one of the guests to whom he'd paid little enough attention that he could not place her by voice alone. "Whoever could it be?"

"I do not know," Gloriana answered, *her* voice as distinct as a ringing bell. There was, however, something hair raising in her tone. "No one else was expected."

He hesitated, peering over the railing to see the grand entrance thrown open to welcome these late-arriving inter-lopers. As the carriage crunched into the pebbled drive, the horses being urged to a stop, he felt a chill of ice creep into his veins. Perhaps it was intuition or perhaps he had devel-oped a heightened sense of connection with the young woman below, whose reaction must be a much more magni-fied version of his own.

Yes, somehow he was not surprised when she said, in a voice stiff with barely disguised horror, "My parents are here."

CHAPTER 19

*I*t was truly unfair, as far as Gloriana was concerned, that such a perfect morning could be shattered so thoroughly, so quickly.

She hadn't yet been able to bring herself to cross the threshold, out into the lawn. Instead, she stood in the large doorway, cool autumn wind teasing tresses free from her carefully styled hair and whipping wrinkles into her carefully chosen dress. Why not destroy all she had planned for the day ahead of her at once, and save herself the pain of ongoing, gradual despair?

Rose had brushed right past her to go greet the carriage, without even a glance of apology or a whisper of concern. Of course she wouldn't think anything amiss, would she? Well, Gloriana knew with utter certainty that she would not be so cavalier and light-footed if it were Rose's mother stepping out of that carriage, unannounced and carrying a grudge.

Rose must have believed she was mending fences. She had always been a particular favorite of Sir Reginald's, perhaps because she had no Papa of her own to dote upon her. She greeted him with a hearty embrace, kissing both of his ruddy cheeks in greeting with her joyous laugh carried on the wind.

Mrs. Polly Blakely, Gloriana's mother, had always been a touch more reserved than her husband and daughter. She descended carefully, her narrow frame wrapped in excessive amounts of fur, as though the lack of padding on her person made her far more susceptible to the blustery winds up north.

With her attention so fixated on her parents, Gloriana didn't notice Alex's approach as he arrived silently at her shoulder. It wasn't until he pulled her hand into his own that she was shaken from her reverie. She clasped the warmth of his fingers readily, a small breath of relief permeating her icy dread.

In return, he'd given her fingers a clandestine squeeze, their forbidden union of hands hidden amidst the folds of her frothy pink skirt and the pleats of his morning jacket. He pressed something cold and narrow into her palm, stepping away before anyone might notice that they were standing suspiciously close together.

She wrapped her fingers around the little gift, the shape of a key immediately apparent between her fingers, and glanced at him curiously with a subtle tilt of her head. "Am I to keep this so you won't lose it again?" she whispered.

"Keep it for many reasons," he responded softly. "Let it serve as a reminder that you are your own woman, no matter what others demand of you."

She softened, something about the sentiment in his voice warming her despite the circumstances. "It shall only remind me of you, Alex."

"That's all right, then," he decided, giving her half a grin. "Perhaps that's the outcome I wanted anyhow."

She slid the key into the ribbon at her waist, taking a deep breath as she prepared herself to face what awaited outside. And here she'd started the morning wondering only how it might be between her and Alex Somers after they had been so intimate the night before.

She had been anticipating all of the variables, the factors that had changed, and steeling herself to behave normally in his presence after he'd seen her like that, touched her like that. If she had contemplated the greatest challenge for the day ahead of her only moments ago, it would have been concern over being in his company, something that somehow still felt as natural as waking when the sun rose.

She knew he stood behind her as she took those harrowing steps out of the protection of Somerton and into the bracing morning air. She put on her most gracious smile, practiced and perfected under the tutelage of Mrs. Arlington herself, and waved to the carriage just as her mama's head turned and spotted her approach.

"My darling girl," Polly cried, opening her arms to fold Gloriana into an extremely well-insulated hug amidst her mother's furs. "We have missed you so!"

"It hasn't been so very long," Gloriana replied, an airy

nonchalance in her tone that grated against the anxiety building in her chest. "Has Papa been driving you mad?"

"Me?" huffed Sir Reginald, bouncing on his heels in anticipation of his turn in his daughter's embrace. "Perish the thought!"

Polly gave an indulgent smile, but did not otherwise comment on her husband's prolonged effect on her nerves. Gloriana had a sneaking suspicion that perhaps they had been enjoying their time alone, despite their sudden appearance in Yorkshire. All the same, it was lovely to feel the warmth of her father's embrace again, to stand in their presence without having to weep or apologize.

As the luggage was carried into the manor and the guests who had gathered on the lawn decided that warm interiors were far more interesting than new arrivals, everyone made their way back into the comfortable embrace of Somerton.

Gloriana remained in the foyer, pointedly ignoring the piercing gaze of the portrait of Heloise Somers as her parents were escorted up the stairs and to their chambers. It was only then that she turned to Rose, who was clasping her hands in front of her, an uncertain smile on her face.

"Are you not pleased?" she asked.

"Why would you think not?" Gloriana replied evenly, careful not to give away the turmoil rolling in her belly.

Rose took a step forward, her brow furrowed. "It is only the tone you took when you saw they had arrived. I thought you would be very relieved to have a pleasant reunion, considering how distraught you were when we left London."

"But I am still guilty of the same crimes I was six weeks ago,

Rose." Gloriana sighed. "I had hoped to write them only once a betrothal was secured, as a means of apology."

"Well," Rose replied, a secretive glint in her eye, "as I understand it, Nathaniel Atlas is a traditional sort. He asked me when and if your parents would be arriving, as he had an important matter to discuss with Sir Reginald."

Gloriana froze, certain that in that moment, her slippers had sprouted roots and anchored her to the spot. For the space of a breath, she genuinely could not move, a strange tension flooding her from her toes to her eyelashes that felt like neither relief nor dread. How odd to experience an emotion one could not name!

"Glory?" Rose said, reaching out to touch her arm. "Are you well? I thought you would be ecstatic! That is why I allowed it to be a surprise."

"I'm fine," Gloriana said in a voice that sounded far more fragile than not. She gave a weak smile of apology. "It is just a sudden shock, several sudden shocks, all at once. Perhaps my fortitude is not as strong as I'd like."

"Nonsense," Rose scoffed, pulling her cousin forward into an embrace of her own.

She did not seem to mind when Gloriana gripped her back with all her might, burying her face in her cousin's neck. For just this moment, Glory was a little girl again, who trusted her brave, strong, wonderful elder cousin to always rescue her from anything frightening or ugly. She inhaled deeply, squeezing her eyes shut as she savored the safety of this embrace, and then pulled back with only a hint of teardrops at the corners of her eyes.

There were a thousand things she wished she could tell Rose. A thousand monsters that would be so much less ferocious if her cousin were to slay them for her. But that time of her life, it seemed, was truly past, and now she had to take up the sword and confront all of the terrors of adulthood herself.

"I am going to dress for luncheon," she said to Rose, hoping that her lips did not tremble, nor her hands at her sides. "I love you very much, you know."

"I know," Rose replied softly. "I love you too, my darling girl."

OF THE MANY surprises that the day had brought, perhaps the one that struck Gloriana as the most peculiar, was the enthusiasm with which her mother greeted the dowager viscountess at luncheon. The two had embraced with delighted squeals, words falling so rapidly from both of their mouths that the rest of the table simply looked on in bemused interest.

"Look at that," Tatiana had whispered behind her glass, "it is the two of us, at a dinner party some thirty years in the future."

"If we're lucky," Nell had replied with a titter.

Introductions were made around the table to those who required it, though Sheldon Bywater, the Marquis of Moorvale, greeted her parents with the enthusiasm of an old friend. Indeed, he had attended Glory's debut ball, she supposed, and even danced with her mother a time or two.

She glanced at Tia out of the corner of her eye while this

reunion was taking place, and noted that rather than uttering a lighthearted comment, her friend had receded into an open scowl. So, then, Nell was right. Tia had some quarrel with the marquis, whom Glory had never observed being anything but aggressively pleasant. How very curious!

Alex arrived fashionably late, his entrance stopping the breath in her lungs in a sudden warm flush. His eyes found hers immediately, a slight curve of his lips serving as secret greeting, and he turned to bow and introduce himself as a gentleman to her mother and father.

He took note of his own mother's presence with a silent nod, which was perhaps not quite the polite greeting that was strictly appropriate, but was such an improvement that Gideon's eyebrows shot up as he turned to exchange a meaningful look of surprise with his wife.

For perhaps the first meal that they'd sat down to since the festivities had begun, Gloriana could not think of a single thing to say to spark conversation with those around her. She thought that this went mostly unnoticed, however, as her father and Gideon both engaged in a rousing bout of ask and answer with Mr. Atlas about his thrilling diplomatic career and what his next adventures might be.

She could see the future as clearly as if the Fool on Tatiana's divining cards had leapt up and performed it in pantomime. Everyone at the table could see it too. She imagined that by tonight, her father and Mr. Atlas would discuss the specifics of her future in a room filled with cigar smoke and the swish of fine port in expensive crystalware.

This was what she'd wanted all along, wasn't it? This was the first step in making a life all her own. Mr. Atlas was handsome and exciting and respectable. He didn't make untoward jests nor cut his hair unfashionably short. He didn't have freckled skin and a penchant for mischief. His eyes weren't warm, sparkling green, and his touch always strictly proper, never scandalous.

For the second time in a handful of hours, Gloriana Blakely had the strangest urge to cry.

CHAPTER 20

*A*lex was mumbling to himself as he walked, clutching his overcoat tight around his ribs against the early evening winds that seemed to get sharper and less forgiving by the day. It had already reached that desolate point at year's end where every day was shorter than the one that came before it. Winter was still a ways off, but already it was pitch-dark well before the bell rang for dinner.

These early sunsets always gave him the feeling that he was running late, even if he had no particular commitments or was perfectly well on schedule. If it were up to Alex, it would be summer all year long and every night would have a big, bright moon to light your way, whatever your deeds may be.

Perhaps that's why he wasn't in charge of things.

He had been running his intended speech in his head over and over for the last several hours. Its origins had begun weeks ago, in truth, when he'd sat opposite Gloriana Blakely on the floor of his bedroom and told her all about the pitiful state of his upbringing.

Heloise always said that Alex was the most like their mother of any of them, and no matter how he scoffed or spurned her, he'd always known that to be true. When he was a child, they had been as tightly bonded as mother and child could be, perhaps more so than Ruthie had ever been with her other two children in their tender years. What Heloise didn't understand was that the ferocity of his love for her was the reason her betrayal had pierced so deeply, had hurt so badly. Wounds like that never completely healed.

He was uncertain exactly what the rift had been between Gloriana and her parents, but the message he'd received from watching them arrive had been a staggering one. The three of them had embraced. They had *smiled*. They had been truly happy to see one another, despite the tone of shock and fear in Glory's voice when she'd seen their carriage arrive.

He knew she was vexed with them. She'd told him so. And yet she'd conducted herself with grace and love in the presence of her family. Astonishingly, it seemed, no spat nor quarrel was severe enough to create a permanent divide.

The dower house loomed up in front of him so suddenly that he was certain he'd been magicked from the drive of the manor house, rather than walking the whole way. The walk had certainly been much longer the last time he'd made it, hadn't it? Perhaps, he thought, he should turn back and try again from the beginning. It would give him more time to practice what he intended to say, after all.

He made an irritated noise and spun on his heel, pacing as

he blew hot air into cupped hands to warm his face. His heart was thumping against his rib cage and all the words he'd assembled so neatly in his head were scattering about on his tongue like incoherent nonsense as he attempted to recite them quickly under his breath.

"Alex?"

His head snapped up, his pulse leaping directly into his throat. The sight of his sister, rather than anyone else, had the charitable effect of only momentary alarm. Seeing her there with her arms crossed impatiently, tapping her foot as she waited for an explanation, sent his anxiety slipping neatly back down his throat and into his belly. "Evening, Hel."

"Good evening," she replied warily. "Is anything the matter? If Rosie sent you to fetch Reggie, he's already gone down for the night, and I think it would be better if he stayed until morning."

"No, it's ..." He cleared his throat, shaking his head against the ridiculous jolt of panic that rang through him. "I wanted to speak to Mother."

He got the impression that he couldn't have shocked Heloise more if he'd shown up in a petticoat and announced his intention to elope with Sheldon Bywater. She did not bother to politely disguise her surprise, her eyes going wide and her mouth dropping open. "You've what now? Do you mind saying again?"

"Oh, Hel, don't make this harder than it already is," he moaned, digging his fingers into his hair and resuming his pacing. "Perhaps it was a stupid idea. I ought to leave and come back later when I'm not beside myself."

"No, no," she said quickly, stepping forward and putting a hand to his arm to still his movements. "No, please don't. I had given up hope that you'd ever come around to speaking to her. I am happy to see you here, Alex. Truly."

He peered at her through slanted eyes, trying to gauge how likely it was that she was winding him up for a punchline, but she was gazing at him with clear, hopeful eyes, and the hand she rested on his elbow was gentle and sweet. Seeing Heloise behave so reasonably clashed in his mind with all the other foolishness in there, and he wasn't sure whether it was a comfort or an exacerbation, all things considered.

"Come inside," she said, giving his elbow a tug. "I'll get you a glass of whiskey to calm your nerves and let you warm up by the fire. How does that sound?"

He nodded, allowing himself to be led into the house like an errant schoolboy being cajoled by a crafty governess. Before he knew it, she'd positioned him next to a hearth, shoved a glass of amber liquid into his hands, and brought around a servant to take his overcoat.

He blinked at her in open admiration. Did motherhood grant such competence? Or had Heloise decided to leave her poor big brother in the dust and glide into adulthood ahead of him?

She gave him a wry sort of smile and shrugged. "You looked like you needed this more than a good ribbing."

He gave a hollow chuckle and nodded in agreement, tipping the whiskey into his mouth. It was an impressive feat that he didn't choke on it or spit it back out, for as soon as he did so, the doors to the drawing room opened, admitting Ruthie

Somers *and* Polly Blakely, giggling together like a couple of debutantes.

Ruthie came to an abrupt halt, her cheeks flushed pink with whatever joviality she was sharing with her old friend, her eyes locking on her son.

"Hello, Mother," he choked, the whiskey burning its way down his body, his eyes watering at the strain of it. He attempted to swallow a second time so as not to burst into a fit of coughs, and said in a croaky voice, "I was hoping we could talk."

"Of course," she breathed, not daring to move from her position by the door. "I was just entertaining Mrs. Blakely. Have you met?"

"Oh, yes, we met at luncheon." Polly Blakely beamed, dipping into a polite curtsy. "He is a very amusing gentleman, Ruthie. You must be so proud!"

"Oh, I am," she replied with a tight little smile.

He glanced at his sister, wondering if she'd known for all these years that the mother of her nemesis was such an intimate of their own mother. From the tightness of her lips, he guessed she did not.

"I must go," Heloise said abruptly, her attempt at a polite smile teetering somewhere on the edge of sarcasm. "I must attend one of the expecting mothers in the village, I'm afraid. You know the timing of these things is never quite convenient."

"Of course, darling." Ruthie nodded. "My daughter has taken a philanthropic position in our local township, training under a midwife and our very handsome local physician," she explained to her friend. "She has become a bit of a folk hero to the villagers."

"Oh, Mama, please stop." Heloise sighed with a shake of her head. "Mrs. Blakely, my horse is tethered nearby. If you'd like to share my saddle, I could take you back to the manor house on my way out."

"You aren't taking a carriage?" Mrs. Blakely asked in surprise.

"She never does," both Alex and Ruthie muttered in perfect unison. The two shot each other uneasy looks at this unintentional alignment.

"How curious," Polly replied, evidently seeing nothing amiss with a bit of mother-son mind reading. "I certainly would appreciate it if Ruthie will be a while. I'm afraid I'm not much of a horsewoman, though."

"Don't worry." Heloise smiled, taking the other woman's arm and leading her from the drawing room. "Boudicea is as gentle as a lamb."

Alex watched helplessly as the door swung shut behind his sister, her voice fading as she made her way from the house. The fire crackled merrily and the cool rivets of the crystal in his fingers urged him to have another drink. At the very least, the first one had slowed his heart a bit.

"Heloise has become a singular woman," Ruthie remarked, crossing the room to pour herself a glass of the same whiskey. She took a long drink, without a hint of discomfort, and sighed, refilling her glass. "I can scarcely believe that is my rebellious little girl talking expectant mothers through childbirth, setting broken legs, and the like. What happened to my little hellion? Where has the time gone?"

Alex bit back the impulse to reply with snark, to point out that time had moved at exactly the pace it always had, but that one must be physically present in order to experience it. The truth of the matter was that for these last three years, Ruthie had spent far more time with Heloise than he had, and if he were being honest, the bulk of this maturation had occurred within that time.

Too bad he couldn't say the same for himself.

Ruthie did not seem to expect him to respond, however. She tapped her thumbnail thoughtfully against her glass, raising it to her lips for a much more conservative sip, and then turned to face him, her eyes wide and wary, the same clear green they had been before everything had gone wrong.

"I have hoped against hope that you would eventually come to forgive me," she said carefully. "Am I to believe this moment has actually arrived?"

"I don't know," he replied earnestly. "Forgiveness seems rather more like a process than an event to me. At the very least, I think I am willing to consider undergoing that process now, where I was not before."

She nodded, taking a deep gulp of air and tilting her eyes upward, as though to prevent them from sprouting tears. "I have had nightmares about the last time I saw you for well over a decade, Alexander. There was so much rage in your young face, so much frustration and confusion. For a long time, I thought, if only he could understand the position I was in, he would forgive me, but of course, you did understand, even then, because you were living with him too."

He gave a curt nod. "I do not particularly wish to venture back in time tonight, Mother. Instead, I thought merely to extend an olive branch and work toward a better future."

"Of course," she said, gripping the glass of spirits in both of her slender hands. "Won't you sit? Perhaps we may talk for a spell rather than attend dinner at the estate tonight?"

"All right," he said, though in truth he felt as though someone else were guiding his movements and his words just now. It was all rather surreal, standing here, talking to her so calmly.

He followed her to a set of armchairs and settled in opposite her, averting his gaze from the overwhelming expression of hope that lit up her face. He didn't know what he was expecting, but he certainly had thought it would be more difficult and strained than a simple sit-down to catch up.

"It was a surprise," he said, shifting awkwardly in his seat, "to see that you were intimate with Mrs. Blakely. What a strange coincidence."

She raised her eyebrows, still chestnut brown, though he suspected she had begun to dye her hair to maintain the color. "Yes, I suppose it is funny how life reminds us all the time of who we once were. Polly and I were dear friends in our first Season, and remained correspondents for some years afterward. When she finally had a child of her own, we had hoped that one day her daughter might marry my son and make us a sort of sisters."

Alex blinked, his throat suddenly dry, and lifted the glass to his lips to avoid responding. Was his mother saying that they wished for him to marry Gloriana? Was such a thing even possible?

"Of course, your father drew up a sloppy sort of contract, never delivered it to Sir Reginald, and in the end, Gideon eloped with the cousin instead. It took me almost a year to piece together that Rose was related to my old friend. How strange to think that if things had gone differently, your brother might be married to the other girl instead."

"You are ... erm, aware," Alex began, "of that girl's fraught history with Heloise?"

"Oh, yes." Ruthie shrugged, as though it were no matter. "But who didn't Hel have a fraught relationship with in her wild years? I hardly think it is a damning mark on Miss Blakely's character. After all, she has been most pleasant during the course of this little country party."

Alex managed to nod in agreement. He didn't quite trust himself to speak, having been entirely unprepared for the subject of Gloriana to arise in this tender reunion with his mother.

She was watching him carefully, seemingly unaffected by that impressive swig she'd taken of the whiskey, as though she did indeed expect him to speak. Perhaps she'd taken notice of a friendship between him and Gloriana, but surely she couldn't possibly be aware of anything more than that!

"I understand that it is a big night for Polly herself," Ruthie continued, that shrewd and piercing gaze of hers unwavering. "Her husband has been in conference with one of our guests, who seeks her daughter's hand."

"Atlas," Alex provided, ignoring the pang in his chest at the thought of it. "I had heard whisper of it."

"Mm." Ruthie nodded. "Polly and I both found our

husbands in that first Season, you know. I thought she was making a terrible mistake and she thought the very same about me. Of course, Reginald Blakely was not yet a knight, nor was he the type of man the girls swooned over, awaiting invitations to dance. He's always been much the way he is now, a little soft around the middle, a little thin of hair on his head, but endlessly boisterous and optimistic. I could not understand why a girl of Polly's standing and looks wouldn't hold out for a better offer."

"Like you?"

She sighed with a begrudging nod. "Yes, like me. Your father was everything Reginald was not. He was devastatingly handsome, rich, and titled, and yet Polly was as concerned for me as I was for her. She knew there was nothing but practical business between us in the matter of our union."

"I daresay that's more often the way of things than not," Alex replied. It caused him no shock or injury to learn that his parents had never wasted time on the business of falling in love with one another.

"She seems so happy that her daughter has finally found the right match," Ruthie continued, her brow furrowing. "When I asked her if it is a love match, like her own, her cheeks pinkened and she laughed away the question, saying she could not possibly know for certain what her daughter's deepest feelings were, only that Gloriana had turned so many men down that it was relief she had finally settled upon one."

"Well, I haven't any daughters," Alex said, "but I imagine fear of never seeing one settled is a disconcerting thing."

"Perhaps it is," Ruthie agreed, though the troubled look on

her face did not ease. "It's only that, seeing Polly again after all these years has been like a new spark on old fires. I remember so clearly the way she'd watch Reg at balls, the way her eyes would sparkle when he approached. Her eyes are that same pale blue as her daughter's, if you've noticed."

"I hadn't," he admitted, an eerie sensation of being caught at mischief beginning to settle into his midsection.

Ruthie set her glass on the table between them, holding her hands out in front of her for a moment, and then wiggling free a pearl and sapphire ring that she wore on her middle finger.

"This was my grandmother's ring," she explained, holding it out to Alex. "Perhaps the only other woman I've ever known who married for love."

He took it, still unsure exactly what was happening or why, and held it carefully between two fingers. "It is lovely," he told her, holding it back out.

"Yes," she nodded, settling back in her chair instead of retrieving it from him. "And meant for a woman who is going to marry for love. Perhaps you will give it to such a woman before she finds herself making a terrible mistake."

Alex blinked at her, a rumble of unease in his chest. "Mother, I—"

"Hush." She smiled, those eyes full of unspoken knowledge. "Now, how would you like to stay for a private dinner, instead of returning to the manor right away, hm? There is so much I want to ask you, now that you're here."

He studied the little jeweled ring, watching the way the

gems caught the light. The blue would compliment her eyes beautifully, he thought.

He looked up at his mother again, slipping the ring into the pocket of his waistcoat. "Yes," he decided, "dinner sounds nice."

ALEX FOUND himself walking back to the manor with an entirely different sort of speech playing in his head. If the fates were kind, he would not be too late. Hell, even if Atlas had already staked his claim, he would try his luck anyhow.

He had nothing to offer her yet. He knew that. Worse, he'd squandered the work she'd done to present him with a fertile field for his future prospects throughout the course of this party, more focused on finding ways to spend time in her company than in any serious endeavor to lock down vocation.

Of course, he could always lean on the excuse of fearing for his life. That was valid, wasn't it? It *sounded* valid, even if it was a bald-faced lie.

He chuckled to himself, his breath fogging in the cool night air as the manor came up before him. At the very least, he'd made a fine discovery tonight. If one had daunting tasks to mull upon, long and boring walks dissipated into mere seconds, with only the mystery of how one could be transported so quickly left in their wake.

The house was already dark. He had missed a small concert performed by musicians from the township tonight, following dinner, but it seemed that this festive task had not unraveled into a late night for their guests.

Perhaps after so many consecutive nights of merrymaking, it was an early slumber in a soft bed that began to seem exotic. He certainly was looking forward to a night of rest himself, though he'd had far more diverting and pleasant evenings in his bedchambers of late than those focused solely upon slumber.

He took care climbing the stairs, his joints stiff from the blustery walk, and shook his head in wonder at the evening he'd just had, laughing over dinner and drinks with his mother—a woman whose very presence had caused him to flee on instinct for the last several years.

He patted the ring in his waistcoat, wondering what sort of woman this great-grandmother of his had been and how she'd come to marry for love, far off in the Americas.

Perhaps he'd ask Ruthie to tell him the story someday soon. At the moment, the future seemed full to the brim with possibility.

He noticed, with a quickening of his heartbeat, that the door to his bedchamber was open, just a crack, but enough to allow a sliver of moonlight into the hall. Could he truly be so lucky? Was she waiting for his return tonight?

He hastened his stride, his heart full to bursting in his chest at the thought of seeing her so unexpectedly and so soon. Damn the speech, anyway. He did not need to take airs with someone who knew him the way she did. He would simply stride into the room, fall to one knee, and beg her to be his wife.

Strangely, when he pushed the door open and stepped inside, all was still very dark, save for one low-burning candle at his bedside. He furrowed his brow, uncertain where she might have gone, and turned to head for his tinderbox and provide some light as a start.

It was only when he intended to move that he took notice of a very sharp point pressed into his back. The world suddenly came into sharp relief, the sound of another person breathing behind him as evident as the workings of his own lungs.

"Don't wish to hurt you," a man grumbled, his words ragged and rough, "but I will if you make a fuss."

Alex nodded, lifting his hands to indicate his compliance with this man's demands. Perhaps he should have been concerned about his mortality after all, he thought. If Gloriana truly had come to this room tonight, with some criminal skulking around, she might have found herself in serious danger.

The thought lodged his panic directly into his throat, like a chunk of unforgiving, ragged ice.

"You left Oxford with something that doesn't belong to you," the man said, a sourness on his breath that seemed to flood the entire room. "Tell me where it is and I'll be on my way."

"Everything I brought back with me is in that valise," Alex said, pointing across the room to the little suitcase he and Gloriana had fruitlessly searched. "Take it."

"Oh, I will." The man chuckled. "Thank you kindly."

There was an abrupt and blinding shock of pain to the back of Alex's head, and then there was nothing but darkness.

CHAPTER 21

The first thing Alex was aware of was the sound of a dog barking, swiftly followed by a throbbing pain just above his left ear. He winced, but that only made things worse. The pain blossomed out over his scalp and shafts of light pierced through his eyelashes in sharp, tiny points, and then there was nothing again for a while.

Next, he was aware of the rumble of voices around him and smooth, delicate hands prodding at his head, which appeared to now be resting on a woman's skirt.

"Gloriana?" he murmured, his voice thick in his throat.

"I beg your pardon!" his sister's voice returned, followed by a rare chuckle from his brother.

"I shouldn't laugh," Gideon sighed, "but I suppose that answers your question as to whether or not the blow to his head addled him."

"Should I fetch the doctor?" Sheldon Bywater asked, his

Scots brogue thicker than usual, perhaps punctuated by panic.

"No," Heloise responded, tilting Alex's head to the side and pressing some sort of cloth to the spot where he'd been hit. "There's always a lot of blood with head wounds. It's not nearly as severe as it looks."

Alex opened his mouth to argue this, but found that attempting to speak only made his head swim. He made a noncommittal groaning sound instead. Through his bleary vision, he noted that Echo the bloodhound was sitting directly in front of him, ramrod stiff, as though she were guarding him from further harm.

It was certainly endearing, even if the sentiment was somewhat tardy.

"Don't fall asleep," Heloise snapped, giving him a sharp tap on the cheek. "I'm just cleaning you up and then you can tell us what happened."

"Can't I tell you tomorrow?" he mumbled. "What time is it?"

"It is two o'clock in the morning," Rose replied from somewhere behind him. "Lord Moorvale here was apparently letting his hound out to relieve herself when she went tearing down the hall at the smell of your blood. She awoke the entire house, you know. I'm sure they all think you've been murdered at this point."

"Hm." Gideon's frown was audible, somehow. "Perhaps someone ought to go out there and reassure everyone."

"Can't rightly do that until we know what happened," Sheldon pointed out. "Best everyone's locked in their rooms until we find the intruder anyhow."

"Atlas and Benton are sweeping the property," Gideon said. "Hopefully they catch the brigand. Alex, are you well enough to tell us what happened?"

Heloise made an irritated click of her tongue. "Fine. Sit up if you can. I don't think you'll need any bandaging. Just don't scratch the wound, all right?"

She gave him a gentle push, helping to lift him from her lap to sitting haphazardly on the floor, his back supported by his wardrobe. The pain in his head was profound, and the room appeared to roll and buck before him, but he gave them a shaky grin anyhow, not wanting to overly trouble any of them.

As they came into focus, it was truly unsettling to him how concerned they all looked. Even the dog looked painfully worried. He put his hand out, beckoning her closer, and she padded over with a whine, flopping her warm head into his lap with what sounded remarkably like a relieved sigh.

"My valise," Alex began, noting that quite a few of his belongings were scattered about the room, perhaps knocked over during the search for the elusive spy parcel. "He was an enemy spy and he took my valise."

"Oh dear," Heloise frowned. "Perhaps he is addled."

Alex squeezed his eyes shut. How to explain? "He had a knife. Thick accent. He wanted the parcel."

"What bloody parcel?" Gideon snapped. "Heloise, I think perhaps the doctor—"

"No!" Alex said, eyes wide. He attempted to lean forward for emphasis, but was stopped both by the wave of nausea that overtook him and the gentle paw that Echo placed on his thigh, as though to discourage him from any foolishness. He sighed, attempting to sort through the muddle of his thoughts, and tried again. "The doctor might be one of them! There are spies at the party, looking for a parcel in my things. They think I'm a spy too!"

"Christ," Gideon muttered, running a hand over his eyes.

"Gloriana!" Alex realized suddenly, looking from his brother to Rose. "Gloriana knows. Get her!"

"Well, at least his delusions are consistent?" Heloise said dryly, bundling up a collection of bloody rags from where she'd tended his wound. "Alex, are you saying Gloriana is a spy?"

"No! Listen to me!" he groaned, aware of how he sounded but unable to do anything about it. "We overheard them. The night of the ball. I'm all mixed up, please go get her. She can explain."

Rose cut in before either of his siblings could react to this bizarre request. "I will retrieve her," Rose said softly. "If she is as confused as we are, perhaps we call for the physician after all."

"Yes, fine," Alex breathed, relief a small comfort against the way he currently felt. What the devil had that man hit him with, anyhow? "Get Gloriana."

"For God's sake," Heloise muttered with a shake of her head.

GLORIANA FLEW from her bed the moment the knock

sounded at her door. She hastened to open it, twisting the key in the lock and wrenching it open.

"What has happened?" she demanded immediately, her cousin's face unreadable. "Is he hurt?"

"He?" Rose replied. "Who do you mean?"

She bit her tongue, realizing her error immediately. When she'd rushed into the hall at the sound of the frenzied barking not an hour prior, she'd known immediately that it was Alex's bedchamber from which the ruckus originated.

"Why, Lord Moorvale," she lied, blinking innocently at her cousin. "I assume there is only one dog on the premises?"

"Sheldon is quite all right," Rose said in a tone that implied she saw right through Glory's attempt at deception. "It was Alex who was attacked, and he is asking for you."

"For me?" she breathed, her heart leaping in her throat. "Oh, Rosie, is he horribly injured? Let me get my dressing gown."

She allowed Rose to take hold of the door, watching her as she rushed to wrap herself in the gauzy robe that Alex had removed from her body only a night ago. She felt tears welling in her eyes and forced herself to breathe.

Would he call for her if he was not grievously injured? Did he simply wish to say goodbye before succumbing to his wounds? Oh, her poor Alex!

She slipped her feet into a pair of slippers and hurried after Rose, not bothering to lock the door behind her. She hadn't even checked her appearance, despite knowing for certain that the thick braid wound about her head for the night was likely in spectacular disarray by now.

Oh, it didn't matter, not when he could be dying!

"He is a little shaken," Rose explained, leading her down the darkened hallway. "He was trying to explain to us who attacked him and claims that you can elaborate on his story, which he is having trouble recounting to us at the moment with the blow to his head."

"Shaken?" Glory replied breathlessly. "Is that all? He is not seriously hurt?"

"Heloise doesn't seem to think so," Rose replied, "though there was a rather shocking amount of blood."

"Oh," she breathed, putting a hand to her chest. "It must have been one of the spies then, who attacked him?"

Rose stopped dead in her tracks, turning to face her cousin with an expression on her face that appeared to straddle amusement and shock.

"Or ... someone else?" Gloriana suggested, uncertain how to read that expression.

"Spies," Rose scoffed with a shake of her head. "Yes, apparently it was these spies that do, in fact, exist. Come along, Glory. The two of you have some explaining to do."

CHAPTER 22

$\mathcal{I}$t had been unspeakably difficult to compose
herself upon entering Alex's bedchambers. All of
her fortitude was required to resist rushing to his side and
investigating him for injury. It was twenty times worse just
now. She was seated on a chair next to his wardrobe, her
hands folded in her lap, eyes averted to nothing in particular
in the far corner of the room, while the other occupants of
the Somers family stared at her in open-mouthed disbelief
at the story she had just recounted.

Of course she hadn't told them *everything*. The story of the
conversation they'd overheard and sparse details of their
conversations about the incident since were enough to paint
a picture of the situation. As far as she was concerned, she
and Alex Somers had navigated a terrifying situation with
grace and care, and it wasn't for any of the assembled
Somers clan to say different.

"Erm," the Marquis of Moorvale began, clearing his throat
rather awkwardly. He was standing next to the window, a
dark-red dressing gown cinched around his waist, and

appeared deeply uncomfortable with everything that had just transpired. "I might just go check in with Benton and Atlas. I'll let them know about the valise and such. Come along, Echo."

Awoo, Echo replied balefully, her tail slapping Alex's thigh as she stayed resolutely in front of him. She locked her brown eyes on her master with a meaningful tilt of her head.

Sheldon sighed and nodded. "Yes, you're right. Keep guarding the fool boy. I'll return shortly."

Gloriana watch his departure from the room. After confessing the details of the conspiracy surrounding Alex Somers, she had determined that staring at that damned corner of carpet on the far side of the room was pertinent, at least until someone forced her to speak again. She assumed that someone would be Rose, as long as it wasn't ...

"So, what you're telling us," Heloise began, her voice slicing through the silence like a slap in the face, "is that both of you have known of a murderous threat within the walls of Somerton for *weeks*—a home with *two small children* present—and did not think to inform *anyone* of the danger?"

"Hel," Alex sighed, "what would spies want with children?"

"Alex, so help me," she hissed, pushing herself up from where she sat with a rustle of skirts.

"Enough," Gideon sighed, the weariness in his voice sparking a pang of guilt in Glory's chest. "Heloise is confused, as are we all, at why we were not entrusted with this information and asked for our aid."

"Because it sounds ridiculous!" Alex snapped. "And because it would somehow be my fault, like everything else, even though I don't have the *faintest idea* what the brigands think I have that's so valuable. Hopefully it's in that valise, or I imagine this whole situation is going to get even stickier."

"What were the two of you doing in the library on the night of the ball?" Rose inquired. She was investigating the state of her fingernails while she asked, carefully keeping her voice even and impassive, though the implications of the question were clear as day.

"Do you recall that morning, how angry I was that Lord Alex did not appear for the arrival of the guests?" Gloriana asked, forcing herself to blink away her haze of avoidance and look at her cousin. "For reasons I did not understand, he vanished from the ball within moments of arriving as well. I was extremely cross about this, and stormed after him to insist he return to the festivities I'd so painstakingly arranged."

"It's true." Alex sighed. "I was acting like a child, avoiding Mother, and Glory followed after me. When we heard others coming, we hid in the linen closet so as not to be caught in a compromising situation."

"Oh yes," Heloise mocked, "the linen closet is *far* less suggestive than a large, open room."

"Oh, are we talking about safeguarding reputations now?" Alex snapped back, making her eyes narrow. "Let's talk about yours, Heloise."

"Enough," Gideon said again, his tone more exhausted than angry. He took a breath, rubbing at the bridge of his nose before speaking again. "I take it the man who attacked you was one of the men you overheard in the library, then?"

"No," Alex replied, firmly enough that Gloriana immediately believed him. He was still propped against the wall, one hand on Echo's back, but his eyes looked clearer now, his voice steadier too. "The intruder tonight had a thick foreign accent. All three of the plotters from the night of the ball were English as English can be."

"What flavor of foreign?" Heloise asked.

He shrugged. "I haven't the faintest idea. I just know he wasn't one of the three from the night of the ball."

"We thought those we overheard might have been members of the serving staff, perhaps some of the temporary hires Mrs. Laughlin brought on for the party," Gloriana added. "We had hoped that after the grouse hunt, when they planned to search Lord Alex's room, that perhaps they had found what they were after and departed. If this were the case, then we need not trouble any of you."

"And you have no idea what it might have been?" Rose asked Alex, still using that terrifyingly even voice that spoke nothing of her inner feelings.

"Not the first inkling," he replied. "I searched through all of my things. Twice. I couldn't find anything of interest at all, and now I've sent some other dangerous nutter out into the world with a caseful of philosophy texts with rude drawings in the margins."

"How have you survived into adulthood?" Heloise muttered with a roll of her eyes.

A sharp knock at the door captured everyone's attention as Sheldon Bywater attempted to squeeze his significant frame into the room as discreetly as possible. His presence sent

Echo's tail thumping into Alex's leg again with considerable fervor.

"The gentlemen have turned up nothing," he said with a shrug, "and no horses are missing from the stables. Suggesting that any horses might have gone missing under his watch sent Graham into such a rage that I took my leave rather than attempt an apology."

"Then it is probably a lost cause," Rose said, rising from her spot. "Whoever the villain was, he is gone now. I suggest we all return to our beds and contact the constabulary in the morning."

"Oh, yes, I'll sleep wonderfully after all this," Heloise scoffed, crossing the room to bend over Alex and check the side of his head again.

"Come along, Glory," Rose said, offering her a hand up from her chair. Her brown eyes were clear and sharp, despite the hour, and seemed to take no small notice of the way Gloriana watched in concern as Heloise inspected her brother's wounds.

"Is he going to be all right?" she asked quietly, accepting the hand and following her cousin to the door. "How badly was he hurt?"

"According to Heloise, he'll be tender but otherwise fine," Rose replied. "He is lucky his most recent dalliance with questionable decision-making did not lead to a darker result."

"You are angry," Gloriana whispered, her heart clenching in her chest.

"I am perplexed," Rose corrected, her back straight and her

stride quick. "I had thought that you trusted me enough to tell me anything, and that I would be your first confidante over something so upsetting and dangerous."

"I wanted to tell you," Gloriana insisted, blinking away an infuriating rise of tears and attempting to stifle the sound of them in her voice. "But Alex did not wish Gideon to know, and telling you would put you in a position of either betraying my trust or keeping a secret from your husband!"

Rose shook her head. "Alex was not thinking clearly, and a man like him occasionally needs a cooler head to urge him in the sensible direction."

"It did not seem my place," Gloriana replied weakly.

In truth, she agreed with Rose. The honest motivation for her secrecy had not been a matter of clear thinking, but rather the heady thrill of being wrapped up in such an intrigue with the handsome and charming man who seemed to haunt her every thought.

Perhaps it was one last foray into childishness before she committed to a life with the respectable Mr. Atlas?

They rounded the corner toward Gloriana's bedchambers to find many of their guests, still wearing nightclothes, gathered in the halls, whispering amongst themselves. Her father, toes peeking out from his nightshirt, had puffed up his chest in indignation and was insisting that he would have been *most useful* during the search of the grounds to a bored-looking Lord Benton.

Rose sighed, leaving her side to approach the gentlemen and soothe tensions that may have arisen in the wake of the incident.

Gloriana was quickly surrounded by Nell and Tatiana, who pulled her by the arm into the shadows, both wide eyed under their lace night caps, their faces pale in the sparse light of handheld lanterns.

"What on earth is happening?" Tia whispered. "I never knew a barking dog could cause such chaos!"

"Is someone hurt?" Nell asked, chewing on her lip. "Are we in danger?"

"Is it Lord Moorvale?" Tia gasped. "It must have been his dog we heard! Oh, Glory, is he wounded?"

Gloriana glanced over her shoulder at Rose corralling the various guests back to their rooms and jerked her head toward her room, taking each girl by the hand and tugging them toward the privacy of a bedchamber. Once inside, she released a heavy sigh and paced through the room to immediately toss herself into her bed.

She rolled onto her back, a strange sensation of relief overtaking her, and turned her head to where her friends stood by the door. "Well, come on, then, there's room for all of us," she said.

Tia and Nell exchanged a glance, an unspoken resignation to the situation passing between them, and approached the large bed in the center of the room, climbing on to sit on either side of Gloriana's supine position.

Nell nudged Glory's side with her bare foot and said, "Go on, then!"

"You won't believe me," Gloriana said, blinking up at the ceiling. "It sounds absurd."

"I believe quite a few things that others find absurd," Tatiana pointed out. "Tell us, please!"

"It was a foreign spy," she said, her voice even and calm, as though she were simply sharing the weather. "Lord Alex Somers has found himself the object of attention from both the home office and the enemy, though he is completely befuddled at why they have taken an interest in him."

"He told you this?" Nell asked, skepticism clear in her tone. "Are you certain he wasn't simply trying to seduce you?"

Gloriana laughed, rolling onto her side to face her friend. "We overheard it together, on the night of the ball. We were having a conversation in the library and heard people coming, so we hid in the linen closet to avoid stirring up any gossip. He was just as surprised as I was to hear that he was apparently an enemy of the Crown, transporting valuable contraband for the enemy troops."

Nell's eyebrows rose, shock clear on her face. "Did you identify those you overheard?"

"Sadly, no." She sighed. "And whomever attacked him tonight was not one of the spies in our midst as party guests or servants. The man tonight was foreign."

"So he was attacked?" Tatiana gasped. "Is he very hurt?"

"No. He took a blow to the head, but seems to be all right. He gave the villain his valise, filled with his things from Oxford, and the man evidently was satisfied with the exchange."

There was a lull of silence, though Gloriana was certain she could feel the questions brimming within both of her friends floating about them in the air. Why had she been alone with Lord Alex? How had she gotten embroiled in this mystery? What would happen now?

In truth, she had pictured her friends gathered excitedly in her bedroom for different reasons tonight. She thought perhaps they would cluster together on the bed, just like this, to squeal and sigh over the proposal she would accept, on the morrow, from Nathaniel Atlas. She had seen it perfectly, had imagined the way she would smile and blush and wave away excitable questions about her future.

Instead, the three of them were collapsed in various ways, stunned silent and gray-faced, after a grisly and unpleasant affair that had unfolded around them.

Nell was frowning particularly hard.

Gloriana reached out to touch her ankle, hoping it was a reassuring pat she had delivered. "They must have what they want now," she said. "Perhaps this is the end of it."

"But Glory," Nell said, "if there was something valuable to Britain in that valise, it sounds as though it has fallen into enemy hands. This could be a tragedy! A major danger to our brave soldiers at war!"

"I think it all must be a misunderstanding," Gloriana said, with complete sincerity. "Alex has no idea what they were after nor where it could be. When the intruder reaches his master with a suitcase full of philosophy texts and old socks, perhaps they will realize their mistake."

"Or return to kill Lord Alex," Tatiana muttered grimly.

"If Lord Alex truly is ignorant to what he had of value, then there is no saying whether or not it is contained in that valise," Nell insisted. "In fact, it seems almost guaranteed that it would be, if all of the spies involved in this affair have mentioned its origin in Oxford!"

"What do you suggest we do?" Gloriana asked, propping herself up on her elbow. "Rose said she will summon the constable from the township tomorrow, and perhaps pass along the issue to those more equipped to manage it."

"Oh, yes," Tatiana said with a roll of her eyes, "a Yorkshire constable is certainly up to the task of unraveling a spy ring related to the war."

Nell was chewing her lip so hard that it had turned red. Her mind seemed to be turning one solution over to the next, trying in futility to find a way to prevent England's enemies from gaining possession of this mystery object of such great importance.

"I must talk to Peter," she decided, her head snapping up. "He will know what to do!"

"Peter?" Tia and Glory repeated in unison.

"My brother is the smartest person I know," Nell replied defensively, setting her jaw. "And he is a man, which means people will listen to him if we derive a solution!"

"Do you think your brother might take issue with you appearing at his door before the sun has even come up?" Tia laughed. "I can see him bleary-eyed and yawning as you pelt him with information about espionage and tragedy."

"Laugh all you want!" Nell huffed, shoving herself from the bed. "He'll be more help than the two of you!"

She marched from the room, her little fists balled at her sides, and let the door swing shut behind her.

The other two girls sighed, knowing it was hopeless to attempt to calm her when she got into a snit.

"Can I sleep here tonight?" Tia asked, already climbing under the blankets, fluffing up a particularly appealing pillow.

Glory only nodded, watching Tia's eyes flutter shut as she settled in for a fitful slumber. She watched with a tinge of envy as her friend's breathing evened out, her mind pulled into the bliss of dreams.

Gloriana knew she would not sleep at all.

CHAPTER 23

S he waited until the grandfather clock in the hallway sounded three chimes to slip out of bed. Surely time enough had passed for everyone to have returned to their rooms and the manor to settle back into the blissful quiet of the night.

It had been torture, lying there next to her soundly sleeping friend, her eyes locked on the gleaming silver key that sat on her nightstand. She had tasked herself with unraveling the messy braid in her hair, then with counting the ticks of the second hand on the clock, neither of which hastened the passage of time.

At first, she was vexed with Tia for staying, thinking that without her, she already could have slipped away to speak with Alex in private. However, being forced to lie still and contemplate the situation had forced her to begrudgingly confess to herself that it was safer to wait a while, anyhow.

She held the key against the palm of her hand, imagining that she could feel some otherworldly power from it, emboldening her to follow her instincts and soothe her nerves. She needed to know for certain, without family as an audience, that he was all right and that he'd told them everything that had truly happened. She knew, somewhere deep in her soul, that she couldn't have resisted the pull to see him again, no matter the risk.

When she left Somerton, and this magical time ended, she thought she might wear this key around her neck on a ribbon. It would be a secret totem to who she was before she became a wife. It was a symbol of the last days of her youth. Her heart hurt to think of it, but she knew it to be true.

She did not knock, instead turning the knob of the door and slipping inside, much more gracefully than Sheldon Bywater had done an hour earlier. "It is only me!" she whispered, as loudly as a whisper could be, into the room, and slid the key into the lock behind her, securing their privacy within the room.

He was sitting on the bed, his back against the headboard and a light still burning in his lantern. He responded with only a smile at her entrance, his eyes seeming to sparkle to life from whatever contemplation had been keeping him awake following his ordeal.

She couldn't help but return the smile, her feet carrying her across the space between them and propelling her into his arms, her head buried into his chest as she gripped her arms around him. "Are you truly well?" she asked, her voice muffled against his chest. "I was so very worried!"

"Were you really?" Alex chuckled, wrapping her in his embrace. "That almost makes the entire ordeal worthwhile."

She tilted her head up to meet his eyes, blinking away tears of relief at finding him well and whole. "I feel so foolish," she confessed. "Rose as much as said that I ought to have known better and that if you had been seriously injured, it would have been at least partially my fault. The worst part is that I see the truth in what she says, and I know I couldn't have borne it if something terrible had befallen you."

"Just a light blow to the head and a stolen valise," he assured her, stroking the line of her back through her clothes. "Perhaps now the worry is finally over, and we can put this business of spies and murder behind us."

"I certainly hope so," she agreed, resting her cheek against the warmth of his shoulder. "I hope that whatever they wanted was in that valise and that you and I were simply not skilled enough to identify it. Oh, Alex, everything has just gone so terribly wrong so quickly. Please God let it be over now."

He rested his chin on the top of her head, his fingers absently sliding along the curve of her body as she nestled into him. "It hasn't been all bad," he said after a moment. "Without the intrigue, it's possible you and I would never have had cause to spend so much time together."

"That is true," she sniffed, "and I shall cherish the memories of our time together for the rest of my life, though they may be bittersweet in your absence."

He was quiet, but did not cease to hold her nor touch her. His steady breaths communicated only that he was contemplating what she'd said, and, God willing, that perhaps he would cherish these memories too, as he pursued whatever life he chose to build for himself.

"Why must I be absent?" he finally said.

"Because when I marry Nathaniel, I will be cleaved to his destiny," she said softly. "I will no longer be the youthful younger cousin of the Viscountess Somers, sent to Yorkshire to contemplate her poor decisions and uncertain future. I will have to follow him, take his name, become his wife."

"So he has proposed marriage?" Alex asked quietly. "Tonight?"

"No, not yet. He spoke with my father at length tonight, and so I expect the proposal to come on the morrow, if the emotions of the congregation have calmed enough to allow it. I will accept and then my parents will love me again, wholly, without those little wisps of disappointment hovering between us every time we speak."

"Are you saying your parents were angry at you because you are not yet married?" he asked incredulously. "What an absurd thing to punish your child over!"

"It wasn't simply because I am not yet married." She chuckled, followed by a sigh. "I have turned down several proposals. More than my parents even know about, truth be told. The last one, I'm afraid, rather embarrassed my father and his standing at White's, as he had agreed to the business with the man rather extensively prior to the offer being made known to me, and I absolutely refused to have him. Alex, he was repugnant. I could not stand to even be in the same room, but they were so, so angry with me. They called me entitled and bratty and short-sighted. If Rosie hadn't been visiting, and made the offer to take me with her, I don't know what might have happened."

"It is your right to decline a proposal!" he declared, gripping her to him tightly. "If your parents love you, they would not force you to marry someone who turns your stomach!"

"Oh, Alex." She sighed affectionately. "You do not know what life is like for a woman, particularly one who isn't from a titled or exceedingly wealthy home. The *ton* is a treacherous maze, requiring careful navigation and foresight. Honestly, I am lucky that Mr. Atlas has retained an interest in me, as I am nearing my fourth Season and the fringes of spinsterhood and becoming a permanent burden on my parents."

"You could never become a spinster," he said seriously. "Are you certain about Atlas? You trust him to make you happy?"

"Happy? I couldn't say." She frowned. "Content, yes, I suppose. Safe. Not miserable."

They held one another in silence for an extended pulse of time, the candle on Alex's nightstand dancing more merrily than seemed appropriate, considering the tone of their conversation.

"What if you married me instead?" he said, his voice so quiet that it hinged on the edge of a whisper. "Could I make you happy?"

Her heart gave a rolling thump in her chest, her vision momentarily a blur of light and color. "Alex, do not jest so," she choked, tilting her head up to give him a stern look. "It is unkind!"

He swallowed with difficulty. "I am not jesting," he said. "I think I am in love with you."

"You think," she repeated, pushing back against his chest to sit up, facing him, her eyes wide. "You *think* you're in love with me?"

He gave a sheepish smile, color fanning over his cheeks. "Well, I have just had my brains shaken about. I'm fairly certain I am. I knew for sure I was, just before all the business with the intruder. I have a ring I wanted to give to you."

"A ring?" she echoed, moisture brimming in her eyes.

"Yes, if you give me just a moment," he began, moving to get off the bed and retrieve this ring he apparently had gotten for her.

"You idiot!" she cried, giving him a shove back onto the mattress. "You fool man! It's too late for rings and proposals! Could you not have come to this stunning conclusion a day earlier? Even a few hours prior to your brush with danger!"

He looked stunned, opening his mouth in an attempt to answer, but failing to summon anything suitable to say.

She gave a choking sob of frustration and collapsed on the bed, clutching a pillow close to her face in an effort to stop herself from dissolving completely into tears.

"It isn't too late, is it?" he asked hesitantly, placing a hand on the small of her back. "You have not yet accepted a proposal from Atlas."

"No, but he met with my father, Alex," she said through the muffled down of the pillow. She heaved a large sigh and turned her cheek to the side, her eyes blinking away tears as she sought his gaze. "Don't you understand? My father has finally forgiven me! He holds Atlas in very high esteem, and in brokering this arrangement can finally return to White's with his head held high next Season, with no chatter about his henpecking wife and spoiled daughter. It is already done, and I'm afraid humiliating him once more would destroy my relationship with my parents forever."

He frowned, considering these words as he stroked her back. "What if I spoke to your father first thing in the morning, before Atlas has an opportunity to propose to you?"

She swallowed the lump in her throat, the look of hope and eagerness in his face almost enough to send her burying her face back into the dark confines of the pillow and crying until she could cry no more.

"What would you say to him?" she asked softly, unwilling to insult a man who had just professed his love for her. She would not be the one to point out the obvious rift in prosperity and position between Alex Somers and Nathaniel Atlas. She could not, for against all her careful planning and sensible thinking, she loved him too.

She slid her hand out to brush over his knee, wanting to return his touch, even as pitifully splayed on her stomach as she was in this pique of frustration.

"With you by my side, I could be just as prosperous as Atlas," he said quietly. "You have the skill to navigate Society, to place us in front of the right people, to find us the perfect vocation. I am biddable and willing to heed your guidance. We would be unstoppable together, would we not? As husband and wife?"

She nodded, forcing the swell of sadness down into her belly. "But how would you get Papa to see a future that does not yet exist and hold it in favor of an established certainty? If only you had asked for my hand first, Alex. It might have been possible if you had done so."

"Well, you've been saying all along that you're going to marry that overly coiffed Mr. Atlas since our very first conversation!" he snapped, eyes flashing. "I've known all along that I'm not good enough for the likes of you. It's only after being knocked about the head that I got the foolish idea to step above my station."

She sighed, reaching up to wrap her fingers in the folds of his shirt, pulling him down to her. He did not resist, though he continued to wear that same expression of a chastened boy, embarrassed by his folly and defensive of his behavior, ever missing the true point of what she was saying.

She kissed him first, before speaking, once he'd bent low enough for her to lift her mouth to his. She kissed him until she felt the hard lines of frustration ease away, his lips softening against hers and his muscles easing from their tension. When she pulled away, still holding his shirt in her grip, she looked upon him as though she might never see him this way again, her eyes hungry and desperate, attempting to lock this moment in time, so that she may never lose it.

He sighed and slid himself into the bed next to her, wrapping an arm around her body and leaning his head against hers. "Would you have me?" he asked. "If this business with Atlas had been avoided, would you consider it?"

She nodded, pressing her face into his shoulder despite the feeling of her tears soaking through his shirt. "Of course I would! Don't be absurd. Surely you know that I am in love with you too."

He squeezed her against him, lifting his other hand to stroke her hair. "Well, then," he said, a begrudging smile tinting his words, "I suppose that will have to be enough."

"No." She shook her head, gripping him tightly to her. "It isn't enough. It will never be enough. I have been looking forward to being secure in my future for so long, and now on the eve of a decisive path forward, I want nothing more than to belong only to myself for a little while longer, free to give myself to whomever I choose."

"Glory, I will still exist after you wed," he assured her. "We need not part ways forever, never to speak again. I would hate to lose you entirely."

"Do you mean that I shall be your friend?" she asked, her grip loosening as she inched back to look up at him. "Or an adulteress?"

He let out a surprised gasp of laughter, biting down quickly on his lip as to not raise the alarm again. "I hadn't considered you might be willing to commit adultery, but far be it for me to discourage you from it."

She frowned, the idea bringing her very little comfort. In fact, the very thought of having to sneak around like this for the rest of her life, under the guise of visiting Rose, put a sort of sharp weight in her chest. She did not like it at all.

"The world is often unfair to the gentler sex," Alex continued, wiping away her tears with a heartbreaking gentleness. "It sounds a sordid thing, but you would hardly be the first woman to seek comfort outside of the bounds of a marriage of convenience. It is not the great sin the clergy would have us believe to find comfort in our lives, in the little places where we can."

She considered this, her brow furrowing in discomfort at the thought. Her parents were so obviously happy together, despite the occasional bickering, that she could not imagine her mother suffered any discontent from the match. Even Rose, having run off with Gideon to save Gloriana herself from being shunted into a marriage too early and without her consent, seemed at peace with her lot, happy and calm. She could not imagine either of the married women in her life considering such a thing.

She realized, lying here in the arms of a man she had come to love, that she would be surrendering the last vestiges of her innocence and childhood to someone else, someone she had chosen strategically rather than emotionally. Even if she found her way back into Alex's arms and his bed in the years following her wedding, she would have lost the part of her that had begun to blossom here in Somerton this autumn.

"If it would not break my parents' hearts," she murmured, "I would insist we follow in the footsteps of Rose and Gideon and flee tonight for the border. I feel I am trapped between misery, no matter what I do."

"You are likely making the wise choice," he said, perhaps more kindly that she deserved. "Even if we did elope tonight, we would have nowhere to live but under my brother's roof, and I would still have just as few prospects as I've had all along."

She shook her head. "You are so much more capable than you credit yourself, Alex."

"It is only a jest." He smiled, leaning down to kiss her eyelids, the tip of her nose, her lips. "If we have only a short time together, let us not spend it in sadness."

"How would you suggest we spend this time together, sir?"

she asked with a little smile. "For we are already in your bed, entwined like lovers."

He chuckled, kissing her again as his hands slid over the column of her throat and over the tops of her arms. "We are lovers, aren't we?"

"Not completely," she said softly. "We have only dabbled."

He hesitated, the green of his eyes seeming to darken at her words. "Are you trying to tempt me, Miss Blakely?"

"Yes," she whispered, her heart thumping in her chest. "Tonight I am still only a maid, with no fiancé nor husband. My body is mine to give for only a few hours more, and I wish to give it to you."

He froze, his eyes widening and hands flexing against her soft flesh. "What is it that you want?" he asked, the words careful if not a bit strangled in his throat.

"I want you to make love to me," she replied, licking her lips in uncertainty. Did she sound ridiculous? Was this not the way to proposition a man? "I want to experience the act of love with you before anyone else has occasion to touch me," she added, hoping that she sounded assured and womanly. "I want it to be you."

There was only a moment of silence as the words left her lips, his eyes dark and intensely locked upon her face. Once the meaning of the things she said reached him, it seemed she had made herself clear after all, for he descended upon her with the most passionate, heated kiss she had ever experienced, as though he would consume her very soul if he were able.

She reached up to touch his face, to pull him closer into her, to return the pure desire that was communicated in that kiss as he pulled her body closer to his. Was she imagining it, or was there the moisture of teardrops on his cheeks as well? Did men cry, and over love at that? Had she brought Alex Somers to tears?

Her heart seemed to surge and break all at once in her chest, the devastation and cruelty of their situation wound up tight in the defiant pleasure of this forbidden embrace. She tore at his shirt, desperate to be rid of it, to touch his flesh and feel his body, warm and alive and all hers, in this stolen hour of the night.

He complied with her unspoken request, tugging his shirt away and pushing her dressing gown back over her shoulders, his lips traveling along the column of her throat as his hands worked to rid her of the burden of clothing.

On instinct, or perhaps the pure and sinful desire to spark pleasure within him, she followed his lead, allowing her hands to travel down the planes and crevices of his magnificent body, over the strings that held his trousers at his hips, and over the rigid evidence of his desire for her, hidden beneath his clothing.

He sucked in his breath, his hips rocking forward into her touch, filling her hand with this forbidden part of him. His mouth descended on the delicate flesh of her neck, his teeth grazing her as he sampled the taste of her. His hands slid down, cupping her bottom with an indulgent squeeze as he gathered up the fabric of her night rail, urging it higher and higher along the curves of her calves and thighs.

She bent her legs, arching her back and pointing her toes into the soft lushness of the mattress as she lifted her hips, her ribs, and finally her arms, allowing Alex Somers to strip her completely bare, removing anything that might have afforded her one last modicum of modesty.

He pulled away from her, his eyes flashing in the candlelight, and knelt over her body as he draped the night rail carefully over his bedpost. He seemed to caress her with nothing but his gaze, admiring this view of her, without the confines of propriety—physical or assumed.

He drew one of his hands over her throat, down between her breasts, and over the modest curve of her waist and hip. He touched her lightly, like she was a valuable treasure to be admired with utmost care. She thought to herself that the way he was kissing her before would shatter a girl who could only be touched this gently.

She propped herself up on her elbows, her hair spilling down her back, eyes locked intently on his. She drew herself up to sitting and reached forward to untie the strings at the waist of his trousers, her fingers quick and nimble, easily destroying the knot and unlacing their hold upon his modesty.

He did not stop her, still and intently watching as she reached around to the back of his waistband and sank her hands into the hidden recesses of his flesh, enjoying the feel of his muscled backside against her fingers. She took her time here, urging the trousers down over his hips, biting down on her lip as she drew out his impressive organ, which she had not had occasion to explore in close capacity the last time they had been intimate.

She could see the muscles of his abdomen clenching, and even, surprisingly, a twitch of movement in his manhood itself as she wrapped her hands around its silky, smooth length, exploring the way it felt beneath her fingers, the way it reacted to her touch.

She glanced up at him, wondering if he would stop her from this task, perhaps under the guise of pulling his trousers the rest of the way from his legs and toppling her back into a submissive position. He seemed to have no intent to do that, and instead reached forward to gently push her hair behind her ear, still gazing upon her as though she were the most precious thing he had ever seen.

On impulse, she leaned forward and kissed the top of his manhood, a little thrill sparking in her stomach at the way he gasped. She rubbed her lips around the top of this part of him that brought him pleasure, the taste of him soft and pleasant on her lips. She slid her fingers over the tip of him, which seemed to become moist much the way she did when inspired by pleasure, allowing the opalescent liquid to coat her fingers before she slid them down the length of him again.

Curiously, she allowed a bead of this mysterious liquid to form and whisked it onto her tongue, wanting to experience its taste.

This seemed to be the breaking point for Alex, who groaned in a way that brought her attention back up to his face with something between concern and wonder.

"We can try that again later," he told her, his voice raspy. "I need you now."

She nodded, allowing him to tip her onto her back, tossing his trousers carelessly away and descending upon her, flesh to flesh, with more of that ravenous, unbearably demanding kissing.

He nudged her legs apart with his thigh, as he'd done those nights prior, and without hesitation or playful teasing, he slid his hand between her legs, stroking her sweetly, as though he were urging her most secret desires out of hiding.

She threw her head back on the pillow, her body aflame with want and wonder, her knees spread for him to explore her to his heart's content. He pressed his cheek against hers, and said with hot breath tickling her ear, "I want to taste you too."

She shivered, her nipples hardening into little peaks as he slid down the length of her, his fingers lingering on her breasts as he made his way down to explore her the same way she'd done to him. She fought the urge to tense up or to squeeze her legs together, banished the sudden surge of concerned thoughts that flooded her mind at the presentation of this part of her.

He seemed to find no flaw in the wealth between her legs, gazing upon it as though it were perfection itself. He leaned forward and used the flat of his tongue to taste the entire surface of her womanhood, once and over again, lingering in it. He flicked the tip of his tongue over a spot that sang with pleasure and sank his fingers into her as he did so, gently thrusting them forward in the way that she imagined he would soon do with his entire body.

"Mm, Alex," she managed, wriggling under his touch, desperate for what came next. "Alex, is it going to hurt?"

"No," he said sternly, rising up on his knees. "No, you are slick and ready. You were built for my cock."

"I ... I was?" she gasped, her cheeks warming absurdly at the sound of this unknown, though obviously ribald word.

He leaned forward, sliding his hands up along her arms and securing his grip around her wrists, which lay on either side of her head. "Is this what you pictured happening when I climbed in through the window?" he asked with a wicked little smile. "The *fun* you thought might occur?"

She nodded, her mouth dry, desperate for kissing. "Yes, oh yes," she panted, her legs sliding up around his where he knelt. "Yes, I wanted you to ravish me."

"Good," he growled, urging his hips forward as the warm, solid reality of his want began to make its way inside of her. "Because that is what I am going to do."

She thought she would freeze, perhaps whimper or close her eyes when this moment finally arrived in her life. She knew, generally, what men expected of their wives. What her mother had never prepared her for was how glorious it felt, being filled up in a place that begged for invasion, being completely overtaken by someone so beautiful and strong.

Instead of freezing or tensing or squeezing her eyes shut, she found herself lifting her head from the pillow to find the delicious kisses of Alex Somers, her hips rocking forward, urging him fully inside of her, urging him to claim from her that which she had chosen freely to give.

He was right that there was no pain, nothing but an adjustment within her to this new and delicious presence. He held her hips steady, pulsing in and out of her with gradually faster strokes as his organ gathered the shared warmth and moisture that both of them were producing, his manhood turning slick with arousal.

"Oh Christ," he muttered, one hand buried in her hair, the other guiding her hips. "You are perfect."

Perhaps they were only perfect for one another, she thought. She could not imagine any other man making her feel this way or so easily becoming a part of her very body, as though he had been crafted for exactly this task. She found herself sliding her legs along his body, testing the sensation of wrapping one around his waist, or pressing against the thrust of his backside with the arch of her foot.

Each time he entered her, it was a new sensation. Her body jolted under the thrusts, each one a little harsher and more desperate than the one that came before. She wrapped her arms around his neck and melded her body into his, burying her face in his neck as he seemed to topple right over the edge of self-control.

As he picked up speed, she felt that incredible sensation building again, that miraculous release she'd only felt once before. He held her close, their bodies wound together in a primal dance of pleasure and satisfaction. She opened her mouth to tell him that she loved him, but found that she could not speak. Instead, her mouth only opened to release sweet little moans as she found herself at the apex of her pleasure, and the shuddering explosion of sensation that followed.

He withdrew from her, seemingly in haste. He locked his eyes on her, his manhood in his hand, and spent a wealth of that pearly liquid onto her bare stomach with a shudder of helpless satisfaction.

They stared at one another in frozen awe, both gasping for breath, both glistening with a sheen of sweat from the intensity of their efforts. Finally, Alex seemed to crumble, his knees buckling as he caught his own collapse on the mattress beside her, allowing his body to go limp and languid, as hers had done.

They lay there together like this for some time, gazing into the world in stunned wonder.

CHAPTER 24

*H*e had slipped from the bed once he felt the world go still again, fetching a cloth with which to clean his seed from her stomach, and a glass of water, this time to share between them.

He had kissed her more times than he could count between every step of this process, unwilling to spend more than the briefest moment without touching her. When he crawled back into the bed, he pulled the large duvet over both of them, tucking her into the curve of his body, his face buried in her hair, arms wrapped around her form. He allowed himself to imagine that this was the life that he could have had, if he'd acted sooner. He allowed the fantasy, for at least a moment, that they could fall asleep together like this at night, and wake up still entwined in the morning.

"I have bedded married women," he said, his voice contemplative and soft. "In fact, it has always been my preference, so that I shouldn't risk ruining a girl's reputation before she could find her place in life."

"Al-ex," she groaned, clearly not interested in hearing tales of his exploits.

He chuckled, dropping a kiss on the back of her neck. "What I mean to say is that the idea of a married woman has never bothered me. I have never felt jealousy toward their husbands or coveted them as my own wife, until now. Until you, Glory."

She was quiet for a moment, perhaps allowing his words to sink in. She snuggled back against him, the warmth of her body a balm for the ache in his heart at the thought of losing her.

She inhaled deeply and rolled over within his arms, the flats of her hands coming against his chest as she tilted her nose up, nearly touching his own. "I have always thought it a romantic and delicious thing to make a man jealous, especially a handsome one," she whispered back. "But I do not wish to inspire jealousy in you. The thought of it pains me."

"Then I will do my utmost to never burden you with it, my love," he promised, his fingers running along the column of her bare back, beneath the blankets. "Nor will I attempt to inspire it in you. In fact, I cannot imagine renewing my affairs with other women, after having been with you. I cannot imagine being able to enjoy it."

She pulled back a touch, enough to give him a look of skepticism. "I have heard your exploits are quite prolific, Lord Alex. It is likely that in time, your ardor for roguish behavior will return."

He grinned, a flicker of amazement rising in him that he could laugh at a time like this, that she could bring so many emotions to life all at once. He twined his fingertips in the tendrils of her hair that floated along her back, overwhelmed with so many things that he wished he could express eloquently.

"The night I left Oxford feels like it happened a thousand years ago," he told her. "I sneaked out of the window of a married woman's house, just as her fairly powerful husband arrived home. I was so careless, so lax and indifferent, that I realized on the walk back that I'd put on the husband's shoes instead of my own! A few days later, I crawled through another window, only to be laid flat on my back by you, perhaps addled once that night and again here tonight. It has been a whirlwind of strange parallels and cryptic lessons, but all I can come back to is how grateful I am to have known you, to have held you, even if I cannot keep you for life."

She giggled, shaking her head in disbelief. "What do you think that man thought when he went looking for his shoes and found an alien pair? I hope his wife was quick enough to dispose of them before he could notice!"

"Bess is very resourceful," he assured her, "and her husband is old enough that I imagine he misplaces things all the time. So in the end, I'm the one with a pair of shoes that's far too big, sitting in the ..." he trailed off, his eyes widening, "... in the back of my wardrobe."

"Alex?" She followed him as he sat up, a sudden flash of eureka sounding in his brain.

"The shoes!" he said, turning to her with his eyes sparkling. "I brought back something from Oxford that didn't belong to me, but it was not in my valise!"

He gave her a quick, hard kiss and threw his legs over the edge of the bed, propelling himself out to hurry over to his wardrobe and fling it open. The moonlight and flickering candles were a poor illumination, and he did feel somewhat ridiculous going about this errand in the nude, but after a moment, he re-emerged from his tangle of clothing, holding aloft a pair of large, rather unremarkable leather shoes.

Gloriana had thrown the covers aside, reaching for her dressing gown, which provided fair to no modesty over her body without a night rail in between, and hurried to meet him where he knelt on the floor with the cuckold's shoes between them.

He handed one of the shoes to her and took the other, inspecting the inside, pulling at the sole, attempting to find somewhere that contraband might be hidden. It filled him with a strange swell of pride to see the woman he loved doing the same, needing no instruction in the endeavor.

"Ah!" she cried, brandishing the shoe forward with her discovery. The heel, which *had* been a little higher than Alex thought strictly necessary, seemed to twist to the side on a hinge, revealing a small compartment within.

This compartment was stuffed with carefully folded documents!

The other shoe, the one Alex held, also had a compartment, but within it were a few gold coins, perhaps payment for a courier along the route of the spies.

"We found it!" Gloriana breathed, her cheeks a bright pink with excitement, her hair wild around her shoulders. "Alex, we solved it!"

He was unfolding the documents, scanning them in curiosity at what had caused so much of a fuss that it had nearly cost him his life. To his surprise, he found that they were rather personal missives, written between a general and the wife of some powerful government official. There were several of them, apparently penned by both parties in this affair, and they were suitably salacious reading for a pair of lovers who had just consummated their own passion.

Forgetting the temporary nature of their affair, Alex recited some of the passages aloud, suggesting that perhaps they might try some of the more graphically described acts and maneuvers for themselves. Despite the unlikelihood of ever having the opportunity, Gloriana seemed sporting to the suggestion.

They read every word of these secret documents, both of them energized by the discovery of this forbidden affair, despite having not the faintest clue as to who the two parties caught in this particular scandal were. The excitement was a contagious electricity, sparking between them as they shared this victory.

"Was the man who owned these shoes someone of great import?" she asked, sitting back on her heels as she finished the last of the letters. "A spy in a chain of spies?"

"Perhaps. He was a barrister, more recently elevated to judge," Alex said, tapping his chin thoughtfully. "It is certainly a position where one rubs shoulders with the powerful and dangerous, but I find it extremely unlikely that he would have known that it was I who made off with his shoes, unless Bess revealed my identity to him at some point."

"She might have, if they were embroiled in something dangerous," Gloriana replied, the missives in a messy stack upon her lap.

He shook his head, something about that scenario just not sitting right with him. "He is an old man, and Bessie insists losing his memory, completely unsuited to the task of his station. It doesn't make sense that he'd be involved with something like this."

"Bessie," Gloriana repeated, the sound of the name on her lips giving Alex a strange jolt of unease. "In Oxford, married to a barrister lately turned judge, you say?"

He nodded, having the grace to blush a little at the revelation.

"Elizabeth Corden née Parrish, by chance?" Gloriana said, unblinking.

"Erm ... yes, actually," he croaked, the flush in his cheeks fully bloomed now. "You know one another?"

"Yes, I knew her at school," Gloriana said with a gust of ironic laughter. "How strange, I was just talking about her with Nell."

She pushed herself to her feet, chewing her lip and tapping on the stack of papers with her fingers. She turned to Alex, her face alight with realization. "Elizabeth—Bess, I suppose —is a general's daughter. She is far more likely to be our spy than the husband, wouldn't you say? Especially as she is the only person who knew for certain how this pair of shoes came to be missing."

Alex considered it, scratching his chin as he watched her

pace in front of him in that very alluring translucent robe. "She would attend many functions with her husband," he said thoughtfully, "which would give her the opportunity to pass along important documents. Hiding them on an unsuspecting, doddering old man is actually a stroke of genius."

Gloriana nodded, "Yes! We have to tell your brother before they call for the constable. It would be much more sensible if we talked amongst a trusted group to figure out how to deal with these documents delicately!"

"I will tell him in the morning." Alex sighed, pushing himself to his feet. He glanced over his shoulder at the open curtains framing his windows and sighed. "I suppose morning is any minute now. The sky is looking awfully purple."

She giggled, tossing the letters onto the floor and wrapping her arms around his neck. "Neither of us have slept for two nights going," she whispered. "And if I could stay, who knows how much longer that would be."

"I wish you could stay," he said, kissing her on a regretful sigh. "Forever, as it were."

She nodded, heaving a sigh of her own. "I must return to my rooms before the servants arise and see me coming out of yours. I will keep the key, if you don't mind, as a keepsake."

"You could take the ring instead," he said, nuzzling her ear. "It is meant for the woman I love."

"Perhaps one day you will love someone else," she said, a sad smile playing on her lips, but a hopeful timbre in her voice. "Judge Corden certainly only has a few years left in him, as it were. Elizabeth is an attractive girl, and apparently a capable spy."

He chuckled despite himself, though the memory of Bessie seemed dim and tawdry in comparison to the things he'd experienced with Gloriana Blakely. He could not summon her face to mind, not with the angelic countenance of Gloriana here in front of him.

"It's funny," she said as she pulled away, floating across the room to retrieve her night rail. "I used to tease Elizabeth Parrish for being such a swooning simpleton, reduced to a fawning puddle over every handsome boy, but here we both are, having fallen for the same one."

"And you both were the cause of me being beaten about the head," he added, pushing down the swell of sadness that threatened to rise in his throat. "That counts for something too."

"Yes," Gloriana said, retrieving the silver key from the lock and holding it close to her heart. "It counts for everything, my love."

ALEX BRIEFLY CONSIDERED ATTEMPTING to sleep for an hour or so, just out of primal necessity. However, it was apparent from his racing thoughts that any attempt at rest would have been an exercise in futility, and so he gathered up the shoes, stuffed their hidden contents back into the heels, and donned a dressing gown to head out in search of the master bedroom.

If anything would cheer him up, it would be irritating Gideon at the crack of dawn.

Sadly, as he approached the end of the hall, where the Viscount Somers had his bed, the door was already ajar, with Mrs. Laughlin standing without, wringing her hands in clear distress. Catching sight of Alex clearly did not allay her anxiety, and she moaned to herself, her foot tapping rapidly on the carpet.

Rose withdrew from the room shortly after, fully dressed for the day already. She stopped short when she spotted Alex, her eyes widening in something that seemed more like exasperation than surprise. Her gaze dropped to the shoes in his hands and rather than express confusion, she only sighed. She whispered something to Mrs. Laughlin as she gathered her skirts up in her hands and motioned for the two of them to march off into whatever melee apparently called to them.

"You might as well just go in now," she said to Alex as she passed him. "He's already awake and riled up, so there's no point in drawing out the experience." She brushed past without awaiting a response, turning the corner sharply with the housekeeper, their conversation in low enough, rapid enough whispers for Alex to glean that whatever was happening was both scandalous and a secret.

He found some small part of him was disappointed to have to share the spotlight, particularly when it came to making Gideon's icy veneer boil over with emotion. Ah well, he thought, these recent life lessons had all been to do with life's little compromises, after all.

He hoped, perhaps against his moral center, that the villain hadn't already been caught just yet. He wouldn't want someone else to go and reveal the secrets he and Gloriana had just managed to uncover. He found he rather wanted credit for this discovery, hard-won as it was, though he didn't particularly look forward to explaining to his brother how he'd come into possession of the shoes in his hands.

The idea of Gideon staying behind so Rose and Mrs. Laughlin could punish the man who'd nearly stabbed him was an amusing enough fantasy to put buoyancy into his step as he rapped on his brother's bedroom door and stepped inside without awaiting invitation.

"What now?" Gideon snapped, frozen midway in the act of pulling one of his boots on. He was seated on the cushioned sill of his bedroom window, his hair still mussed and unstyled from the night, shirt hanging open, and sans cravat.

If Alex were not entirely certain that this was the right room, and that irritable voice wasn't Gideon's, he might not have recognized his brother in such a state of early-morn disarray. "You look wrong," he announced, grinning like an idiot with a pair of shoes held to his chest.

"I haven't much slept." Gideon sighed, reaching up to pat at the fluffy mess of auburn hair on his head. "It's just been one thing after another over the last few days, hasn't it?"

"It has," Alex agreed, plopping down on the side of the bed across from his brother. "Care to tell me what's got Rosie and Mrs. Laughlin marching to war?"

"I don't entirely know," Gideon confessed, his boot thumping onto the ground as he finally got the thing buckled on properly. "Rose just said there was something urgent she had to attend to and took off, but I gathered that

I should probably be dressed and ready to involve myself on the event of her return."

"Maybe not," Alex said with a shrug. "Rose is rather good at fixing problems all on her own, isn't she?"

"Hm." His brother grimaced. "When you're too competent, problems start to seek you out, I think."

"Problems like a prudish lord with a pregnant, unwed sister?" Alex suggested, suppressing the urge to laugh at the way his brother's eyes narrowed. "She's just competent enough, I think."

"Is there a reason you've brought me a pair of old shoes?" Gideon grumbled, shoving himself up to cross the room to his mirror, unaware of the way the back of his shirt stuck out of its half-tucked position in the back of his trousers. "Perhaps you're still addled from your blow to the head."

"Perhaps!" Alex agreed. "I've brought you the shoes because they don't belong to me."

"Wonderful," Gideon grumbled, raking a comb through his hair.

"You see," Alex continued pleasantly, "I took them on accident when leaving Oxford and I've noticed, presently, that there are hidden documents and currency in the heels of these shoes that would likely have a bit of value to a knife-wielding ne'er-do-well."

Gideon lowered the comb he was holding, carefully placing it on the table in front of him with a resounding *clack*. He turned on his heel to face his little brother, his eyes falling to the shoes Alex held in his lap, and he gave a great, beleaguered sigh. "Whose shoes are they?"

"Judge Corden's," Alex said, as matter-of-factly as he could manage. "I took them by mistake, as they quite resembled my own, and by the time I realized the error, it was too late to swap them back."

"Should I inquire as to why you were without shoes in the judge's home?"

"I'd rather you didn't."

The two men looked at one another for a beat of early-morning silence, a perfect understanding of the unspoken passing between them. Gideon shook his head and turned back to the mirror, retrieving his comb and returning to the business of grooming himself. Without taking his eyes from his reflection, he asked, "What would you like to do with the treasure, now that you have discovered it?"

"Well, I think it would be a damned mistake to hand it over to the constable. The man's post is to manage farmland disputes and petty crime. I can't imagine he's equipped to handle the issue of wartime espionage."

"That is a valid point." Gideon frowned. "Did you happen to parse the contents of the documents?"

"I did," Alex nodded. "It is a series of salacious letters between the wife of an important man and another impor-tant man, to whom she is not married. They are extremely descriptive."

"Of course they are." Gideon sighed, flicking droplets of water from his comb as he urged his hair into its customary perfection. "Perhaps Sheldon would know the proper person to pass the information along to, though I rather get the impression that this is information that was meant to be used as leverage."

"It certainly was," Alex confirmed. "There is also the issue of the money. There is a sizable amount in the left shoe. Honestly, I'm surprised I did not notice the weight difference for the short time during which I wore them!"

Gideon nodded at his appearance, evidently pleased with the result of his aggressive grooming, and turned back to his brother as he went about the business of tucking his shirt fully into his trousers. "I think we need not act in haste," he said. "Let us find out what chaos Rose has uncovered, and when that is resolved, we can convene as a family and decide what action to take."

"With Gloriana as well," Alex said quickly. "She is as embroiled in this as I am."

"Well, yes," Gideon said with a tilt of his head. "Gloriana *is* family, remember? She is Rose's cousin."

Alex felt heat rising to his cheeks. Damn his perfect complexion! Always giving away his emotions. "Yes, of course," he said, clearing his throat. "That is what I meant."

Gideon shook his head, heaving out a heavy breath through his nose, and rather than continuing to dress, he crossed the space between them and sat next to Alex on the bed, placing a firm hand on his shoulder. He needn't say it, Alex realized. The truth of the matter was as obvious as the rays of sunlight peeking over the horizon.

"If you are going to propose to her," Gideon said, "I have it on good authority that you ought to do so post haste."

"I already have," Alex confessed with an ironic smile. "She

feels her parents would never forgive her if she humiliated her father again, who has already struck an accord with Nathaniel Atlas."

"Rose thought that the Blakelys would never forgive her for running off with their daughter's intended," Gideon replied. "They seem a forgiving pair, particularly where the young ladies of the family are concerned."

Alex, despite himself, felt a little spark of hope ignite in his chest. "Should I tell her that? Even though she has already refused me?"

"Yes," Gideon said without hesitation. "Do whatever you must, Alex. I have never seen you so focused and sincere."

"What about that spring when Heloise was the size of a horse?"

"It was close, but not quite the same," Gideon allowed with a little smile. "Do not jest to change the subject. Please. Heed my words, Brother."

"I am listening," Alex said, chastened. "I am simply lacking optimism at changing the whims of fate."

Gideon patted his shoulder, nodding in understanding. "My own foolishness and pessimism almost lost me Rose. She is the only woman who has ever made me feel fully whole, and I was more prone to resign to defeat, not once, but twice! I could have lost my chances with her forever. Do not waste years in passive hope or despair and regret. I promise you, the way you feel about her is not a thing that will strike you often in your life, and her future is not yet set in stone."

"So what do I do?" Alex asked, unable to stomp out that damned flicker in his chest, unable to kill the sudden hope that all was not lost. "I am not a viscount. I have nothing to offer her."

"Do whatever you must," Gideon replied with a shrug, then, apparently considering his words, he added, "within reason, of course, Alex."

CHAPTER 25

*I*t was with a muddle of clashing emotions that Gloriana finally crawled into her bed, just as the first hint of the sun crested over the Yorkshire moors.

She had always been very good at containing her tears until she was either alone or with those it was permissible to collapse in front of. Tonight, Alex had seen her cry, but he had not seen the torrent of pain that had roiled and raged within her as she was forced to deny his proposal of marriage. He could not know the way her heart cracked in two as she casually suggested that Elizabeth Parrish may become an available widow with whom he might heal his heart someday in the future.

Mrs. Arlington had taught her too well.

Almost as though she sensed the need for it, Tatiana rolled over in her sleep, slinging an arm over Glory's waist as she flopped onto her stomach. It wasn't necessarily an embrace, nor even intentional, but Gloriana took comfort in it all the same. She took a shaky breath and swallowed down the tears that threatened to boil over from within her, instead telling herself she must sleep, for today was the day she would win her parents' love back.

She allowed her eyes to flutter shut, conjuring thoughts of making love with Alex to the forefront of her mind, locking into the secret places in her heart the overflowing of perfection that had been spent in his bed this night, aside from all of the other things that had transpired. So, so many things had come to pass, she realized, in such a short amount of time.

When she left Somerton, not so long from now, likely in her parents' carriage, headed toward Devonshire where they would plan her wedding to Nathaniel Atlas, she would need these memories to be crystal clear. To remain sane and happy, she would need to summon the taste of a kiss from Alex Somers, and the warmth of his hands upon her skin. She needed to memorize the particular timbre of his voice and the way it sent a pleasant shiver of warmth up her spine.

She pressed her lips hard together, forcing the cry of distress deeper within her. She had made the only choice she could. She had done the right thing, even if it killed her a little, deep inside. She would always have this precious memory of her first experience of lovemaking, which she chose freely and happily, with someone she indeed loved. She had that, if nothing else.

Somehow, despite the cacophony of thoughts and feelings leaping and tossing within her, she found herself beginning to drift off into slumber. There had never been a greater relief in her life than giving herself over to that oblivion.

"Glory!" Tia's voice rang out, her hand gripping Gloriana's shoulder, giving her a rough shake. "Glory, please, wake up. Oh, Glory, he's gone. He's gone!"

"What?" she whispered, her head swimming as she attempted to claw her way out of much-needed sleep. She blinked her heavy eyelids, focusing on the panicked face of her friend. She winced against the sunlight, attempting to shake herself from the shroud of sleepiness. Some hours must have passed since she was last aware of the world around her.

She lifted a hand to shield the light from her eyes, squinting up at Tatiana. "What are you saying?"

"He fled in the night, the scoundrel." Tia sniffed, her eyes brimming with tears. "He's left you."

Like a wave of icy water had flooded over her, Gloriana's senses snapped to life, her body surging forward from the bed to where she stood on two feet, gripping her friend's shoulders with wide eyes. "Where has he gone?"

"Oh, he's eloped," Tia moaned. "He's run off with ... with *Nell*!"

Gloriana thought for one hysterical moment that she might faint. She swayed on her feet, her head suddenly swimming with confusion. "He's done what?" she managed, sinking down on the mattress with her fingers to her forehead. "With Nell? Our Nell?"

"I know, I know. It's terrible," Tia replied, sinking down next to her with tragedy etched all over her pretty face. "Who could have thought him capable of such a thing, and only hours after asking your father for your hand!"

Gloriana shook her head, her thoughts spinning as the world refused to steady around her. "Wait. Tatiana, wait. You're saying that Nell eloped with ..."

"With Mr. Atlas!" Tatiana cried, looking fit to burst into tears. "Oh, I take full responsibility for it, Glory. I told her to embrace her lustful urges, remember? That night with the cards, I told her to, but I had no idea that she'd do *this*. I cannot imagine it! And him! Oh, I don't know whose betrayal is worse, Glory. Can you ever forgive me?"

"Tia," she said, unable to repress a relieved bubbling of laughter that caught in her chest. She reached out to pat her friend's shoulder, a dizziness still swimming about her at the shock of it all. "Tia, how could it be your fault? Can you imagine Nell staging an elopement! I am ... dare I say it? I am proud of her!"

"You're ... what?" Tatiana gaped, her dark eyes wide with shock. "Darling, I don't think you understand. Our Eleanor has eloped with your intended! He is gone!"

"Oh, Peter must be beside himself," Glory breathed, shaking her head. "I would have never suspected she had such scandal in her!"

"Gloriana!"

"What? Oh, I know." She sighed. "Atlas is gone, and good riddance. Why should I want a man who would run off with one of my dearest friends?"

Tia blinked in surprise, perhaps still suspecting that

Gloriana was in a state of shock, not quite understanding that she had just been jilted, in a way.

"He hadn't even proposed yet," Gloriana continued. "It is only a betrayal in the loosest perception of the word. And now ..." Her eyes widened, a smile blossoming on her lips. "Now, I can marry who I please!"

Tatiana's expression of concern seemed to deepen. She reached out, cupping Glory's cheeks and looking hard into her eyes. "You desired Atlas, didn't you?" she said slowly. "You have been scheming toward a proposal for him for almost a year!"

"I did," she laughed, a joy bursting in her chest that she did not know possible as she reached up to hold Tia's wrists. "But now I've fallen in love with someone else. Isn't that silly?"

She stood, Tia's arms falling uselessly at her sides while she watched Gloriana fly to her wardrobe and pry open the doors. "I must get dressed! I must ... I must find a way to tell him. I must hope he still wishes it!"

Tatiana did not respond. She watched her friend in silence, her expression a mixture of bemused awe, as Gloriana flitted about the room, preparing herself for this incredible, unexpected opportunity to perhaps grasp the life she wanted and hold onto it forever.

CHAPTER 26

*P*erhaps three cups of coffee had crossed the threshold into too many, Gloriana pondered, all the while lifting the invigorating liquid to her lips. Perhaps in a handful of minutes, she would regret her overindulgence, her heart already beating a fair deal faster than she thought it ought to be.

If someone had reached back in time, and told her at the genesis of this endeavor, some months back, that her party would devolve into a bunch of sleep-deprived, panicked gossipmongers milling around the dining room while she calmly sipped a beverage she did not enjoy the taste of, she would have most likely found the news devastating. If the entirety of the context had been revealed to her—that she would be relieved at the flight of Nathaniel Atlas because she had fallen in love with the younger, untitled, unlanded Somers brother; that she was hoping to marry him and become sister to Hellish Heloise after all, she very well would have burst into hysterical tears.

All things considered, and despite the (perhaps alarming?)

increase in her blood pressure as she made her way through this drink that apparently dissolved the need for sleep, she considered herself to be handling everything rather well. The most difficult thing this morning was waiting for Alex, who was likely dead asleep in his bed, and still under the impression that by the time he woke, she would belong to another man.

There were far too many people wandering the halls today, or she might have simply tossed caution to the wind and gone to wake him herself. Good lord, how she wished that were an acceptable thing to do! She had even considered simply passing by his door and "bumping" into it hard enough to rouse him, though she suspected this maneuver would be difficult to execute in a convincingly accidental fashion.

"So was *that* the cause of the chaos last night? Lord Moorvale's dog caught them eloping?" one of Lord Benton's daughters asked her father, who shook his head grimly in response, mumbling something vague about an unrelated home invasion.

"Goodness!" the other cried, her eyes sparkling with keen curiosity. "Was anyone hurt?"

It should have irritated her, she knew, that the Benton girl seemed so eager to hear about someone having their blood shed, but she couldn't bring herself to care much for their silliness with all that had happened.

She did not even feel her ire rise when Heloise Somers swept into the room, looking refreshed and well-rested in a flattering cut of ivory brocade, her blazing red locks caught up about her head in a dignified chignon.

The two locked eyes, amidst the scramble of movement and the hurried voices, and Heloise, for some reason, chose to approach the chair next to Gloriana's, and then sit, and pour her own cup of coffee, filling a cup nearly to the brim, with no room for milk or sugar whatsoever.

The two sat in silence for a moment, each sipping at their brew, as guests milled in and out, whispering and casting nervous glances at Gloriana herself. Both watched the doorway, from which Alex Somers did not deign to emerge.

"I suppose you think I'm experiencing something akin to schadenfreude just now," Heloise said, her tone casual and calm, but low enough for only the two of them to hear it.

"Naturally," Gloriana responded with a shrug. "I shouldn't blame you for the reaction. Goodness knows I'd feel the same in your place."

Heloise chuckled to herself, sipping at her coffee as she turned to face her nemesis. "You know, I don't believe you would. I think it would rather disappoint you if I fell directly into the role you predicted for me in school. A brooding wallflower or tragic jilt would be so very boring for me, because it wouldn't be a surprise."

Gloriana considered this with a tilt of her head. "True enough," she allowed, setting down her cup and turning to face Heloise, the sunlight streaming in through the windows almost confrontational alongside her childhood tormenter. "Is it strange that I'm proud of Nell? I would have never predicted her doing such a thing."

"Nor I," Heloise confessed. "I was going to ask her to consider becoming a governess for us, in fact. I had assumed she would simply never marry."

"Well, that is rather harsh. She's not unattractive, just ... eclectic."

Heloise bit down on a guilty little smile. "Ah, I'm just as bad as you are, in the end. All the same, I'm proud of her too. May we all continue to surprise each other for as long as we live."

"Mm." Gloriana nodded, noting that this conversation in and of itself was somewhat of a surprise. "Did she give you that book before she left, by chance?"

Heloise shook her head, a faint amusement about her freckled features as she indulged in her coffee. "Not that I recall. What book is this?"

"Oh, just another surprise, I think," Glory replied with a sigh. "We might as well go fetch it, while I'm thinking of it. It's tardy enough in reaching you that I shall feel badly if it remains forgotten."

"Well, I am intrigued now," Heloise decided, pushing her chair back, but retaining her cup of coffee. "Lead the way."

The two of them swept from the dining hall, passing by Rose and Gideon, both of whom cast befuddled looks in their direction as they walked, side-by-side, down the halls of Somerton. Gloriana thought their balking rather an overreaction. It wasn't as though she and Heloise had linked arms and were giggling with their heads together. No, this was simply a formal errand, and something to occupy her time while she awaited Alex's appearance this morning.

The waiting was driving her insanc.

"It looks like a tomb in here," Heloise commented as the two made their way into the guest chamber that Tatiana and Nell had shared.

It was indeed dark and gloomy within, the curtains still drawn and a pile of night clothes abandoned in a corner where Tia had hurriedly dressed that morning, before returning to Glory's room to shake her awake. Heloise crossed the room to throw the curtains open, allowing in a stream of sunlight from without that at least provided a little visibility, if not a particular aura of cheer.

Nell's side of the room was neatly packed away. She had evidently left with only a single bag of necessities, with the rest of her things left behind for her brother to retrieve on her behalf. Glory wondered if she had left a note for Peter, alerting him to her plans, or if perhaps he had known ahead of time that she had intended this.

She knelt and lifted the lid on the chest at the foot of the bed, questions brimming in her mind. Nell had gone in search of her brother last night, hadn't she? And by morning she'd fled into the unknown with Nathaniel Atlas. Had she ever made it to Peter's room? What had happened between her departure from Gloriana's bedroom and her departure from Somerton itself?

"Ah, here it is," Gloriana said softly, lifting the book from the carefully arranged stack of Nell's belongings. "I'm afraid it arrived for you some years ago, shortly after you departed Mrs. Arlington's, and Nell has been keeping it for you all this time."

"Well, that *is* quite tardy, isn't it?" Heloise said curiously, holding a hand out for the book from over Gloriana's shoulder. "What on earth?"

Gloriana pushed herself to her feet, brushing her skirt down and lowering the lid on the chest, still deep in thought about what had occurred in the shadows last night that resulted in this strange and unpredictable outcome.

She turned to Heloise, resolving herself to simply ask the wretch for her opinion on the matter, but found herself stunned into frozen silence at the look on Heloise's face.

She was standing, haloed in the late-morning sunlight, holding the book open to its inside cover, where the inscription still stood bold against the page. Her mouth was open in surprise, and her eyes, to Gloriana's horror, were brimming with tears.

"Heloise?" she ventured, unsure if she should step forward or, dare she consider it, reach out to touch the other girl's arm.

"Oh," Heloise blinked, a tear escaping down her freckled cheek as she looked up. She appeared to have, for a small moment, forgotten that she was not alone in this room. She gave a wan smile, brushing away the teardrop on her cheek, and clapped the book shut. "I am just surprised is all. I thought he had gone off to war without a single backward glance, and now ..."

"I had no idea," Gloriana began, biting her tongue on the barb that rose so easily to her. What she had instinctively begun to say is that she'd no idea Heloise was capable of tears, nor that she knew how to cry, should the occasion arise. It struck her that perhaps Rosie had been right that day in the carriage, as they left London, and the two of them had grown quite a bit since leaving Mrs. Arlington's.

"That I had a beau?" Heloise replied with a shy sort of smile.

She seemed to crumple, gently, onto the edge of the bed, holding the book in her hands so delicately, as though it might crumble to dust if she made any sudden movement. "Oh, no one did. Except, I suppose, Nell, since she's had this book for all these years. She couldn't have known that this was the only missive he's ever sent me since leaving England. I cannot tell you how ... well, honestly how *confusing* it is to find out that I've been wrong for all these years. I was so angry with him!"

"I would have been angry too," Gloriana said, hesitating only a moment before crossing the space between them and sitting next to her one-time enemy. "In fact, I rather think you still have a right to be. One gift in three years is hardly fitting, and with such a short message within."

Heloise smiled, another teardrop escaping the corner of her eye, which she quickly whisked away. "He has good reason for not writing me here at Somerton. Besides, with no response from me in all this time, it is very likely he thinks I have moved on with my life. In fact, I suppose I have."

"Are you going to marry that handsome physician?" Gloriana asked curiously, remembering the gossip from the ball.

"Are *you* going to marry my brother?" Heloise shot back, that old sparkle of challenge in her eye. "I think perhaps that's a more pertinent question to the day."

"Would you hate it very much if I did?" Gloriana asked, a sudden spark of concern firing in the back of her mind. She had not played wicked tricks on Heloise, no, but she had certainly been unkind to her. She had teased and taunted her for her freckled skin and bright hair, for her lack of elegant manners and her unseemly knowledge of masculine things. She suddenly regretted this very, very much.

Heloise inhaled deeply and released a long sigh. "I think, after everything, that I can be frank with you, Gloriana. After all, you've just seen me in a moment of rather embarrassing vulnerability."

"I would appreciate candor," Glory replied.

"I love Alex very much," she said, lowering her eyes to the book in her lap. "Enough to wish him happiness and direction. For all the nonsense that passed between us years ago, I believe you bring out the best in him, which is often buried under his penchant for reducing everything in life into a jest or an obstacle to avoid. Even if I hadn't seen the hope in his face last night, when he woke from his attack and asked immediately for you, I would have known he was smitten. And so, if you'll allow me the freedom to tease the both of you about the match in the days to come, I will, in confidence, give you my blessing. It is more than I ever expected for him, to be sure."

Gloriana found herself oddly touched, a pang in her chest at this endorsement from the least likely of people. "I love him too," she said, uncertain how else to respond to such a lovely speech. "I truly do."

Heloise nodded, pushing herself to stand. "I know. A sister knows these things."

"Does she?" Glory wondered, something regarding Nell still scratching at her mind. "Do you think Peter Applegate knew his sister planned to elope?"

"Doubtful," Heloise replied. "Though he probably had an

inkling of her attraction to the bloke, if that's what you're getting at."

"It's just so strange. Last night, Tia and Nell came to my room to find out what the ruckus had been about. I gave them a very abridged version of events, and Nell insisted on taking some sort of action to retrieve the lost intelligence, or whatever it was, from the vagabond. When Tia and I were reluctant to join in this fantasy, she stormed out, claiming she was going to speak to her brother."

Heloise gave a slight roll of the eyes, failing to repress a smirk. "Yes, because if anyone is going to cower a knife-wielding foreign agent into submission, it's Peter Applegate!"

Gloriana giggled despite herself, drawing out laughter from Heloise as well. Perhaps it was a little unkind, but Peter was truly a bookish sort, with a slight frame and a gentle disposition. "Perhaps she realized en route to Peter's room that Atlas is much more the sort who could stand up to a villain?" she suggested.

"And in a fervor to restore honor to the Crown, he not only set out after the thief, but took Eleanor with him?" Heloise continued, skepticism writ large on her face. "I didn't even know they had a rapport to begin with. That is a strange leap to take, isn't it?"

"Yes. It makes very little sense!" Gloriana made a click of annoyance, shoving herself up to pace the floor. "Even if she ran into him as he returned from the search, how would it have culminated in running off together? It seems so outlandish!"

"That night in the library," Heloise said slowly, thoughts

clearly whirring in her brain. "You said you overheard a woman and two men, isn't that right?"

"Yes ..."

"One of them would have had to have come from Oxford, where the item that Alex supposedly apprehended was taken. Peter Applegate was at Oxford, was he not?"

"You think two of those voices were Peter and Nell?" Gloriana said, stunned momentarily into a frozen position.

"And the other Atlas," Heloise said excitedly. "Yes, it makes sense, doesn't it? You said one man argued with the other pair, and who better to stand united on an issue than siblings, much less a set of twins?"

"She called him cold," Gloriana recalled, a chill finding its way along her skin. "She was concerned that I was considering marrying a man I did not truly know. Yes, that follows!"

And, she thought to herself, Nell brought up Elizabeth Parrish. It was not mere coincidence at all. Bess must have been Peter's contact in Oxford.

"We have to tell Alex," Heloise decided, turning on her heel and hurrying to the door. "Come on! Don't dally!"

Gloriana did not need to be told twice. She gathered her skirts in her hands and rushed after Heloise Somers, her heart racing in her chest. Whether it was the prospect of finally seeing Alex, the excitement of solving another element of their puzzle, or perhaps simply the result of too many cups of coffee, she would never know for certain. What she did know was that it was the most exciting moment she had ever experienced in her life.

CHAPTER 27

*A*lex Somers had not intended to fall asleep. In fact, he had been rather hard at work penning a list of arguments that could be used to convince all three Blakelys that he was a better fit for Gloriana than that foppish Nathaniel Atlas. It was not yet a very long list.

When the rapping at his bedroom door startled him from his slumber, his body jerking to alertness amidst a nest of discarded papers and smudges of ink, he momentarily felt his heart lurch so violently in his chest, he was certain it was going to pop out of his mouth. The sun was already well into its journey across the sky, and his plans of intercepting Sir Reginald before he could break his fast were certainly no longer valid.

Oh, damn him and his incessant need for sleep! Couldn't he, just this once, forego inconvenient biological necessity?

"Yes, yes, I'm coming," he shouted, shoving his blankets to the floor as he stumbled to his feet. A wave of dizziness sent him flopping back onto the bed, holding a hand up to his bruised head, and on second thought, he called out, "The damned door is open! Come in!"

The knob turned, and in slipped his sister, looking fit to burst with some new horror she'd brought to crash down on his head. He opened his mouth to tell her to go right back to whichever realm of hell she was most enjoying these days, but clapped his teeth back together when Gloriana appeared just behind her, slipping through the crack in the door and shutting it carefully behind her.

What in God's name was this, then?

"Good morning, Alex," Gloriana said softly, hovering next to the door.

"Afternoon," Heloise corrected. "Alex, while you've been dozing away in here, you've missed quite a lot of excitement. Glory and I have solved the identities of the spies you overheard!"

"You ... have?" He winced, raising a hand to touch the throbbing point at the back of his head. Perhaps he was hallucinating. "Did you not have rather more pressing business this morning, Miss Blakely?"

She blushed, casting her eyes down to the floor in a way that made him immediately regret asking so churlishly after something he knew she no longer truly wanted. He wished his damned sister would disappear so he could call her over to him to apologize in the way he truly wished to, but alas.

"Atlas has run off with Eleanor Applegate," Heloise blurted out, her words as effective as a sharp slap across the face for the purposes of clearing his groggy head. "He's gone, she's gone, and only one person is left who makes sense as their third."

"Oh, for God's sake," Alex grumbled. "Is it too early for a drink?"

It was difficult to prioritize just what to do first, especially with this pounding in his head. He did not put half the effort into comporting his appearance that Gideon had, significantly earlier in the day, and as a result he still had a rumpled look about him, with his hair sticking up in various places as he made his way to the little library where they'd agreed to convene.

Heloise had lingered in his bedchambers after Gloriana had departed, a gloating smirk on her face as she watched him heave himself forward in search of clothing for the day.

"What in God's name were you writing here?" she asked, picking up one of the papers on his bed with a snicker. "On this one, you wrote '*duel to the death!*' and then scratched it out several times. Just as well, it is a terrible idea."

"So I came to realize," he muttered, snatching up the waistcoat he'd worn yesterday from its place on a chair. Surely no one would notice a repeated waistcoat.

"Atlas is gone," she said, repeating the information he'd very well taken in the first time, "but if you dally, she'll slip from your grasp again."

"What do you care?" he clipped, fumbling with the buttons on the damned waistcoat. "Don't you hate her?"

"Don't be an idiot, Brother." She sighed, strolling up and assisting him with the buttons. "I'm going to go make you a willow bark tincture for your headache, but I think otherwise you'd best leave me out of your dealings with agents of the Crown. I've got quite enough to deal with already."

"Yes, fine," he said, but she had already gone.

He had the strangest compulsion to knock upon the door of the library, even though it was a public room and in his own damned house besides. He had a flash of regret for not remaining a few moments longer and adjusting his appearance into something more dapper and presentable, but there was nothing for it now. He was already here.

He pressed the door open, flashes playing in his mind of that night he'd spoken to Gloriana in here, with her form silhouetted by the fireplace. How had such a silly little room become such a central hub of the universe?

She was there, seated primly on the couch he'd lain on with a compress to his cheek after she'd smacked him with that ledger. She looked poised and elegant, her back straight and her face turned toward the window, where she appeared, for the briefest moment, lost in thought.

His entry, however, drew her attention immediately, and she rose to her feet, the fashionable lines of her sky-blue gown falling in lovely folds about her hips. She looked so divinely composed, so utterly perfect, that he thought his heart might actually break on the spot, particularly in light of his own slovenly appearance.

"Alex," she said softly, raising her clasped hands to her heart. The shoes she'd taken from Alex's bedchambers sat tucked against the ottoman, much like her own slippers had been on the night they met.

A thought arose, unbidden and unwelcome to his mind, that perhaps she had never truly meant that she'd accept him as a husband. Yes, she loved him, perhaps, but that did not mean he was a suitable spouse. He was, after all, still no one of import, with an uncertain future ahead. He swallowed hard, rooted to the spot with this new and horrible fear resounding in his head like the clanging of cymbals at a symphony.

"Heloise brought you a drink," Gloriana said, his own uncertainty seemingly reflected in her face at his lack of a greeting. She lifted a teacup filled with chalky liquid and crossed the room to bring it to him. "She says it will help with the pain from your injuries."

"Thank you," he managed, painfully aware of how distant and cold his own voice sounded leaving his lips.

"Is it very terrible?" she asked, those lovely, big eyes turned up at him with anxious curiosity. The sunlight glimmered on the blonde lashes that framed them, and his own face reflected in their icy blue depths was enough to make him wish he could wither away to nothing just now.

"It is worse this morning for certain," he confessed, accepting the tincture from her soft, graceful hands. "Though perhaps my impromptu nap has alleviated something even more dire."

"I slept very little myself," she said softy, hovering just a breath from him, the sweet smell of lavender blossoming around them. "Much has happened. Much has changed."

"Indeed," he replied warily.

She took a shaky breath, wringing her hands in front of her. "Alex, did you mean what you said last night? I know it is oft said that a man in the grip of desire is prone to say things he does not necessarily mean, to profess things he cannot necessarily—"

"Me?" he blurted out, cutting her off mid-sentence. She gazed up at him wide-eyed, pressing her lips together in surprised silence at the interruption. "I thought perhaps it was you who was professing sweet words with no consequence!"

"I have never done such a thing," she whispered back, a sharpness coming into her words. "In fact, *Lord Alex*, the light of day has illuminated upon me just how much I wish to—"

She was interrupted again, this time by the door swinging open and revealing a haggard-looking Peter Applegate, who blinked at the two of them in surprise as they quickly took steps away from one another.

"Lady Heloise said you wished to see me?" he said awkwardly, seemingly uncertain if he should step out of the doorway. His eyes darted between Alex and Gloriana, uncertain who to address directly. He decided, instead, to simply speak to the empty space between them. "Miss Blakely, perhaps you have some news of my sister?"

Glory straightened her shoulders, seemingly stepping into the skin of a practiced social player, and gestured to the couch she'd just risen from. "Please come in, Peter. If you wouldn't mind shutting the door behind you, I believe it is best that we conduct this conversation with a degree of privacy."

"Oh, yes, of course," he said with a furrowed brow, hastening to click the door shut in its frame.

Alex crossed the room and took a seat, crossing one of his ankles over the opposite knee and leaning back into the cushioned embrace of the couch. It wasn't precisely that he was looking forward to a confrontation, but discovering a sordid secret under the professorial veneer of Peter Applegate, after all those years of coaxing him into simple revelry, was something that did spark a degree of anticipation in his soul.

Peter took the seat next to him, folding his clasped hands between his knees and anxiously watching as Gloriana settled into a stuffed armchair opposite the couch, her regal bearing on par with a reigning fairy tale queen.

Alex took the opportunity to gulp down the remainder of the bitter-tasting tincture Heloise had made for him. It had already gone cold and was unpleasant enough in tiny sips, but the gulp did momentarily render him pucker faced and regretful.

"Did Nell come to your chambers last night?" Gloriana began, her tone so even and contained that it rather reminded Alex of the way Rose had sounded the previous night during their confession.

Peter shook his head, clearly distressed by this business with the elopement. He removed his spectacles under the guise of clearing dust from them, but Alex rather suspected he was fighting off tears. "I have not seen her since supper, at which time, I am certain nothing was amiss."

"So she did go immediately to Atlas," Gloriana said to Alex, "or perhaps she ran into him along the way. I believe he was about the estate searching for the intruder."

"Intruder?" Peter repeated, sliding the lenses back onto his nose. "What intruder?"

"We're onto you, Applegate." Alex sighed, reaching down to pull the shoes into his lap, attempting not to overly enjoy the bafflement on Peter's face. "We know it was you and your sister on the night of the ball, casually discussing having me murdered."

Peter's eyes widened, his mouth dropping open as he attempted to stammer a response.

"Alex," Gloriana chided, "come now, we know it was Peter who was against that suggestion, though perhaps not vehemently enough."

"A foreign agent broke into Somerton last night," Alex continued easily, grinning at his old classmate. "He held me at knifepoint and demanded the parcel I'd removed from the Corden household. In the end, he absconded with my valise, and we believe your sister and Atlas have gone after him in an effort to retrieve the stolen goods."

"God Almighty," moaned Peter Applegate, dropping his forehead into his hands, his body shuddering with disbelief and shock. "Nell can be so reckless!"

"Well, she's secured herself a rather eligible bachelor in the gambit," Glory pointed out. "For Atlas will have no choice now but to marry her, no matter the true purpose of their departure."

"The good news," Alex said, giving Peter a smack on the

back, "is that the villain made off without the actual goods, which we have here in this room."

"Peter, you must understand that handing the money and the letters over to you must come with a guarantee that there is no hint of suspicion hanging over Alex Somers and his loyalty to the Crown. He risked his life to trick the foreign agent into taking the wrong items, and I rather suspect his life will be even more at risk when the man realizes he was duped."

"I have always maintained his innocence!" Peter replied with a sudden ferocity that startled them both. His head came up, his cheeks flushed with fervor or perhaps it was simply frustration with the situation at hand. "It was a stupid thing you did," he said to Alex, "you and Nell both! What is wrong with everyone?"

"I didn't *intend* to steal Judge Corden's shoes, Peter," Alex replied defensively. "It was erm ... a moment of immediate necessity, and I simply took them by mistake. Perhaps if you'd simply approached me about it, we could have avoided all this nastiness?"

"Oh, right, yes," Peter snapped, "just approach you out of the blue with knowledge that you had been cavorting with Mrs. Corden and had stolen her husband's property, which for some reason, I urgently required the return of. I'm sure that wouldn't have raised any inconvenient questions!"

"It would have saved everyone a great deal of trouble," Gloriana replied calmly. "But what's done is done, Mr. Applegate, and I'm sure a man of your intellect can appreciate that there is no going back on any of our choices now."

"Atlas is *dangerous*," Peter said, frustration tinging each of his words. "And Nell is alone with him, God knows where, on a fool's errand! Who knows how he will react when they discover their flight was in vain!"

"Nell is brave and intelligent," Gloriana said with a lift of her chin, "and Atlas is many things, but reckless he is not. You must trust your sister to navigate her own life with cunning and care. I daresay she's just executed a master-stroke in improving her own lot."

"At your expense, Miss Blakely," Peter said miserably.

Gloriana smiled, her eyes turning to the rumpled, irreverent form of Alex Somers on the far end of the couch. "You're wrong about that, sir," she said softly. "It has been at my great gain."

She really was exquisitely beautiful, Alex thought, his insides alight at what her words implied. He was utterly under her spell, unable to tear his eyes from her gaze. He realized with a start that the ring his mother gave him was in this waistcoat still, just over his heart.

"You'll find the documents and the coins in that pair of shoes just there," Gloriana continued, forcing herself to turn her focus to Peter, her voice picking up an air of zealousness as she spoke, "and with your victory, we expect word of Alex's bravery in the face of danger to reach your point of contact within the royal arms. He is an educated, loyal man willing to devote his life to the betterment of Britain, and such talent and devotion ought not be overlooked."

Peter nodded, lifting the shoes with the tips of his fingers and a look of light distaste. "The documents are in a pair of shoes?" he asked with a curl of his lip.

"Mm, in the heels," Alex replied easily. "A clever enough hiding spot, wouldn't you say?"

"An introduction would be a suitable reward," Gloriana continued, as though such a thing had already been agreed upon, "and perhaps an option of positions befitting of Lord Alex's talents and his devotion to the Crown."

"Yes, fine," Peter said, pushing himself to his feet. "I must go write a series of letters. Lord Alex, Miss Blakely, please accept my thanks and my apologies."

"Don't worry, Peter." Alex laughed, coming to his feet to extend his hand to the other man. "I never really believed you'd let them kill me."

CHAPTER 28

*M*embers of the Blakely family had always prided themselves on their ability to remain calm through all manner of storms. Gloriana, with her penchant for being quick to tears, had long boded a concern that she did not live up to her parents' example of dignified British steadfastness. If she needed further examples to concern herself with, her nervous pacing in the halls of Somerton provided ample evidence of her breaking point.

Perhaps it had been the coffee, after all. Or the confrontation with a real, honest-to-God spy? Perhaps it had been her soon-to-be fiancé running off with Nell Applegate? No, she knew it was none of those things.

The silver key bit into the palm of her hand where she clenched it in her fist, her footsteps taking her from one end of the hall to the next, over and over, as Alex and her father hid behind the door to the drawing room. For goodness' sake, they might have at least had the decency to leave the door cracked, so that she might listen in on this discussion of her future.

Rose was nowhere to be found, off with Peter Applegate, helping him secure his things for his return to Oxford and whatever manner of explanation he must offer up to his family about losing his sister at a country party. Depending on the sort of people the Applegate parents were, it was just as likely that they would be thrilled as horrified. Considering the other matters Peter currently had at hand, and the particular pair of shoes that had found their way into his things, she thought it better to simply not inquire about such sensitive matters.

She had, of course, attempted to find Tia, who had long been her confidante and conspirator in matters of the heart. However, upon pushing open the door to the room she'd shared with Nell, she came very close to interrupting what appeared to be a passionate embrace between Tatiana and none other than the Marquis of Moorvale, who was kissing her most thoroughly!

With her present fond feelings for trysts behind hidden doors, she did not wish to intrude, nor to interrupt what looked to be a satisfying conclusion to Tatiana's strange dislike for the man. Perhaps it had simply been begrudging attraction all along? Or better yet, the dislike may have been a ruse to disguise a passionate affair! One could never know for certain with Tatiana.

For the first time since her departure, Gloriana felt a tinge of annoyance at Nell's absence, for this certainly would have made for a juicy and enjoyable conversation.

She must write to Nell, once her whereabouts became known, and assure her that she held no grudge for what she'd done. In fact, she was rather grateful, and eager to hear the story of how it had come to be, particularly concerning their work together as agents of the Crown! If Peter followed through with his promise to make appropriate introductions, and if her father was reasonable about this latest proposal for her hand, she might soon find herself in a world of intrigue and secrets, after all.

At last, the door hiding her beloved and her father opened, revealing a bedraggled-looking Sir Reginald, who walked out muttering to himself. Alex did not appear behind him, likely still within the room gathering his thoughts.

"Papa?" Glory said, rushing to his side. "Is all well?"

He turned to her with a mysterious little half smile and patted her hand. "My Gloriana," he sighed, "I have come to realize that no matter what happens, the offers for your hand in marriage will never cease. The young Somers lad has decided he wishes to make an offer, even though you spurned his elder brother, which I did mention as a matter of necessity."

"Oh, Papa, that was not necessary," she whispered, perhaps a little more harshly than intended.

Sir Reginald shrugged, a laughter bubbling up within him that sounded just a little bit hysterical. "My point, darling Glory, is that I am no longer concerned that you must leap upon the next offer made to you or face a future adrift. The offers will simply continue coming, well into your dotage, and it is up to you to ensure you choose the right one. I told the lad just that. He's welcome to try, but she'll only have who she's decided is worthwhile!"

"I certainly hope your phrasing was more tactful than that!" she scolded, uncertain if she wanted to frown or smile.

"I cannot say for sure that I was tactful," he confessed, "only that I did not deter him from his task. I look forward to hearing your decision, my love."

And with that he wandered off down the hallway, whistling to himself.

His daughter stayed behind, watching him go with an air of befuddlement that she suspected would linger for quite some time.

It had been foolhardy, perhaps, to risk sneaking about in the dead of night again, though at worst, they would be caught and forced to marry, which was all rather redundant at this stage, wasn't it?

Gloriana lay on Alex's bare chest, her own clothes strewn about his bedroom, and admired the flash and sparkle of the antique ring upon her finger. Her head was still light from the copious champagne they'd had at dinner, perhaps poured in excess to provide a bit of relief to the guests and the Somers family after such a rapid-fire sequence of distressing events.

He had asked her privately first, a strange sort of nervousness about him, as though she might have changed her mind in a matter of hours. She had kissed him rather than providing an answer, hoping her enthusiasm to be in his arms was answer enough.

Over dinner, they had been placed together and celebrated, with Rose moved nigh to tears and Tatiana hovering somewhere between befuddled and elated, whilst also carefully avoiding the gaze of a particularly smug-looking Sheldon Bywater.

The silver key was on Alex's bedside table, reflecting the light from the single candle as they held each other in the glow of hope for the future. It was strung through with a ribbon, which Gloriana had decided henceforth to wear around her neck, hiding this little token of their love against her heart.

"I shall sleep the entire day tomorrow," Gloriana decided, stifling a yawn into the warmth of Alex's chest.

He caught the yawn himself, craning his neck to the side with a sigh. "That sounds splendid," he decided, "though I wish we could laze the day away together."

"Soon." She smiled, displaying her hand out to share the admiration of the ring upon her finger with her intended. "A Yuletide marriage, perhaps? If we begin planning now, it ought not take more than a month or so, and we can marry while the snow falls outside."

"Mm, and have incentive to keep the other nice and warm," he agreed, pulling her into his side. "But then what?"

"Oh, Alex," she sighed. "We'll have a Season in London and collect on Peter's promise. I predict by the end of next summer, our lives will be filled with untapped possibility and potential. We will be ever so happy."

"That sounds delightful." He chuckled. "I hope I can keep up with you in Society."

"You will," she said, certainty in her tone as she turned up her face to solicit a kiss. She nuzzled into his side, knowing she had only a few more minutes before she must dress and return to her rooms under the guise of propriety. Alas, it was good practice for diving into a world of discretion.

"Are you absolutely certain you wish to marry me?" Alex teased, curling a strand of her platinum ringlets around his finger. "After all, it sounds as though you'll be doing the bulk of the work in making us respectable."

She giggled, aglow with the perfection of the moment. "You'll be wonderful, my love, and we'll have the world at our feet. I expect we'll find many doors open to us. After all, spies know all the best people."

"Well," he decided, dropping a kiss on the tip of her nose, "they certainly will, soon enough."

AUTHOR'S NOTE

Thank you so much for reading! This one was a lot of fun, and it was hard to wrap up and say goodbye to Alex and Glory.

Next on in the Somerton Scandals is Heloise's reunion with Callum Laughlin in *The Hero and the Hellion*, which will finally resolve the scandalous secrets that started in the free prequel novella (available at the end of this book).

Nell's adventure with Mr. Atlas is now available as well, *Unmasking the Silver Heiress* is the first in a new series called The Silver Leaf Seductions.

As an up-and-coming indie romance author, reviews can make or break my future as a writer. If you have a moment, please consider leaving me a review on Amazon, Bookbub, or Goodreads. It would mean the absolute world to me!

I love to hear from my readers! If you have feedback, questions, or ever just want to say hi, you can reach me at Ava@AvaDevlin.com

FREE EBOOK

Discover the Scandal that Started Them All ...

Lady Heloise Somers has always been wild, despite the best efforts of a dozen governesses, a posh finishing school, and her exasperated brother.

Callum Laughlin is the son of a housekeeper, whose dreams have always been of greatness—riches, glory, and, most of all, a red-haired hellion born far above his station. He would give anything to have Lady Heloise at his side and in his bed.

As the summer sun blazes over Yorkshire, Callum and Heloise can't resist the heat that draws them together, no matter how forbidden their passion may be. Secret trysts, rumbling storms, and dreams of something more weave together this sweet and steamy prequel to The Somerton Scandals, sparking the romance that changed House Somers forever.

Click Here to Get Your Copy Today!

(Or head to BookHip.com/BPKWKS to claim your exclusive copy)

Printed in Great Britain
by Amazon

43823925R00192